LINCOLN CATHEDRAL

J. STEPHEN THOMPSON

FriesenPress

Suite 300 - 990 Fort St
Victoria, BC, V8V 3K2
Canada

www.friesenpress.com

First Edition — 2018

ISBN
978-1-5255-1713-6 (Hardcover)
978-1-5255-1714-3 (Paperback)
978-1-5255-1715-0 (eBook)

1. FICTION, WAR & MILITARY

Distributed to the trade by The Ingram Book Company

ALSO BY J. STEPHEN THOMPSON

Novel

The Aftermath

Editing & Reissuing

Bomber Crew, Second Edition by Jack E. Thompson

Short Story

Aubergine – in the red line on-line magazine

Photography

Reflections Through a Special Lens:
The photography of Jack E. Thompson

Collaborative Novel

Tales from the Raven Café – with various authors

Anthologies

Kawartha Soul Project – with authors from
the Canadian Authors Association, Peterborough Branch

Kawartha Imagination Project – with authors from
the Canadian Authors Association, Peterborough Branch

This book is written with admiration and affection for my late parents. It is not their story. However, their involvement in the Second World War, both serving in England with the RCAF, their letters and notes, my father's memoir, helped guide me in my research. Certainly, as others my age have found, whose parents served their countries, they seldom spoke of any of their experiences.

ACKNOWLEDGEMENTS

I wish to thank many others for their contributions to the otherwise solitary exercise of writing, especially my friends and family who read all or part of one or more versions of the manuscript and/or listened to sections read aloud: Fred and Trudy, Merv and Andrea, Christine, Alex and Catherine, Susan, Bob, Malcom and Rachel, Alan and Anthea, Dan and Katie, the Troupe of Seven – Bob, Rhonda, Jim, Marilyn, Mike, Janice, Donna and the members of my Canadian Authors Association, Peterborough Branch.

Very big thanks to my writing coach and mentor Prim Pemberton and the individuals who participated in her workshops, *Creative Writing in Cabbagetown*. They critiqued and offered suggestions and encouragement along the way: Barb Nahwegahbow, Josie Mounsey, Ilene Cummings, Sylvie Daigneault, Ann Bjorseth, Mel James, Philip Jessup, Lindsay Ure, Pippa Domville, Mary Bennett.

My deepest gratitude to Dan and Katie Ralph of Burghead, Scotland who advised me on the Scotland section and tutored me in the Doric Scots dialect. Also to Malcolm Handoll and Rachel DuBois who toured us on Orkney. Most especially, I dedicate this book to all my Scots friends, who unfolded stories and interpreted a complex history.

Especially, I wish to thank my wife, Donna, who is included in most of the groups above as my greatest friend, supporter, advisor and editor throughout the process of writing this story.

DEDICATION

To the memories of my parents,
Jack and Dorothy Thompson

To my wife, Donna

To my children, Ondine, Michael,
Alex, Bryce and Graham

To my grandchildren, Emiline,
Nicholas and William

To my great-grandson, Gavin

1

AUGUST 1943 – HALIFAX, NOVA SCOTIA

Jack Borden had come to love the yellow Tiger Moth. Its forgiving nature in the air and low stall speed allowed a neophyte to acquire a sensitivity for flight without the awkwardness of fear or panic. He was initially disappointed when he arrived at Victoriaville, impatient to learn to fly that plane, only to find all the trainer aircraft had been fitted with cockpit canopies. His expectation, based on photographs he'd seen before enlisting, was to take off with an open cockpit, to emulate Billy Bishop and other Great War flying heroes. Those photographs, newsreels he'd seen in movie theatres, and books like George E. Rochester's *The Scarlet Squadron*, provided his only knowledge of flight. He was soon thankful, however, when he realized how much protection this Canadian modification provided against the ravages of a Quebec winter.

He loved the initial surge of power sitting with the canopy ajar, opening the fuel cock, switching the ignition and holding the throttle steady while the ground crew flipped the propeller until the engine caught with a full throaty roar.

At first, he felt anxious that he was blocked from seeing directly ahead when he taxied – characteristic of this tail-dragging biplane. Once up in step, however, ready to take off, he could see everything he needed to. The plane's susceptibility to cross-drafts was disconcerting. Of course, he'd never flown. Had never even been a passenger. He really didn't know what to expect but wanted to fly so badly he was determined to get used to anything.

Then his first solo takeoffs and landings. Troubled sleep the night before. Woke up wondering why the RPM gauge was mounted askew then remembered his instructor had pointed out it was to allow room for the all-important oil pressure gauge. Of course, it and the other six gauges on the instrument panel only came to life once the engine was started. Now as he closed his canopy cover, his autonomic understanding took over. He absorbed rather than read his gauge information – altimeter, air speed, inclinometer, turn and slip, RPM, oil pressure, compass.

. . .

Jack had arrived in Halifax about a week ahead of the other pilots he'd first met at Initial Training School near Victoriaville. He, Wally Stanhope and Bill Walker were together there only a few weeks but they connected, young men away from home for the first time in their lives, their first flights in the De Havilland Tiger Moth. Then, as quickly as they were put together, they were split up, assigned to different Elementary Flying Training Schools – Jack to Cap-de-la-Madeleine – before reuniting now in Halifax to await transport overseas.

. . .

Now Jack watched a tall, slim brunette in blue RCAF Women's Division service uniform walk into Y Depot recreation hall. He left Wally and Bill to continue setting up a makeshift card table. The playing surface was just slightly higher than knee height because they had grouped three end tables together. The regular card tables were all in use. They decided to create their own casual setting for a few sociable hands of bridge.

"We still need a fourth," said Wally. "See anybody you know?"

"That girl coming this way …" Jack inclined his head slightly her way. "She's our fourth."

"Sure, I bet she is. Isn't that the same girl you tried to screw up your courage to talk to at the dance?"

"Today's a new day. Watch this." Jack moved away from the improvised card table and stepped decisively toward the woman.

"Excuse me, ma'am," he said. "You look lost."

"Me, Sergeant?" She looked directly at him. "Why would I be lost?"

"Just trying to be helpful."

"You're new around here." She paused. "This is my base. What could you possibly help me with?"

Jack didn't reply.

"Then, if you'll excuse me Sergeant, I'll just continue to check out the rec hall. See what it has to offer today."

"While you're doing that, we need a fourth for bridge. You do play bridge?"

"Yes, of course … of course, I play. Just a little rusty is all. I've never played with sergeants before." Aircraftwoman 1st Class Pearson laughed as she appraised the three men and their improvised playing surface.

They laughed along with her. Bill and Wally insisted she join them.

"No money on the line," Bill Walker said. "Just a friendly game."

"You'll be my partner." Jack pulled a chair out from the table. "Sit your pretty self down here."

"Okeydokey, Sergeant. But remember, I told you I was rusty."

"Jack. Call me Jack."

"Shelagh."

Jack indicated the others. "Billy. Wally. We fly." They all wore the grey-blue uniform of Royal Canadian Air Force pilots, wings above the pocket on the left breast.

Shelagh joined the game. After the first hand, Jack asked what she did. "I'm with meteorology," she said. "Posted here in Halifax. Or are we allowed to call it that?"

The three men looked at each other.

"I mean officially it's just called *an East Coast Port*."

"I didn't know that," Wally said. "Is that code?"

Shelagh looked sharply at him. "I wouldn't know," she said.

2

FEBRUARY 2006 – *LA MAISON ENSOLEILLÉE*, OTTAWA, ONTARIO

Jack didn't want to open his eyes fully. It was too bright. He squinted at the two women observing him. Their talking woke him up. He wondered what they wanted.

"When will the staff physician see him?" Dr. Suzanne Best asked the nurse.

"Wednesday. That's the day for this floor," Gladys responded.

Suzanne glanced quickly back to the chart she held, frowned, shrugged her shoulders almost imperceptibly. "Wednesday should be fine. I'm concerned about his weight loss."

"He's been refusing to take his meals in the dining room. That's new behaviour – last week or so. We bring trays to his room. He doesn't eat much."

Where's Shelagh?

Suzanne was sure Karen would be upset, wouldn't like the way he looks. "Have either of his daughters visited recently?" she asked.

"Dr. Borden comes fairly often. Mainly weekends. I don't remember her this weekend. She's from Kingston, I think," Gladys said.

Karen. Where's Karen?

Suzanne hung Jack's chart on the chart hook. "Karen and I are friends," she said. "From med school. About thirty years ago." Suzanne laughed and struck her forehead in mock despair. "Actually, probably closer to forty. Wow! Where does time go?"

"Shelagh ..." Jack said in a whisper.

Suzanne stepped closer to his bed. "Mr. Borden … Jack … It's Suzanne Best … Karen's friend …"

What's she talking about …

"… I'd like to check your heart."

No, no. Jack suddenly thrashed. With his left hand he knocked the stethoscope away and grabbed Suzanne's wrist with his right.

"Shelagh," he shouted, almost screamed. "Shelagh!"

"Shelagh's not here, Jack." Suzanne extricated her wrist from Jack's weak grasp. She turned away from the bed toward Gladys.

"I'm sorry, Dr. Best. He's never been violent," Gladys said. She moved to Jack, stroked his hand gently as she did with her dementia patients. She smiled warmly at Jack as his tension dissipated and she felt his arms relax. His rigid grimace softened.

"It's okay. He startled me. I didn't expect that from him." Suzanne rubbed her wrist. "You seem to have good rapport. Let's not agitate him further. Check his respiration and heart signs later. Once they stabilize."

"Sure thing. Was Shelagh his wife?"

Suzanne nodded. "Dementia protects him from reality."

"This is new. He's often been quite lucid, memory coming and going. Always easy to get along with. A gentleman," Gladys said. She glanced at Jack then returned her attention to Suzanne.

"I've known him a long time," Suzanne said. "I see deterioration. Have you observed any swallowing difficulty? I'm just wondering about him not eating."

"I'm not aware of anything. I spend a fair bit of time with Jack. I haven't seen him cough or choke."

"I'll order an assessment for dysphagia. What's your process to have a Speech-Language Pathologist see Mr. Borden?"

"We can make a referral to Community Care," Gladys said.

Makes me … still talking about me … makes me … I'm hungry. I wanna go home.

3

SEPTEMBER 1941 – PETERBOROUGH, ONTARIO

"Jackie, there you are," Rose Borden said. "Happy birthday, son."

"Thank you, Mom." Jack stooped to receive the small woman's peck on his cheek.

Rose grabbed both Jack's hands and leaned back to consider her son. She understood his dark hair but often marvelled how she and Iain, both short people, could have produced such a wiry, athletic six-footer. "You left for school so early. I wasn't even up."

Jack nodded.

"I'm glad you're more enthusiastic than you were last year."

"That's something I want to talk about. When Dad gets home."

"Won't be long. He said he'd be home early so we can have a proper eighteenth birthday dinner. What did you want to say?"

"Let's wait for him." Jack grinned nervously.

Rose watched Jack while he kept watch through the bay window. She wondered about his nervousness.

"There he comes now. Almost home," he said when he spotted Iain Borden walking up the hill from Water Street. Jack went to the front door to welcome his father.

Iain Borden smiled when he saw Jack and, while still moving toward him, extended his hand. "Happy birthday, son," he said as they shook hands.

"Thank you, Dad."

▪ ▪ ▪

Rose served a roast chicken dinner with mashed potatoes, gravy and boiled carrots.

"Where'd you get the chicken, dear?" Iain asked.

"From Market Hall. The chicken man."

"Douglas Smith, isn't it?"

"Yes, yes. That's his name. He saved one of his larger birds for me."

"It's delicious, my dear. So moist."

"You know, Iain, come January, if rationing proceeds as the government has planned, this chicken will be about half our meat ration for the whole week."

"We'll get by. John Cousins said he's sure he can get us chickens from his neighbour. He's got a backyard coop. Maybe even some beef from one of his friends in Smith Township. And, you know, I still have a couple of clients who couldn't possibly pay me if I don't continue to accept farm produce as currency."

"Then we'll certainly get by."

"But," Jack said. "Isn't that contrary to the whole philosophy of rationing? Spreading things around so everyone can have enough."

"Let's not get started on that again," Iain said. "I have some thoughts about this Liberal government. Really, I think rationing does the opposite – encourages people to worry about themselves when we should be relying on each other. The city has made some vacant land available for Victory Garden plots. People should do that. Grow locally. Fuel's in short supply."

"We don't have a Victory Garden."

"We do our part. We save paper, tin cans and glass." Rose went back to the kitchen and emerged with a small cake platter. "Jack dear, you know I'm not a baker but I made what I think is a pretty decent birthday cake. I still had some sugar from before Christmas so even with rationing I wouldn't have needed to use up coupons." She put her hand on Jack's arm.

"It's delicious, Mom." Jack smiled. He knew they wouldn't lack for anything. They'd talked about this before. He knew his mother felt she should practice in advance of an eventuality like rationing.

. . .

After Rose had cleared the dessert dishes from the table, Jack remained seated.

"You wanted to discuss something with us, Jackie. Shall we have coffee in the sitting room?"

"Actually, Mom, I'd rather stay in the dining room." Jack tapped his hand nervously on the dark oak table top.

"If you like."

"Sure thing," said Iain. "Our man's eighteen and wants to talk."

Stick with the plan, Jack thought. *Start with school. Don't stammer. Just like I rehearsed.* Jack pulled his hands onto his lap then spoke. "You know how I had Old Man Thomas for English last year?"

"Yes," Iain said. "I know that put a damper on your year."

"Well, I have him again this year. I'd feel better if it was Mr. Wells who I had in Grade 11. I write well but Thomas …"

"Mr. Thomas."

Rose grimaced at the correction.

"Right. Mr. Thomas is so strict in his marking that I give up." Jack paused. "I quit yesterday."

"But that's your best subject. You need that course."

"No, mother, I didn't just quit English. I quit school."

"But …" Iain began.

Rose appeared aghast. "Then where were you today? You were gone all day."

Here we go. Jack hesitated. He could feel a red flush quickly progressing from his neck to his cheeks. But he knew there was no backing down, however anxious he felt. This was it. "I took the morning train to Toronto." Again he faltered. "I… I joined the RCAF."

"You what?" Rose's hands flew to her face. Her eyes widened as she regarded her son in dismay. She shook her head as if trying to determine whether Jack had actually spoken those words. She couldn't hear what was being said but Iain seemed to be listening to Jack. She always thought Iain let Jack do just anything. Never imposing discipline.

"But Jack," Iain was saying. "You could finish your year and graduate, then sign up."

"It's my duty." Jack tapped his fingers on the table. "They need me *now.*"

"You've been listening to government advertising. You know it's all propaganda."

"I want to fly."

"There's no guarantee you'll be a pilot. Now that you've enlisted, they'll deploy you wherever they think they need you. They could make you navigator or gunner."

"No!" Rose broke her perplexed silence after what seemed to her an inordinate amount of time had gone by. "Iain …"

"What?"

"You're a lawyer. Do whatever it is you do. Get it annulled or –"

"For goodness sake, Rose." Iain glared at her.

"Iain –"

"Rose, please think about it." Iain touched her forearm. "Jack became of legal age today. When a man of legal age signs the papers, there's nothing anyone can do to change it."

"You know how I feel about war."

"I know how much your family has sacrificed." Iain reached for Rose's hands but she pulled them back to her lap. "We should talk about this later. Jack wants to do this. We must support him." Then, turning to Jack he said, "I'm proud of you, son."

"Thank you, Dad." Jack smiled briefly, stopped fidgeting nervously in his seat and glanced to his mother hoping for the approval he knew might never come. Jack excused himself from the table and announced in a low voice he was going for a walk.

Iain often joined Jack for an after-dinner stroll but tonight he stayed with Rose.

Rose instinctively glanced to the plate rail above the dark oak wainscoting. She stood, walked over and picked up the 'Great World War' Peace plate. She stared at it. Full sized dinner plate. Central grouping of flags – Union Jack, Stars and Stripes, Tricolours of France, Italy and Belgium. Dove of Peace and the word *Peace* inscribed above the date November 11, 1918. Her father had been too old to serve. She remembered both her older brothers – their fervour to enlist. Her father instilled a sense of duty in all three of his children. As a seventeen-year-old herself she'd been so excited when George and David signed up. Months later both were dead. Both killed at Vimy Ridge. Their bodies presumably buried on the battlefield. She had been devastated, her parents overwhelmed. Thank God for Iain. Her compass. Six years after the boys were killed, her father bought that Peace plate to commemorate Jack's birth. His only grandson as it would turn out. "Never again," she could still hear him say as clearly as he had eighteen years ago.

Now Iain and Rose were alone. Iain said, "Think about it Rose. Jack has a plan. He chose the service he wants to join. That's far better than waiting to be conscripted."

"But Iain, you of all people know there is no conscription."

"But it's inevitable. It's coming. You know the government's considering it. When Mackenzie King won't respond to opposition questions about conscription, you know he's planning something. This way Jack's got choice."

4

MARCH 2006 – *LA MAISON ENSOLEILLÉE*

Gladys stroked Jack's shoulder. "I know you're awake, Jack."

Jack stared tenaciously at the ceiling, paying no attention to Gladys until her touch and voice became firmer. He tugged the bedclothes tighter around his body.

"Jack. It's Gladys. How 'bout you get up now?"

"No."

"C'mon, Jack. You'll feel better up and dressed. Eat some breakfast."

"No." Jack lay on his back, holding his legs and arms rigid as if in the unyielding resistance of *rigor mortis*.

"C'mon darlin'. I've got your meds. How 'bout some juice?"

"No."

"Maybe water?"

"No."

"Jack, honey, you need to take your meds. Do you want us to give them by needle?"

"No."

"Big needle in the bum. I know you don't want that."

"I want to go home," he intoned softly. "You drive me home. Please. Take me home." His pleading became louder, desperate.

"Now then, Jack, everything's going to be fine. You're okay."

"No."

"Just sit up then." She offered him her hand. "There, that's it. Let's take your meds – That's a good fella."

Jack began to sob quietly. Gladys rubbed his back tenderly, reassured him with gentle words. Poor guy, she thought. *He's frustrated about giving in. Not being able to hold his ground. He always seems such a nice man.*

. . .

Later that morning, Karen Borden's office telephone rang. The direct private line. She glanced at the caller identification and sighed deeply. They never call me, she thought as she reached to answer. This can't be good.

"Good morning, Dr. Borden. It's Gladys at *La Maison Ensoleillée*. Just want to give you a head's up. Your dad hasn't been responding well for a few days. You asked us to notify you of any changes."

No, not that, Karen thought. *Please don't move him to the enhanced care floor. Not yet.* Then she said, "Tell me how he's acting, Gladys."

"Well, he says no to everything. He resists any attempt to assist him. He just goes rigid. We can't even turn him."

"He's not getting up?"

"No, and he's not eating."

"So you're saying he's not doing any of the activities that were stimulating him?"

"No, nothing, Dr. Borden."

"Has the geriatrician, been to visit him?"

"Yes, she has. I'd have to check the chart but Dr. Best's been here on two occasions I know of."

"Okay, I'll be there tomorrow or the next day. Thank you for calling me, Gladys." *What's going on? Is it Mom? He can't continue to deny reality.*

. . .

Later that day, Roberto Gervais pushed the door fully open and stepped into Jack Borden's room. Because of the reports, particularly from Gladys, at staffing change-over, he hadn't expected to see Jack out of bed and sitting in his chair. "Hello, Jack. How ya doin' today?"

"Fine thank you, Robbie. I'm fine. You washing floors?"

"Not me. Housekeeping does that. They keep old Sunshine House shiny and bright. Sunshiny bright, eh? Get it?" Roberto teased. *Joke may work better in French,* he thought.

"Be careful. You wouldn't want to get AIDS or anything."

"Oh, that's all under control, Jack. They use bleach. Besides, the latest research says you don't get it from floors."

"Get what?"

"AIDS."

"Now why would I want to get AIDS?"

Jack's room's always neat. Roberto glanced around as he often did when he checked on Jack. *His family has really made his space homey. Floral-patterned fabric-covered loveseat. Throw pillows of the same pattern. Two small wood-framed accent chairs, a small wooden desk. Looking much better than nursing home standard issue. Nicer than a lot of residents' rooms. Much brighter. More personal. Familiarity's important. He always keeps his blinds up. Lets sunlight in. Not like some of the others, content to exist as hermits in their dark caves.*

"You doing okay, Jack? The staff are worried about you." Roberto watched closely, evaluating Jack's status for himself. They bantered almost daily, something the younger man enjoyed, wordplay with residents, clients as the home termed them. Often though, conversations had a sameness, same words, same pattern, same responses. That didn't really bother him. In fact, he was expanding his own theories about the importance of maintaining mental agility while aging.

"Are the nurses worried about me getting AIDS?"

"No, not that. They just want to be sure you're doing well. Me, I'm not so concerned. But then, I'm not a doctor," Roberto replied.

"Neither are the nurses."

"What?"

"Not doctors."

Roberto laughed. He picked up the framed eight-by-ten photo of a man and woman in uniform. "This is a great picture." He glanced at their young faces before returning the picture to its place of honour on the desk. *It's great he has so many family photos. Must be comforting.* "It's good to see you up and about again," Roberto continued.

"What do you mean?"

"You haven't been out of bed since last Friday. You wouldn't talk to me yesterday or the day before."

"No … I … I don't remember."

"Are you thinking about your wife?"

"I want to go home. She's waiting."

"But Jack, you know she's …"

"Robbie, drive me home. I'm ready right now." Jack whispered in a conspiratorial tone while pointing to his neatly folded jacket and packed overnight bag on the chair, laid out to go.

5

MARCH 1942 – VANCOUVER, BRITISH COLUMBIA

Betty Pearson sat on the white wicker chair on the front porch as she watched her nineteen-year-old daughter walk across Hastings Street from the bus stop. I wish she'd be more careful, she thought as the tall, gangly girl crossed the road without looking. "You're home early," she said as Shelagh came up the front walk.

"They came for Mr. Tanaka," Shelagh said.

"What do you mean?"

"The RCMP took Mr. Tanaka away."

"Your boss? Jim Tanaka?"

"They said he didn't register as an alien," Shelagh continued. "He was supposed to register last year."

"Jim Tanaka was born here. He's Canadian. His father was born here, for goodness sakes. He's a member of our church. I'm more alien than he is."

"But, Momma, we're on the right side. We don't need to register."

"I thought you liked working for him," Betty said.

Shelagh shrugged. "Yeah," she said. "I guess he's been good to me – teaching me photography so I can be more than a shop assistant. He says it's important for women to take over good jobs while the men are away."

"He took Elspeth's wedding photographs. Such a nice gentleman."

"The law is the law." Shelagh spoke flatly. "He should have registered. Especially after Pearl Harbor. What was he thinking – he could just live here like nothing happened? Serves him right."

"What are you talking about, daughter?"

"He's a spy, Momma."

"Who says that?"

"He takes pictures along the coast."

"He's a photographer. Everybody takes pictures along the coast, lass. It's beautiful." Betty shook her head.

"He gives pictures to his fisherman friends and they take them to the Japanese submarines off the coast. They go right to Japan."

"What rubbish!"

"That's what the Mounties said."

"Such blather. The Japanese could just buy postcards. Imagine if the Prime Minister took a dislike for Scotland. Then we lot would be rounded up too."

"Now, that's just silly, Momma."

"What about your job?"

"I don't know. Mr. Bruton said not to come back until Monday. He said he needs to arrange things. I think he's a spy too."

"Alan Bruton? Where do you get this nonsense?"

"They were talking together yesterday and the day before."

"Mr. Tanaka and Mr. Bruton?"

Shelagh nodded. "They spoke quietly. I didn't hear anything."

Betty didn't offer a reply.

"And this morning … well, they changed the sign on the shop. Now it says Alan Bruton, Photographer."

Betty patted the arm of the matching chair beside her. "Sit you down, lass. Sounds like you need to relax. I've got fresh tea made." She stood without waiting for a response. As she opened the door into the house, she turned to smile at Shelagh. "And we've got fresh scones."

▪ ▪ ▪

Shelagh was peeling potatoes when she heard the front door open and Elspeth announce she was home.

"We're in the kitchen, sweetie." Betty never yelled but raised her voice enough for Elspeth to hear her now. Elspeth and Shelagh usually checked the kitchen when they came home if their mother wasn't sitting on the front porch.

"Did Aunt Marjorie come over?" Elspeth asked.

"Marjorie's coming tomorrow for tea."

"Is Gareth upstairs?"

"He's next door. He and little Susie play so well together." Betty looked after her four-year-old grandson while Elspeth taught history to eighth graders.

"I'll get him just before supper then. Any mail today?" Elspeth asked the same question every day. Her husband, Bob, was stationed in Ottawa.

"Nothing today," Betty replied.

Elspeth stood quietly a moment before she spoke. "Before I forget," she said. "I brought something home to show Shelagh." She removed a rolled-up paper from her school bag. "We had an assembly for the Grade 12 girls during the activity period. Look at this." The fourteen by sixteen-inch poster showed a uniformed woman standing tall in the foreground with male aircrew figures in the background. *She serves that men may fly,* it said. *Enlist today in the RCAF.*

Shelagh dropped her final potato pieces into the water-filled pot, dried her hands and took the print from Elspeth.

"It's brand new," Elspeth said. "The WD, Women's Division, I mean. They're recruiting women to be support workers. To be in the Air Force with actual rank. It's no longer the Auxiliary."

. . .

Shelagh's eldest sister, Irene, came by to visit that evening as she often did after work.

"Look what Elspeth brought from school," Shelagh said, brandishing the recruitment poster. Irene, fifteen years older than Shelagh, took the artwork to look at it more closely.

Elspeth described for Irene's benefit what she had explained earlier about the WD. "It's brand new," she said again.

"Wow!" Irene said. "If I were younger, I'd be right down there to enlist. With bells on."

"It would be exciting." Elspeth agreed with her sister. "I'm almost sorry I can't volunteer. Being a mother, I mean. And with Bob already a colonel."

"Wouldn't that be a hoot? Bob reprimanded for consorting with enlisted personnel – his own wife."

"You're silly, Irene." Elspeth laughed. Shelagh stared at the poster, seeming to miss the joke.

"I may not have a job anymore." Shelagh explained for her sisters' benefit what had happened to Jim Tanaka.

"That's ridiculous. I went to school with Jim," Irene said. "He's my age. He spoke better English than I did. I still had my Scottish accent then."

"Well, he was born here," Betty said.

"If you won't have a job, what's to stop you?" Elspeth turned to Shelagh. "It would be so exciting."

"And just think of the men you'll meet." Irene winked at Elspeth. "All those dances and concerts."

"Oh, shush, such nonsense," Betty said. "Shelagh will not be traipsing off to war! She's too young."

"Actually, Momma, she'd probably be based in Ottawa. Bob says that's where they need support personnel," Elspeth said. She turned to Shelagh and whispered, "You could even find good prospects for marriage." Although Betty couldn't really hear the exchange between Elspeth and Shelagh, she scowled in their direction to further emphasize her displeasure with this talk of enlisting in the military. Not for girls.

"And Momma," Irene said. "Shelagh was a top student at Western Commerce. Office skills are what they need most. And, once they move, Elspeth and Bob will be in Ottawa. She'd be close to family."

...

Next day, Shelagh and her best friend Katy took the bus downtown to the stop near Waterfront Station. Shelagh explained about Jim Tanaka.

"That's awful," Katy said. "They're sending them to camps in the interior."

"They're the enemy."

"You surprise me, Shelagh Pearson. You sound just like the newspapers."

"Well, it's the truth. And it's the law."

"The government is taking their property – their boats, their houses, their shops."

"If they don't cause trouble, they'll get everything back after the war's over," Shelagh said. "Besides, Katy, you never shop in Little Tokyo anyway."

"That doesn't matter. Anyway, it's not the same as it was. Most of the shops I knew are closed now."

"That's what happens when you're on the enemy side."

"Stop it, Shelagh. It's just wrong. And you're wrong. They're Canadians, like you and me."

"We were born here."

"Them too," said Katy. "Mr. Tanaka's photo shop isn't in Japantown anyway."

"You're starting to sound like my mother," Shelagh said.

When they reached their stop, rather than wait to transfer to another trolley, they walked in silence the three long blocks up Burrard Street to the address listed on the recruitment poster. There, long tables were set up in the plaza in front of the Court House on Georgia Street, across from the Hotel Vancouver.

"I've never been in there." Shelagh pointed toward the new, palatial hotel with its greening copper roof.

"It's not really for our kind," Katy said. "Imagine us going for high tea."

"We'll do it after the war, Katy. Believe me, this is going to change our lives."

They were thrilled with how easy it was to sign up. Each swore she was of age and was asked a list of obligatory questions in a rather perfunctory manner by the recruiting sergeant.

"That sergeant really wasn't happy signing up girls," Katy said as the two of them rode the bus back home.

"I guess he was just following orders." Shelagh laughed. "My mom doesn't think much of girls joining the Air Force either."

Katy quickly turned her head toward the window.

Three days later, Shelagh was surprised to receive a letter addressed to *Aircraftwoman S.M. Pearson* ordering her to report to the RCAF base at Jericho Beach for further processing and her medical exam. She was excited to think she might be based so close to home. *Momma will have a chance to get used to it before I'm shipped away.*

When she ran next door to share her good news with Katy, Mrs. Burns answered the door and wouldn't allow her to talk with Katy.

"You … you have no right," Katy's mother began. "You and your wild adventures. You cannot take my baby. Mr. Burns is talking to the authorities. Katy will not be going with you."

Shelagh had no idea Katy hadn't talked with her parents about recruitment.

▪ ▪ ▪

"Where will I be living, sir?" Shelagh asked the clerk when she reported to Jericho Beach, suitcase in hand.

"Corporal," he said. "Call me corporal." He slapped the two chevrons on his sleeve. "Look at the tapes. It's corporal, Aircraftwoman."

"Oh, I see. Sorry, sir."

"Greenhorns." The corporal shook his head and glared at her. "Save your *sirs* for the officers."

"But where will I live?"

The corporal continued to shake his head but now he was grinning. "This isn't an airbase now. The last seaplanes have been moved out. We just use this compound to process you west coast greenhorns." He glanced at the paper in his hand. "You're from Vancouver. Until further orders, you live at home. Enjoy your mom's cooking. That's not what you'll get in the Air Force. Report here every morning at 0800 hours."

Shelagh looked puzzled.

"Eight o'clock in the bloody morning. Now off with you."

"Where am I supposed to be?"

"Go back home. Come back here tomorrow morning at 0800 hours."

6

DECEMBER 1941 – VICTORIAVILLE, QUEBEC

"This is crazy. Ordered to report here just before Christmas." Jack was sitting on the edge of his bed. Bill and Wally were the only others in the barracks.

"What's the matter?" Bill asked. "Worried you won't be getting your presents?"

"Aw leave him alone," Wally Stanhope said. "Poor boy's never been away from his mother."

"Cut it out guys." Jack laughed. "I just meant we're going to be away a long time. You'd think they could leave us home until the new year."

"There's a war on, chappie," Bill said. All three laughed this time.

"You know what I mean. I enlisted in September," Jack said. "Then sat around for three months. Now, suddenly it's urgent to report here December twenty-second. What's a few more days."

"Well, Airman Borden, two words: Pearl Harbor." Wally puffed out his chest and stood at rigid attention. "The war doesn't hold for Christmas, you know."

Bill clapped. "Yes, Prime Minister, we know."

"Yeah. On top of that, we're lucky," Wally said. "We're learning to fly in winter conditions. Not everybody gets such a sterling opportunity."

"We'll be lucky if the props keep turning."

"What would you be doing at home anyway, Jack? Other than decorating for Christmas," Wally asked.

Jack smiled. "You boys know the routine – report to the armouries once a week for about an hour."

"Yeah," Bill said. "I had to take the bus to Regina every Tuesday."

"I was lucky," Jack said. "I could report to the armouries in Peterborough even though I enlisted in Toronto."

"Why enlist in Toronto if you're from Peterborough?"

"I wanted to do it on my birthday. Not have to wait two weeks for travelling recruitment personnel to show up."

"Had to be right on the day, eh?"

"Yep. I didn't want anybody to try to stop me."

"Your momsie and popsie didn't want their baby to go, I'd say."

"That's about it. At first anyway."

"You must be an only child," Bill said.

"Yep. They didn't like when I quit school and took a job as a photo assistant. Just waiting for call-up." Jack said. "My dad always hoped I'd become a lawyer and take over his practice. I like the thought of photography better."

"My old man wants me to take over the farm. There's plenty of time for that after the war." Bill looked toward Wally.

"I'm kinda like Jack," Wally said. "My old man wants me to follow him into medicine. But he understands – he was in the Royal Flying Corps."

"Mine was infantry. He didn't like it but he says we have to do it – serve our country when needed. He came home wounded from Vimy Ridge. Wants me in the air."

Vimy Ridge, thought Jack. *There with the uncles I never met. Poppa didn't enlist.*

"You bring a camera, Jack?" Wally asked.

"No. Cameras aren't allowed."

"You coulda brought one of those little spy cameras," Bill said. "Being a photo assistant and all."

"A Minox you mean. I've never even seen one. Besides, it's German."

"Maybe not a good idea then."

7

APRIL 1942 – VANCOUVER

Shelagh settled quickly into a morning routine of reporting for duty, being assigned sundry tasks such as being fitted for uniforms, although she laughed whenever anyone called the process a fitting.

"Issued," Pamela, one of the other recruits had said. "That's definitely not a fitting."

The twenty or so female recruits soon began to watch the bulletin board in the small canteen shack the corporal had referred to as the mess. In the second week, orders appeared posting Shelagh and a list of about a dozen others to No. 3 Manning Depot in Edmonton.

"How do we get there?" Shelagh said to the group standing looking at the lists.

"Oh, you silly girl." Pamela always had the answers. "The train. Or are you expecting star treatment?"

Shelagh blushed. *Stop asking stupid questions*, she thought. *I'll ask the corporal. He'll know.*

8

MARCH 2006 – KINGSTON, ONTARIO

"That's okay, Suzanne, they've already told me," Karen said into the phone. "I'll come to Ottawa tomorrow." She thought about how long she'd known Suzanne, about how they'd helped each other out of jams. She remembered how they met.

"You Borden?"

"That's me, Karen Borden."

"Best." The stocky brunette stuck her hand out. "We're lab partners. Put 'er there, pardner."

Karen had stared.

"You know – Best, Borden. We're paired up alphabetically." Suzanne laughed. "Are you as nervous as I am?"

From that point on, Karen was aware of Suzanne's false bravado and came to her assistance whenever she sensed Suzanne needed help in new situations. Sometimes she wondered how Suzanne had developed into such a self-assured diagnostician.

Now Suzanne said, "You know, Karen, I'm not certain your dad has Alzheimer's – definite signs of dementia, yes – but you know how it is, family physician sees an older person with diminished physical and mental abilities, it's automatic Alzheimer's. It's not that way in your clinic. I know you have an older patient register," Suzanne said. "Look, when do you expect to be here?"

"It's usually best to visit Dad late morning. He's generally pretty good then."

"Plan to stay over with me."

"I can't but thanks. I have office hours the next morning." *Funny*, Karen thought, *we both live alone but that doesn't mean we're free of obligations.*

"Sometime though, you'll stay?"

"Sure thing. Thanks."

"I'd like to visit Jack as a friend. Is that okay with you?"

"That'd be great. Thanks, Suzanne."

. . .

Karen walked into Jack's room two days after Gladys had phoned. "Hi, Dad," she said.

"Hello." *Who is this?*

"It's me, Dad. Karen."

"I know."

"Usually you're happy to see me."

"Well, okay. Give us a kiss then, *luv.*" Jack puckered his lips, pantomiming a kiss.

She smiled at him, bussed his cheek and pulled him into a hug, surprised once again how fragile her father felt, as if he might break if she squeezed too hard.

It's Karen. He silently berated himself for his hesitation. "It's good to see you, my dear."

"I'm happy to see you too, Dad. I'm sorry I couldn't come on the weekend."

So, what day is it? He scrunched his eyes and scowled.

"Anything you'd like to do today? It's beautiful out there. A lovely spring day. How about a drive or a walk?"

"Are you going to take me home?"

"We can talk about that later, Dad. But let's go out. It's a great day."

"I don't want to go out. I don't feel like it."

"Well," Karen patted his hand. "Let's go to the sunroom for coffee."

"No." Jack screwed up his nose. "I don't like coffee."

"Then maybe a Pepsi? You like Pepsi. Let's go. It's just a short walk," Karen insisted.

"No, thank you. Not today."

Karen watched Jack squirm in his chair. "Do you want to use the washroom before we go? I can help you."

"No," Jack almost hissed.

"It's okay … I'll get the nurse."

Jack nodded his agreement.

. . .

About an hour later, when they returned from the solarium, Jack's compact room was bathed in morning sunlight streaming through the one large window. Karen enjoyed visiting at this time of day. She appreciated the unrestricted view of the Rideau River and the surrounding green space. It upset her when she heard people suggest this prime real estate was too beautiful to be wasted on old people. *Surely society owes the aging the right to beauty, peace and serenity. And expert care,* she thought. *The room's really quite homey. I'm glad we brought the writing desk.* He'd loved it. She knew he didn't particularly like the fabric on the loveseat.

"Too flowery," he had said when Shelagh had it delivered to their home from the furniture store. "Hope you like it 'cause I'll never sit on it." But he did when he watched hockey games on Saturday night.

A compact oak corner cupboard displayed some of Jack's photographs and mementos.

"Gee Dad, you have your own solarium right here," Karen exclaimed. "I've always liked your room." *Neat, not crowded. Absolutely ideal. He was always so organized,* she thought.

"It's okay."

Karen focussed on the small photograph of her father in his RCAF uniform. Handsome, impeccably groomed, dark-haired young man seated in formal portrait mode, feet on the floor, hands clasped on his lap, leaning a little forward with shoulders turned slightly to face the photographer, eyes looking into the lens. Canada flashings on his near shoulder. Wings displayed on his chest. A single stripe on his epaulets signifying his rank. A Windsor-knotted tie and peaked officer's cap. That photo's about sixty years old now, she thought.

They sat awhile, mainly in silence until Karen picked up another World War Two photo, this one a Lancaster bomber in flight, and handed it to Jack. He considered the picture judiciously, as if noticing detail he hadn't seen before. *Lanc. Good old Lanc,* he thought. *Not mine though. We weren't allowed to take pictures.*

"I brought something with me today I thought you'd be interested in. Remember, your friend wrote *Bomber Crew*?"

Tommy's book. "Yeah," he said. "Tommy."

Karen handed her father the thin volume. Jack accepted the book carefully into both hands. He concentrated on the cover, the photograph of a World War II aircrew.

"*Bomber Crew*," he eventually said. "I like that."

"You remember you flew from the same base in Lincolnshire?"

"Of course, I remember. I'm not stupid," he snapped.

"Dad, there's no reason to be angry."

"Sometimes you don't know what you're talking about."

"That's certainly possible. Would you like me to read some, Dad?"

Jack gazed at the small bookcase beside his bed. *I used to read all the time.* He looked back to Karen, then realized she was expecting a reply. "Yes," he said. "Reading would be nice."

Karen paged through the book until she discovered a bookmark. "Here's a spot you've marked. Chapter 11 …

> Our flying experience while on operations was not all grim. In fact, we had some very interesting and pleasant times mixed into the more serious aspects. Probably the most rewarding part of any flight was when we came in sight of Wickenby, our base, once again. In daylight, we could see the magnificent towers of the ancient Lincoln Cathedral, high on a hill in the City of Lincoln, just ten miles from Wickenby. The cathedral was a comforting

and reassuring landmark, a reminder that we had come home unscathed from another sortie against the enemy …

Karen continued to read but Jack's mind remained with Lincoln Cathedral. *Not just daytime,* he thought. *We saw the twin … things … um, things … oh for crying out loud … Can't get to Mick. Bleeding to death. Trapped.*

Karen stopped when she realized her father's attention was not on the words she was reading.

"You want me to get you some tea, Dad?"

A cuppa, Jack thought. "Yes, my dear. That would be nice."

9

APRIL 1942 – MANNING DEPOT, EDMONTON, ALBERTA

The initial weeks of basic training left Shelagh wondering why she'd been so excited to enlist. Her sisters both spoke confidently of her using her business and clerical skills, that they'd be in demand. Instead she learned to march.

"Can anyone here type?" the drill sergeant finally asked at one morning parade. None of the women so much as flinched. During their first three weeks training, they had clearly learned not to move when standing at attention, that push-ups would be ordered to punish even minor transgressions of deportment.

"Stand easy," the instructor said. "I asked a simple question. Can anyone type?"

About two dozen hands stretched into the air. "More than twenty words a minute?" Most of the raised arms dropped. Shelagh was surprised when she was one of only three who kept their arms extended. And even more surprised to see Pamela was one of the three. *Pamela is such a know-it-all snob,* she thought. *She's upper class. High society. I can't believe she's a typist.* She wasn't surprised by Lillian, a woman capable of performing any task thrown at her.

"You three come with me," the sergeant said. "The rest of you are dismissed."

▪ ▪ ▪

The three women were introduced into the administrative and clerical milieu. Trial by fire – immediately initiated into the policies and procedures necessary to run the base office – typing daily orders, procurement requisitions, assignment and training schedules.

On the second day, Captain MacAndrew, the staff officer, designated Pamela in charge of the six-person office. "Please join me in congratulating Leading Aircraftwoman Burroughs," he said.

I haven't even seen her type, Shelagh thought.

The captain was still speaking. "She will communicate daily duty assignments and keep this office ship-shape." MacAndrew laughed. "Perhaps, we should use our own Air Force terminology but you lasses know what I'm saying."

Captain reminds me of my dad before he died, Shelagh thought. *About the same age. Fifty-five, maybe.*

▪ ▪ ▪

"Pearson, Captain wants you to do a typing test." Pamela proffered a handwritten page toward Shelagh but pulled it back before Shelagh could touch it.

"My typing's been tested every which way. I passed every time with flying colours."

"Oh, Pearson, you know ours is not to reason why."

"You're right. I'd rather do than die."

The two women laughed at their repartee. Shelagh was beginning to hold Leading Aircraftwoman Burroughs in higher regard than she had initially. *She treats us women with more respect than the others do,* she thought. *Certainly better than the drill sergeant or the officers. Captain's okay though.*

"So, the test," Pamela said. "I'm to administer it immediately."

"Sounds like a medicine."

"Serious now, Pearson. You have two minutes to look at this page and five minutes to type everything on the page as is. Don't correct anything or change spelling. Okay?"

"Got it, ma'am."

"Sit at this typewriter and let's get started."

Shelagh pointed at another desk across the room. "That's the one I'm familiar with."

"Sit here and let's go." Pamela handed Shelagh the paper.

Shelagh looked at what was written. *This is gibberish. What's the point?* But she had done well in every typing challenge in school and since enlisting. She enjoyed what she'd come to regard as a contest.

"Start typing now."

Shelagh finished well ahead of the five-minute time limit, rolled the paper out of the typewriter and handed it to the hovering Pamela.

"How'd I do?"

Pamela shook her head. "Captain will mark this one."

"Mark a typing test?"

Pamela walked toward the Captain's office. When she returned a few minutes later she said, "Pearson, report to Captain MacAndrew *tout de suite*."

▪ ▪ ▪

Shelagh saluted. "Aircraftwoman Pearson reporting, sir."

"Ah, Pearson. Stand easy. I'm working on placement orders. It seems you may have an aptitude to serve in the M."

"The what, sir?"

"Meteorological service. Weather, you know."

"You could tell that from the typing test, sir?"

"Decisions are not made that lightly, Pearson. You are posted immediately to RCAF Station Uplands in Ottawa. You will be trained to become a weather observer. You leave Friday. Burroughs will handle the details. That's all, Pearson."

"Friday sir? Day after tomorrow?"

"You're dismissed, Pearson."

Shelagh saluted then turned to leave the office.

"And Pearson," Captain MacAndrew said. "Good luck."

10

MARCH 2006 – *LA MAISON ENSOLEILLÉE*

Roberto knocked softly then stepped just far enough into the room to glance around the edge of the door toward Jack.

"Just checking on Jack," he said to the guy sitting in the bedside chair. Seeing Jack was asleep, he was about to leave but looked back. He decided to introduce himself. "Roberto Gervais," he said. "I know you from somewhere."

"Jeremy Goode. I recognize you from the graduate student lounge."

"Yeah, of course. You're the one they call Goody."

"Some do." Jeremy rose from his chair and extended his hand toward Roberto. "But I prefer Jeremy." Roberto stepped further into the room to shake hands.

"So, Jack's your …?"

"Grandfather."

"Dr. Borden's your mother?"

"No, no. My aunt. Aunt Karen."

"I always enjoy talking with him. He's an interesting man. "

"Yeah, me too. But he doesn't even recognize me today." When Jeremy had walked into Jack's room, Jack seemed confused, frowned at Jeremy. "Whadda you want," he'd said before Jeremy could greet him.

"It's me, Grandpa … Jeremy."

"Oh." Jack had turned his back to Jeremy and fallen back to sleep.

"That's tough," Roberto said when Jeremy described what had happened.

Jeremy shrugged. "I guess that's the way it goes. *C'est la vie.*"

Roberto nodded. "Shame it has to be that way."

"Aren't you in a PhD program? How do you have time to work here?

"I work as an orderly a few hours a day. It's a break. It's a few bucks in my pocket. Besides it's basically my field," Roberto said.

"Sorry?"

"I'm in behavioural neuroscience."

"That's heavy."

"Well, more the behavioural end. I never had a science background so it's a struggle."

Jeremy looked at him. "Are you collecting data here?"

"No, no. Can't do that," Roberto replied. "Ethics. Can't use a captive population. Lots of residents can't understand enough to give informed consent. The dementia patients. The ones I'm fascinated by."

Jeremy nodded, understanding.

"I use my time here to kind of verify to myself that my projects aren't way off base."

"I'm in biotechnology myself. Science is my field."

Roberto turned back toward the door. "Good to talk with you but I'd better carry on." He paused and pulled a card from his pocket. "All my contact information's here." He gestured toward Jack. "I hope Jack knows you when he wakes up. You know, maybe it doesn't have to be this way. There's a large body of research out there …"

II

MAY 1942 – RCAF STATION UPLANDS, OTTAWA

Vancouver BC
May 14, 1942

Dear Shelagh:

I'm so pleased you've been able to meet Bob for dinner. I presume he told you about the house he's arranged off-base for us. I'll be moving to Ottawa next week. I'm excited to join Bob, although I know he's terribly busy. Gareth can't stop talking about being with his father. I suppose I shouldn't have told him this far in advance of the move. But I think he could feel my excitement.

I offered to stay until the end of the school year but the principal said they would find a substitute teacher for the remaining weeks.

I know you are probably very busy with your training. Imagine, weather observer. You always did seem to have your head in the clouds. Just joking! Mother sends her love.

Sincerely, Elspeth

Shelagh was elated to hear from her sister and welcomed the prospect of living in the same city as Elspeth and Bob. She had met Bob twice for dinner since arriving in Ottawa. The first time he sent his driver to pick her up.

"I'll take you to Colonel Stewart now, ma'am," the driver, an Army sergeant, said.

Ma'am, Shelagh thought. *This is awkward. He outranks me.* "Thank you, Sergeant," she said. She sensed him appraising her. *He thinks this is a … a tryst.*

"The colonel is my brother-in-law."

"Whatever you say, ma'am." Embarrassed, the sergeant turned his head away from Shelagh and didn't meet her eyes.

The driver delivered her to Central Ordinance Depot near Somerset Street, close to downtown Ottawa. Although Shelagh was pleased with her posting to the nation's capital, she hadn't realized Uplands was both far from downtown and not easily accessible.

Bob Stewart was waiting for her. Shelagh wondered whether she should salute. He is a colonel, she thought. So she did. "Colonel. Wonderful to see you."

Bob smiled. "Hello, Shelagh. It's wonderful to see you too. Come here." He hugged her rather than return her salute. "I'm still Bob. But thank you for being formal in front of Sergeant Meadows. We're going to the Officers' Mess for dinner."

Shelagh didn't respond.

"C'mon kid," Bob said. "Forget the uniform. It's me. You'll see plenty of these uniforms tonight. How's the weather business?"

"Fine, sir."

Bob glared at her then laughed.

"I'm sorry, Bob. I feel uncomfortable." Back home her brother-in-law was always easy to be with. This was their first encounter since she enlisted.

"It's okay, Shelagh. We'll get through dinner just fine."

12

APRIL 2006 – *LA MAISON ENSOLEILLÉE*

Jeremy pedalled effortlessly across the bridge that spanned the Rideau River and on toward the six-storey red brick building. A great spring day, warm, not hot. Ideal after a brutal Ottawa winter. This afternoon it was good to be back on the bike.

He cut the wrong way across the traffic circle to turn into the driveway and immediately noticed a man kneeling on one knee near the rock garden at the base of the entrance sign. When he realized the man was Roberto, he dismounted and walked his bike over.

"Hey, Roberto." Jeremy realised Roberto had two cameras slung around his neck and seemed to be studying the flowers bed.

Roberto looked up. "Hi … uh … Jeremy, isn't it?"

"Right." Jeremy used his foot to engage his bike stand. "What's up?"

"Just taking a few shots." Roberto pointed to the display of daffodils. "These ones won't last more than a couple more days."

"It's been a long winter," Jeremy said. "It's good to see colour."

"Me, I like those ones." Roberto pointed to the double daffodils, brilliantly yellow, each with its deep gold trumpet corona. "It's a shame but they're going to droop and brown-up soon."

"Both those cameras digital?"

"No." Roberto showed Jeremy the one with the long lens. "This one's film."

"Yeah, I recognize the Nikon," Jeremy said. "My grandma was a photographer. She gave me her last camera – Nikon F-601. It'd be older than yours."

"Would that be Jack's wife?"

"Yeah, Shelagh. She taught me a lot about photography."

Roberto lowered himself until his elbows rested on the ground, supporting his camera like a tripod.

"Grandma was a professional. Shelagh Pearson. Kept her maiden name." Jeremy wasn't sure why he was telling Roberto this. Except that he had seen how Roberto seemed to have developed rapport with his grandpa so he continued, "She didn't even like us kids calling her Grandma."

"Really? That's not like my grandma at all." Roberto shifted around and stood again, brushed soil from his pants.

"She was very definite. She did not do weddings or portraits. Nature, landscapes, that was her. Anywhere she could tramp around. She was great – used to take me hiking." Jeremy laughed. "She taught me to find art in minutiae."

"Feel like grabbing a beer later?"

"I was planning to go back to the lab." Jeremy shrugged his shoulders. "Beer sounds better."

"I'm working here 'til about eight," Roberto said.

"You know the pizza place at Cobourg and Rideau?"

"Yeah, I know where it is. Why don't I text you when I get off?"

"I'll visit Grandpa awhile now. Meet you there," Jeremy said. Then he pointed to the sign and grinned. *La maison ensoleillée*. "Funny thing. One of the residents was talking to my grandpa yesterday and he called the home *La maison du soleil levant*." Both men laughed. The House of the Rising Sun.

13

NOVEMBER 11, 2001 – CHURCH HILL, ONTARIO

"Jeremy," Shelagh called upstairs to her grandson. "You're going to be late."

Jeremy surprised her by appearing at his bedroom doorway almost immediately, fully dressed, not his usual early morning dishevelled self. "It's okay, Grandma," he called down to her. "I'm not going anywhere today."

"Oh."

"Remembrance Day," he said.

"Oh, of course," Shelagh said. "You have it off?"

Jeremy shrugged. He came out of his room onto the loft balcony overlooking the lower part of the house. He could see it had snowed overnight with an accumulation that looked significant.

Shelagh joined him. "So you want breakfast?"

Jeremy hesitated. Not normally a breakfast eater, however the idea of a relaxed start to the day appealed to him. "Mmm breakfast. Maybe. Do you usually do something for Remembrance Day?"

"Nothing special," she said. "But I was thinking I might phone your grandfather."

Jeremy was stunned. *They don't even live together.* He was curious but didn't feel it his place to ask. He knew his grandfather had never visited this house in the two years or so since his mother bought it. He'd wait until he could ask his mom when she came home from Kosovo. *Kosova,* she said. Call places by the names the people living there use.

"I'm going to take my camera and head into the bush while the snow's still untracked," Shelagh said. "Care to join me?"

He'd accompanied her once before while she looked for osprey nests to photograph. It had been late August, very much still summer.

"I want to find a nest that's not on a hydro pole," she'd said. "Maybe we can get close enough to see into the nest."

"There won't be any chicks this late in the year."

"I realize that. I want to scope out something for next year. Maybe there's even a cliff face overlooking a nest."

Sure, Jeremy thought, *a cliff face. Grandma's going to start rock climbing.*

"We'd be looking for something different, out of the ordinary," Shelagh said. "Something unique. I'm always looking for that."

Jeremy was a purely academic student, studying maths and sciences at his high school. He felt out of his league when someone wanted to discuss the arts. Yet, there was something intriguing in Shelagh's compositions – rocks, clouds and water, all black and white, all unusually textured. *She wants something unique,* he thought. *I know just the spot.*

As they drove about ten kilometres south inland, away from the Ottawa River, Shelagh talked about the work of a British photographer. "Fay Godwin, she's about ten years younger than me, but she has many of the same interests. Her portraits – did I tell you I went to Ottawa to try to get a job doing portraits? But I got hired because of my landscapes. Anyway, I was just looking at one of her books. Black and white landscapes. I like her work but sometimes the images are too stark. I like to soften my rocks with clouds. I can't think of what you call that right now but I'll show you at home."

"We're here. That's where we start." Jeremy pulled into the small but empty parking area. He pointed out the large green sign at the end of the lot that described the area as part of a nature conservancy. "My friend Daniel and I were out here last winter. This is part of the local snowmobile trail system trail. We came here with his sled. That's the first time we saw the nest I'm going to show you."

Shelagh looked back to the sign and noticed the multi-use trail designation. She'd used various forms of transportation to get her into remote photo shoots – four-wheel drive trucks, ATVs and, yes, snowmobiles – but she considered her use strictly transportation. She was sure Jeremy and Daniel had whipped around, on- and off-trail, as boys would.

"It'll be about three kilometres in. You game for that?"

"Fine with me, Jeremy. Lead on." She almost added "Macduff" but wasn't sure today's teenagers would understand the reference.

They tramped along a well beaten trail lined by cedar and spruce trees with a few birches in the mix. Across flat rocks that Jeremy called limestone pavement – flat bare surfaces left by retreating glaciers.

Jeremy pointed. "There," he said. "That old windmill."

As they approached, an adult osprey took off from the huge nest perched on top of the now non-functioning windmill. There was room for a nest because the four-sailed head of the windmill had toppled and was hanging, precariously suspended, held by a piece of pipe caught on the structural cross-beams of the remaining construction.

Shelagh quickly realized there were two large birds, one circling the nest on a short radius, the other soaring much higher and maintaining a much larger circle. She took a few quick shots with her digital camera.

"This gives me a general idea of lighting. I'm looking for shadowing and features I can enhance."

"Should we wait for the birds to come closer?"

"This is really good, Jeremy. I had a concept of being right on top of a nest but, you know, this is terrific. The possibilities are amazing."

"Great!"

"You knew exactly what I was looking for. But we're intimidating the birds. They'll never come close enough with us standing here. I want them to come to the nest like there's no danger."

Shelagh walked toward the bush then came back. "Here's what we'll do," she said. "We'll build a blind."

"A what?"

"We have to drag some of the fallen stuff outta the bush."

Jeremy wished he hadn't worn a T-shirt and shorts but he'd dressed for the August heat. *Even if I'd brought a pair of work gloves,* he thought. But for the next half hour, the two of them hauled fallen branches and small logs from the bush, heaping them high along the side of the path in front of the windmill, supporting the wall with larger branches they pulled out along with the smaller boughs. All the while, they could hear the high-pitched whistling calls of the osprey. Then the series of chirps rising and falling in intensity as they voiced their displeasure with intruders so close to their nest. At one point Shelagh ducked behind the brush pile and sighted the nest through a square frame she made with her fingers.

"No, this isn't right."

"Looks good to me. Good place to hide."

"We'll have to move the pile just over here to the right."

"Okay." He already knew she was a perfectionist.

Twenty minutes later it was rebuilt. Then Shelagh sighted through her fingers once again.

"Perfect," she said. "Tomorrow I'll bring my real camera and tripod."

"I'll be in school tomorrow." He'd been enjoying this, intrigued to see his grandma at work. He knew she was almost eighty years old yet she tramped along overgrown trails with single-minded purpose.

Shelagh hadn't realized how invested Jeremy was in her project.

"Will you use a big lens?" he asked.

"My four hundred millimetre." Shelagh looked at him. "Were you smirking when I said real camera?"

Jeremy raised his arms as if in self-defence. "I know your opinion of digital cameras."

"They're good for what I told you – lighting, texture. There's a long way to go before they can compete with film."

"Mom uses one in Kosova."

"Your mother's not a photographer. Hers is fine for snapshots. I'm told a seven-megapixel camera is equivalent to 35 mm. I don't see it. They'll need something better than that before I'm convinced."

. . .

Remembering their previous outing, Jeremy stood in the kitchen, looking out the window and surveying the mid-November snowfall. "Yeah," he said. "I'd like to come with you."

Shelagh was pleased. "You'll need your boots."

In the field back of the house, they soon stopped. Shelagh dropped to one knee, brought her camera to her eye in front of a small evergreen sticking about half a metre out of the snow, its crown covered in fluffy snow. "Look at this," she said.

Jeremy knelt beside her to grasp what his grandmother had seen – the snow on the crown diffused the bright morning sunlight backlighting the tree. The effect was a halo. *I would have walked right by it*, Jeremy thought. *Probably trampled it had I been on a snowmobile.*

"Scotch pine. See how the needles are in bundles of two." Shelagh moved the palm of her hand up and down in front of the tree. "It's a fully decorated Christmas tree," she said. He saw what she meant – the feathery effect of the snow garlanding the branches. And that light effect on top like a star.

Jeremy nodded, newly appreciative of his grandmother's genius.

"You know what, Jeremy? That's going to be my Christmas card."

14

APRIL 2006 – OTTAWA

Roberto Gervais
Message
Fri, 8:13 PM

Done work. Leaving now. CU at pizza joint

When Jeremy walked into the restaurant and looked around, he assumed he'd arrived first until he realized Roberto was sitting in a far corner booth. *Funny to see someone out of context,* he thought. *We've really only exchanged a few words in Grandpa's room.*

Roberto was looking down but glanced up as Jeremy approached his table. Jeremy realized he was texting.

Roberto nodded in greeting. "*Ça va?*"

"*Bien, merci. Très bien.* Good to see you." Jeremy eased into the booth facing Roberto.

Roberto lifted his phone toward Jeremy. "One of the first-year students doesn't understand his assignment. Due tomorrow, of course." He laughed and waggled his head in disapproval. "Just give me a minute."

Jeremy raised his hands in a Gallic shrug. "Must be a keener," he said. "It's only eight o'clock, not midnight." He looked around the restaurant. Not busy tonight. Only one table occupied. A man and woman had several empty beer mugs but no food plates in front of them. *Those two must be regulars. They've been here every time I've been here.* He nodded acknowledgement when the man looked over and made eye contact with him. Jeremy was amused. *He probably has me pegged as a regular too.*

Roberto replaced his phone on his belt. They ordered beer. The waiter brought two dripping pints of Beau's Lug Tread Ale, drawn perfectly, crowned with a thick head of foam.

"Cheers."

"*Santé.*"

They clanked their mugs together. Each drank deeply.

"Maybe we should order pizza."

"What's good?" Roberto asked.

"I like the Mediterranean." Jeremy pointed it out on the menu. "Zorba the Greek."

Roberto read the description aloud. "Sounds good but I prefer traditional crust. Thin crust is not real pizza."

"My thought exactly. We could go cheap and share."

"We could arm wrestle for the leftovers if there are any."

"Or we could bet on the game." Jeremy inclined his forehead toward the TV in the bar area. The Leafs were playing the Senators. "Who do you like?"

"Neither."

They both laughed.

"Not a hockey fan?"

"Not those teams," Roberto said. "My team's Edmonton. I grew up in Yellowknife. "

"French? From Yellowknife?"

"I'm Métis."

"Métis! I didn't realize there'd be Métis in Yellowknife."

"My God, Jeremy, who'd you think lives in the Territories?"

"I just didn't know. I've never been north."

"Well, it's my heritage. But me, I grew up in town."

The ice broken, they sat in easy conversation, each ordering another beer. They hit upon areas of mutual interest like cycling and skiing, talked about how they liked the Ottawa specialty sports shops.

"I got a clearance special on parabolic skis after Christmas. Last year's model," Jeremy said. "I used to wear racing skis. The new short ones took getting used to."

"You have time to ski?"

"Not really but it's what I do. I've skied since before I could walk."

"Me, I'm more cross-country. There's something about being out in the bush working up a sweat."

"I actually don't get out that much." Jeremy shrugged. "Been to Tremblant twice this winter. With my mother and Tom, my … uh … stepfather."

"Your mother, eh? You know, I had the impression it was just you and your aunt."

Jeremy laughed. "No, no. You see Aunt Karen visiting Grandpa. My mom's working overseas. Kosova."

"What's she do?"

"She and Tom are helping re-establish the public health lab system."

"They're doctors?"

"Microbiologists."

The conversation stopped while the waiter delivered two fresh beers to the table.

"So …" Roberto paused. "What else keeps you busy?"

"I spend a lot of hours in the lab."

"What area?"

"Molecular medicine," Jeremy replied.

"Then you'd know Ben Aziz."

Ben Aziz. Ben Gay. "Sure, he's a fixture in the department. You know him?"

"We used to run for the same track club. Hung around with some of the same people. Still grab coffee occasionally."

Same social circles. Same flamboyant social circles?

The pizza arrived – herbed tomato sauce topped with feta cheese, slices of fresh tomato, green and red peppers, whole Kalamata olives and spinach leaves.

"This looks good," Roberto said. "I'm glad you suggested this place." He glanced around at the nearby tables as if determining whether anyone was within earshot before going on. "Here's a question. Have you ever considered how inefficient food is for delivering nutrients?"

Jeremy stopped eating. *That's what food is. Nutrition.* He knew this must be a joke and waited quietly for the punch line.

"Sorry. You look confused. I'm not talking meat and potatoes. I mean what herbs could deliver as extracts."

When Roberto had looked up double daffodils on-line to have something to talk about tonight, he'd become distracted by the description of illness caused by ingestion of lycorine, an alkaloid poison found in the bulbs and leaves of daffodils and all other members of the Narcissus family and the reference to this compound in Japanese herbal medicine. He was fascinated with the medicinal properties of dilute poisons. What he considered the basis of modern pharmacology.

"I don't know much about that kind of medicine," Jeremy said.

"What's your research?"

"Nanoparticle technology. My niche is preparing uniformly sized testing material. Especially antibodies," Jeremy said. "What was that about herbs and extracts?"

"Take this pizza. I taste oregano. But does it really deliver its medicinal attributes? Any good is likely destroyed when it's baked at such a high temperature."

"You really pay attention to this stuff?"

Roberto shrugged dismissively. "Folk remedies have a basis, you know."

"I'm open-minded but I like to think my basil vinaigrette is just that – a salad dressing."

Roberto ignored Jeremy's quip. "Herbs taken orally. Not efficient. Susceptible to stomach acids. Can't predict effective dosage. Suppose you could deliver the full measure right to the inflamed site?"

"Like an enteric coated capsule?"

"Curcumin in turmeric is useful for a variety of ailments including arthritis."

▪ ▪ ▪

I wonder about Alzheimer's and dementia treatment, Jeremy thought later as he walked toward his apartment on Montreal Road. He'd seen reports but no scientific proof. *Turmeric dissolving amyloid plaques. Roberto didn't talk about that. Maybe even unravelling neurofibrillary tangles. All speculation so far. Anecdotal evidence.* He developed a cadence, evoking synonyms to match his steps. *Subjective. Colloquial. Skewed. Sketchy.* Then abruptly he halted on the bridge over the Rideau, suddenly comprehending his exchange with Roberto differently. *He could be talking about Grandpa.*

15

AUGUST 1942 – RCAF STATION UPLANDS

The sergeant called across the room to catch Shelagh's attention and signalled her to come to her desk. "Pearson, I have a test for you."

Shelagh was becoming uncomfortable with endless testing but after thirteen weeks on base she knew not to express annoyance; she'd come to accept it as part of her training.

"This is a typing test. To see if you can still type up to standard."

Shelagh didn't respond. She wondered why she, probably the best typist on station, seemed to be singled out for testing.

"You haven't typed for weeks since you've been here."

"Oh."

"Two minutes to look at the material, five minutes to type it. Type exactly what you see. Make no corrections."

Same stuff as Edmonton. Handwritten note. Shelagh knew better than to ask for an explanation.

After she was finished, the sergeant told her to remain seated at the typewriter, then left. She returned within minutes. "Pearson, report to Section Officer immediately," she said.

I'm sure I didn't do that badly. She marched quickly to the Section Officer's office. "Aircraftwoman Pearson reporting, ma'am."

"Stand easy, Pearson. Sit." The Section Officer motioned vaguely toward the chair in front of her desk. "Your typing skills have helped identify you."

"Ma'am?"

"Tomorrow morning at 0800 hours you will report to transportation. The driver has orders to deliver you to RCAF Station Rockcliffe. You will be interviewed by Wing Officer Roberts at 0845. You are to tell no one of this."

"Ma'am?"

"You're dismissed, Pearson."

Shelagh jumped up. "Yes, ma'am. Thank you, ma'am."

■ ■ ■

Shelagh did not sleep well that night. She was aware of disciplinary interviews, of women subsequently discharged. But, in the instances she knew of, the rumoured charges were of conduct unbecoming. *Something like that is dealt with on base by the Section Officer,* she thought. She continued to revisit rough patches during her five months in the RCAF. She was certain her work was done well but worried she'd been frequently reprimanded about her rough manner. She wasn't good with interpersonal contact. *Maybe,* she thought, *it's Bob. Maybe I need to explain Bob's my brother-in-law. Somebody must have reported me being picked up by a colonel's driver.*

Jocelyn Roberts was experienced enough to recognize Shelagh's anxiety. "Relax, Aircraftwoman Pearson. This is a job interview not a corrective enquiry."

"Yes, ma'am." Shelagh remained rigidly at attention.

Over the next fifteen minutes, Roberts drew out details of Shelagh's home life, her father's employment and political views before he died, her sisters' jobs and political views. She already seemed to know most of this including that her sister was married to Colonel Bob Stewart. She seemed particularly interested in Shelagh's skills in photography, that she knew her way around a darkroom.

"The driver from Uplands will transport you here Tuesday and Thursday afternoons beginning next week for advanced training."

"Is this about my typing test, Wing Officer? I don't understand."

"It is indeed about your test, Pearson. Your typing is satisfactory."

"Thank you, ma'am."

"You are reassigned for advanced training here at Rockcliffe. When you are not at Rockcliffe, you will continue with Met Service at Uplands. You are to talk to no one about what you do at Rockcliffe under penalty of dishonourable discharge. Is that clear?"

Shelagh was startled. "*Yes*, ma'am."

"Because I know it will be difficult, you may say you are here for advanced meteorological training. Measuring conditions high in the atmosphere. But nothing else."

▪ ▪ ▪

The following Tuesday, Shelagh was assigned to Sergeant Burroughs. When she realized it was Pamela Burroughs approaching, her shoulders tightened. She was afraid her anxiety was visible, being telegraphed to the entire room through her taut expression. How could Pamela be a sergeant so soon after recruitment?

"Pearson," Pamela said. "Sit there for a typing test."

Typing test. What's wrong with my typing?

"Relax, Pearson. You don't know why you're here and that's part of the plan. Today's test is full of codes the enemy uses in their messages. You must score at least ninety-five per cent to continue in this program."

"The enemy uses code in their weather reports?"

"Affirmative. And in every other message they send. Before the test, you must sign the Oath of Secrecy. I am certain Wing Officer told you the penalties for breaking the Official Secrets Act are severe."

Sentenced to death for disclosing a weather report, Shelagh thought. *As if that makes sense.*

▪ ▪ ▪

Indeed, Shelagh's colleagues at Uplands questioned her about her new assignment. They were a small group and had become close-knit learning *weather natter* as Angus George, the self-appointed joker of the group, termed it.

"Well, well, Pearson," Angus said. "First you're picked up by an army driver once a week. Now he's sending for you weekdays as well. Whatever you're doing, keep it up."

Shelagh wished she could learn to control her blush response, so her matter-of-fact answer would be believable. "It's advanced met training at Rockcliffe."

"If that's what you've decided to call it."

"No, I'm serious. I'm training to use newer equipment for weather forecasting."

"What? Like radar or something?"

Shelagh paused before replying. Angus George hit too close to the mark. How could he know Rockcliffe was experimenting with radar weather detection? "Oh, I don't know what it's called. I'm just being trained in advanced techniques."

"*You* get special assignments? Why you?" Angus laughed, his thought that the colonel might be pulling strings remaining unspoken.

▪ ▪ ▪

Her second Tuesday at Rockcliffe, Shelagh was summoned by the Wing Officer.

"Oh, Pearson. Welcome to Code and Cypher."

"Excuse me, Wing Officer?"

"Your new assignment. You will continue with Met Service. That is your cover. That is the cover for the whole group."

"Cover, ma'am?"

"That is the only story you tell. You will continue because you need to stay up to date with meteorology."

"They're already asking questions at Uplands."

"You need to finish training at Uplands to establish the skills of that service. You must always remain qualified. In three months, you will move to Rockcliffe with a new rank."

"Why me, ma'am?"

"You were identified at recruitment. Sergeant Burroughs is our recruiter. That too is top secret."

"Where is Sergeant Burroughs this week, ma'am?"

Wing Officer Roberts looked at her. "Dismissed, Pearson."

16

MAY 2006 – *LA MAISON ENSOLEILLÉE*

Jack looked at the file folder Karen placed on the small desk. "What letters are you talking about?"

"We found them when we were sorting Mom's stuff. Cassie found them. We thought you might like to see them." Karen pushed the folder toward him. "Maybe, they hold good memories." When Jack hesitated, she opened the folder and handed Jack a piece of paper.

RAF Condover
Shrewsbury
Shropshire

"I really like this letterhead," she said. "Would it be standard issue? Or would it be something you had to buy?"

"I don't know … it's a long time ago … I don't remember."

"That's okay, Dad. There's lots I don't remember either."

Jack looked at Karen in apparent disbelief. She accepted the page Jack handed back and began to read aloud:

September 5 1943

Dear Shelley (ha, ha), I sent an aerograph a few days ago but I wanted to say so much more I decided to follow up with a longer letter –

"I never heard you call Mom Shelley. Was that a nickname?"

"I … don't know." Jack shrugged. "Maybe."

"Maybe you were writing to someone else," Karen teased.

"There was no one else."

"Before you met Mom, I mean."

Jack repositioned himself in his chair. "No one else. I can only speak for me." He closed his eyes momentarily as if he needed to peer into his brain to discern whether what he was saying was true.

Karen continued to read the letter. "Here's an interesting part. You talk about bicycling everywhere … You know, I'll be sixty next birthday. Haven't been on a bike in years. You would have been twenty in 1943. *Only* twenty."

"Guess so."

"Should I read more?"

"I'm tired. Time for bed."

Karen laughed. "It's still morning, Dad. And such a beautiful day. Wait until after lunch. You can have a nap after I leave. Let's enjoy our time together."

"Okay."

"There're about seventy letters here. Maybe you'd rather read them yourself when you feel like it. They're sort of personal."

"Yes," he said. "Personal."

■ ■ ■

Next afternoon, Roberto, on his rounds, once again stepped into Jack's room.

"Good afternoon, Jack."

Jack sat on the edge of his bed, fumbling with a sheath of papers. Roberto was about to speak again when Jack handed him several sheets of paper.

"Look at all this, Robbie."

"What is it?"

"They're my memories."

"Like memoirs?"

"My daughter brought them. Karen. She reads them to me."

"Oh, they're letters." Roberto sifted through the pages. "From you to your wife?"

"It's like the only memories I'm allowed – the past. Isn't that a dilly! The past! What other memory is there?"

"I hear you, Jack. What other indeed?"

"Gladys says it's not the far past they worry about. It's the … the close past. That's not the right word, not close." Jack paused. His eyes swept up as if to retrieve the word from the ceiling.

Roberto listened without offering any help. He generally avoided finishing residents' sentences or offering sought-after words. He was pleased to see even the slight improvements he'd observed in Jack.

"It's like not remembering what I had for breakfast," Jack said. "That's not so important. I never ever remembered what I had for breakfast when afternoon rolled around. Nobody ever asked me that before. You think *immediate past* would sound good?"

"Bang on! *Bien, c'est ça.*" Roberto loved to insert a few words of French into his conversations with Jack. He was always delighted to watch Jack's eyes brighten as he raised his eyebrows and smiled in response to phrases barely remembered.

"You could say *recent*," Roberto continued.

"Oh, yes, recent past. Thanks, Robbie."

"Well, I need to get back to work now. Before I go, here's your secret potion." Roberto handed him a yellow capsule that Jack swallowed with a sip of water. "See you tomorrow, Jack. *À bientôt.*"

Jack nodded goodbye, wanting to but not confident enough to offer *au revoir*.

. . .

Jack held the pile of papers on his lap. *Karen brought these letters,* he thought. *She said effects. Shelagh is dead. That's what effects means. I thought it was another bad dream. I should remember.*

They're written both sides. There's quite a pile here. I called her Shelley. Maybe I didn't hear with the noise in the rec hall. Maybe I thought everyone was calling her Shelley. Maybe the women all had those, uh, damn it … that other way to call them. I was never Iain or Jack with the crew, always Bords or Bordsie. Doesn't even make sense. Jack all my life. Should have been nickname enough. Ah, nickname, there's the word. Oatmeal, I had oatmeal for breakfast.

Halifax. Waiting to ship overseas. Getting ready to embark – I remember that word. To England. Always said overseas, never England or Britain. Like code – maybe unlucky to name the place. Went over on the Queen Mary. Must've been thousands on the same ship. But Halifax, that's where we … we started, no, not started … Damn it! We met in Halifax. Met, that's it. Saw her at the dance, Wednesday night. Don't remember the date. And then the next night I saw her again. We had three for bridge.

We were all waiting. Hurry up and wait. I think that's all we did. Not training, just lingering. Waiting to go to war. Shelagh was in uniform too. The Women's Division, the WD. Waiting too. We didn't always care about names. We were being shipped out soon, maybe we would never meet again.

17

AUGUST 1943 – HALIFAX

A few days after the bridge game, Jack watched Shelagh walking toward him on South Street. She hadn't noticed him yet. She'd been coy about her RCAF duties but Jack knew she was attached to Y Depot and lived in the Gorsebrook Barracks. When he had nothing assigned, he hung around the area, sometimes strolling the short distance between the barracks and Eastern Air Command headquarters. Sometimes smoking a cigarette on the bench outside the tobacconist's. Always hoping he might bump into her.

"Well, hello again, Sergeant," she said when she saw him. "You seem to have discovered where I work. But don't ask me what I do. I'm not going to tell you. Don't you badger me." She laughed. "Security, you know. As if the Germans want to know what I do."

"Don't worry, they'd need to use torture before they'd get anything out of me. Besides, you already know what I do."

"Well … you seem very proud of the wings on your chest. Obviously, you're a pilot. And you're waiting to go."

"How about we hike up to Citadel Hill? If you've got time, that is," Jack said.

"All right."

They walked toward Barrington Street until Jack grabbed her hand and pulled her toward a cobblestone street. "Let's get some local colour," he said. "This looks more interesting."

Shelagh slowly drew her hand away, glancing around to see whether they were observed. She self-consciously brushed her uniform tunic.

From Sackville Street, they entered the long road toward the Citadel structure expecting they might be rebuffed at any point. Shelagh had mentioned this was the city's anti-aircraft defence headquarters. When Jack asked how she knew that, she said the gunnery always needed up-to-date weather forecasts.

An army guard barred them from accessing the Citadel buildings. So, they were content to follow the perimeter of the old fortifications around to the easternmost point. They climbed onto a parapet to view the lower city and the harbour.

"That's Bedford Basin." Jack leaned toward Shelagh to show her where he was pointing. When she didn't pull away from his touch, he grasped both her shoulders, gently turning her to face him. She leaned into his embrace and kissed his cheek and then his lips.

"I'd like to get to know you better, Shelley." Jack kissed her again.

"Really?"

"Absolutely."

"Okay. Start with this. I'm Shelagh." She laughed and pulled back to look at him. Then laughed again at Jack's crestfallen face. Then she leaned in to kiss him again, tenderly inserting her tongue into his mouth and running the tip of it across his teeth.

18

MAY 2006 – *LA MAISON ENSOLEILLÉE*

"This letter has pages missing. It starts in the middle. Christmas Eve 1943." Karen showed her dad the letter. Jack nodded.

> When we catch up with each other, we'll be able to make plans. Tonight we have to fly, even if it's Christmas Eve. Tomorrow our Christmas dinner is at two p.m. It all sounds okay but what I wouldn't give to be eating with you! At least I know I'll be seeing you soon, darling.

"This could be the first letter. I should have paid more attention to the dates when I sorted them." Karen held up the flimsy sheet of faded blue paper. "Here you mention bread and gooseberry jam for a midnight snack."

Gooseberry jam! Such good gooseberry jam! I call her Shelagh here. Maybe Shelley was a nickname or a joke. Not crazy after all. Everybody still uses nicknames. Me, too. Don't need to worry about a faux pas sixty years ago. That's it, isn't it? The old mind recycles this stuff, worries it to death until you believe it's gospel.

"Do the letters bring back memories, Dad?"

You've only read me three. And two had bits missing. But here we are another day. The sun's shining. I feel good. "They bring back memories, I'm not sure good or bad, yet." *Where's the other one? The other girl. Oh, you can't say girl anymore. It's woman, Shelagh says. Where's the other woman. That's funny, the other woman. My daughter, Karen's sister.*

"Where's your sister?" Jack asked, proud of his ploy.

"Cassie's back in Kosova again." Karen sat on the edge of the bed immediately next to Jack's chair. "You remember, she's helping set up a lab."

Cassie, that's it, Cassandra the scientist, always busy. They both are. Cassandra the scientist, Karen the doctor. They're good daughters.

"You do remember Cassie's in Kosova?"

Jack replied abruptly, "Of course, I remember. What's she doing there?" He paused a moment then asked, "Is it dangerous?"

"I think it's quite safe now, especially where Cassie and Tom live."

Good. My daughters don't need to be in danger. We fought the war for them. So the world would be better. So they wouldn't need to fight. We gave up years of our own lives so they could be free. Cassie brought gooseberry jam back from Newfoundland. We hadn't tasted it for all those years. Who's Tom?

...

After Karen left, Jack sat awhile in his occasional chair, in the dappled afternoon sunlight, just thinking, reflecting, remembering. *Always dances and entertainment in the small towns and cities near the base. Kept us busy so we wouldn't have time to get into trouble. Was there a bus into town? Did we walk? I hope Karen doesn't ask. Questions, questions that one. How did you do this? It was so long ago. We were young. As if I could remember. Who ever worries about anything when they're young? We were training. Lectures, always lectures. All day. Like going to school. I quit school to join. Still like school, like going to college.*

Sounds from the corridor – shuffling gaits and tapping canes of his fellow inmates, as he called them, the click-click of the medicine trolley, the constant PA announcements of activities he wasn't interested in – didn't intrude on his thoughts. Except when Amy checked on him and brought a fresh glass and water pitcher. Pitcher, he thought. *Isn't it funny how many still mispronounce picture as pitcher? Wish I had some pictures, PIC-TURES. Not those ones. Ones from the base, my buddies, my crew. But they didn't let us, they didn't want us to take ... photos. Afraid we'd send them somewhere in a letter.*

19

JANUARY 1944 – YORKSHIRE, ENGLAND

Wally interrupted Jack's letter writing. "Hi-de-ho, Bordsie! You still writing to Shelagh or is this a new one?" He pointed at Jack's blue Air Mail writing pad.

"Where've you been, Stanhope? Haven't seen you since Friday," Jack said.

"I'm sworn to secrecy. Can't say what I've been doing." Wally grinned. "Tell you what, buy me a pint tonight and I'll spill the beans."

"Too high a price. It's not that important to me."

"All right, you win. We were over to Hixon. Flew over late afternoon. Dropped in for dins but stayed overnight."

"We're flying over there today."

"By the by, tell Shelagh I'll be up to Allerton Saturday and I'll look in on her. Ask her to say hello to Lorraine."

"How do you know Mac?"

"Mac?" Wally scrunched his forehead.

"Lorraine Macdonald."

"Oh yeah, Lorraine – the brunette."

Jack threw a crumpled piece of paper at Wally. "You're incorrigible," he said.

Wally feigned ducking away from the projectile. "Incorrigible, me?" he laughed. "Well maybe I'm not so good with names. But I sure like a girl in uniform. Mmm … that Lorraine. Lo-raine, sweet Lo-raine."

"You must have something better to do than hang around bugging me."

Wally wandered away singing, "When I met my sweet Lorraine, Lorraine, Lo-raine …"

20

JUNE 2006 – *LA MAISON ENSOLEILLÉE*

"Wally was my best friend at the time. From Saskatchewan. We did lots together – pub nights, movies. Gee, we had good movies."

"When Wally used to come to the house, sometimes Bill came with him. What was Bill's last name, Dad?" Karen asked.

Questions, questions! Do ye ken John Peel, with his coat so gay? "Are you testing me, Karen? Of course I know. Bill Burgess, just like Diefenbaker. From Saskatchewan, I mean. Dief the Chief cancelled the Avro Arrow."

"It's not a test. I remember hearing Bill's name a lot. I don't remember hearing a surname."

"Oh, he was no sir –"

"That's funny, Dad. That's what you've always said about Wally, too."

"Then didn't he just build the Diefenbunker? Right near Ottawa. If he kept the Arrow, he'd not be needing a bunker. Shoot bombers right out of the sky. We designed them to do that. Do you remember the cottage?"

"The one on Georgian Bay or the one on Stoney Lake?"

"Damn it, Shelagh. Don't confuse me." Jack paused, his eyes opened wide in panic. *I called her Shelagh.*

"Sorry, Dad, just asking," Karen said, ignoring his discomfort. "I remember two cottages. But yes, Huckleberry Island."

"Georgian Bay. Yeah, that island. We lived in Nobel. Diefenbaker screwed that up. Closed the factory. There was nothing in the area for us after Orenda Engines shut down."

"But we kept the cottage."

"Your mother liked it. But she thought it was too far to drive."

"It wasn't that far from Sudbury."

"I never lived in Sudbury."

21

AUGUST 1956 – HUCKLEBERRY ISLAND, GEORGIAN BAY

"Tell me honestly, Jack, is this job really you?" Leon Buck asked.

"Honestly?"

"Yeah."

"It's formulaic, if you know what I mean." Jack walked over to the window, gazed across the water toward Elizabeth Island and the mainland just beyond. "But at least I get to live around here. It doesn't get any better than that." He looked back at Leon. "There's certainly no room for style or creativity. But as someone once said, writing is writing."

"Yeah but what do you actually write?"

"I create step-by-step instructions so any dolt on the assembly floor can follow the directions. I can't say I like it much but it's a job that needs to be done. And, you know Leon, it pays the bills better than the *Star* did."

Leon waggled his head as if weighing options. He paused before he spoke again. "Actually Jack, I'm quitting the *Star*. Heading back to Halifax. There's a job for me at the *Chronicle-Herald*."

"So back home you go."

"I like Toronto fine but I miss Halifax – the smell of the sea air. I put in seven years. I've only been home when editorial needs somebody to give a real east coast take on a story."

Karen and Cassandra entered the cottage running. Shelagh followed close behind and caught the screen door before it slammed.

"Daddy, Daddy." Cassandra, wrapped in a towel, came directly to Jack. He lifted her onto his knee. "There was a big fish under the dock and he bit me."

Jack looked to Shelagh for confirmation.

"A perch this size." Shelagh indicated about six inches with her hands. "And I think he just nibbled at your toes, Cassie."

Jack unwrapped the towel to expose her feet. "Let's see, Cassie."

"There, Daddy. See my toes are all red."

"We better count them. Make sure they're all still there."

Karen looked at Cassie dismissively. "Boy, is she ever a story teller. It was just a little baby fish."

"Was not."

"Was too."

"Okay girls. That's enough. Uncle Leon doesn't want to hear you fighting," Jack said. "Into the bedroom with you and change out of those wet suits."

"If you're going to be here," Shelagh said to Jack, "I'll show Leon around the point."

"Are you going to change first?"

"No. We won't be too long. And I may want to go back in for a swim. C'mon Leon."

▪ ▪ ▪

Shelagh showed Leon the property lines. She explained how the island had been Crown land, how they'd only paid a dollar a foot to buy the property.

"It was a good buy," she said. "Then we were required to build a cottage as part of the deal. Of course, with Jack working at Orenda and not those cheap newspapers, we could well afford to do all that."

"Jack actually built the cottage?"

Shelagh scoffed. "Jack? Are you kidding? Jack's not the least bit handy."

"Then, you hired a contractor?"

"No, I should be fairer to Jack. He was a go-boy while his friends built. He got their tools, bought the lumber they said they would need. Stuff like that."

"Friends?"

"Three engineers from Orenda – Germans."

"Oh."

"They all built cottages too. On the other side of the island. Jack did joe jobs for them too."

They walked carefully over the glacier-smoothed granite outcroppings. Leon wondered how the majestic windswept white pines could possibly be anchored where there was obviously very little actual soil. Although it certainly wasn't the ocean but looking out at the whitecaps and hearing the waves crash the shoreline, he felt at peace.

22

APRIL 1944 – NEAR SHEFFIELD, ENGLAND

Wally walked into the Nissen hut. He opened the door then knocked as, Jack had come to realize, only Wally would. *Such a formal bearing, he looks really good in uniform. Suave,* Jack thought. *The rest of us look good for parade. Wally looks really good every day.*

"Hey, Bordsie, you flying today?' Wally asked.

"No, I'm off 'til tomorrow." Jack buttoned the shirt he'd just changed into.

"We're taking the bus into Sheffield to catch *Du Barry Was a Lady.* Wanna come?"

"Who's going?"

"Just me and Watsie. It's Red Skelton."

"And the Tommy Dorsey Band. Yeah, I'll go." *I'd go anywhere to see Tommy Dorsey even just on film.* Jack looked at Wally. "Just give me a minute. If I'm going with you I'd better press my pants." Wally gave him a dirty look.

After the movie, the three of them went on to the Baxter Arms. Watson had one beer then headed back to base while Wally and Jack ordered another pint.

"Poor Watsie. Doesn't have a woman in his life," Wally said. "Guess he doesn't want to sit around listening to us."

"Watsie's okay. He's married, you know."

"I just meant he doesn't have a woman over here – a local."

"I know what you mean but if I were married, I'd be the same way."

"Least he could have stayed for one more. How is Shelagh, by the way? I'm sorry I didn't get to see her when she was here."

Jack paused a moment. He'd practiced what he wanted to say, but now he wasn't sure how to phrase it. In the end, he just blurted it out, "I want you to be my best man."

"Serious? You're getting hitched?"

"Yeah. In about three weeks."

"That's great." Wally smiled then paused. He turned his beer mug on the bar. Wiped at some spilled beer. Took a sip. Set the mug down then looked at Jack. "You don't have to, do you?"

Jack laughed. He knew that would be Wally's first thought. "No – but thanks for your concern."

"Just that it's frowned on, you being higher rank and all."

Neither man said anything for a moment. Each seeming to study the rich head drawn perfectly on the draught beer.

Jack raised his mug to take a sip but put it back down. "Truth is Wally, I don't know if it's the right thing to do."

Wally looked at him in surprise. "Whadya mean? You love each other, don't you?"

"Well …" *This is awkward but I need to say it.* "We start flying over Europe soon. At least, I hope so. They don't tell us much, do they?"

"It's so we don't spill the beans in the pub. Like now. They keep telling us walls have ears," Wally said. "What's your concern?"

"We both know lots of crews don't make it back. I don't know if it's fair to Sheils if I don't come back. Maybe a POW. Maybe …"

"I know what you mean but – well … if you love her …" Wally paused.

"Of course, I do."

"Then, maybe that's all that matters. You know, Bordsie, some guys got married at home before they shipped out in case they didn't come back."

23

JUNE 2006 – *LA MAISON ENSOLEILLÉE*

That Shelagh, always the planner. I get tired just thinking about it. Always. Our whole lives. Gotta figure this out. We got married end of April. Be about sixty years, no, sixty-three years now. I miss Shelagh. Don't remember her funeral. Maybe they didn't let me go. Wouldn't miss my wife's funeral …

Jack stood from his chair and walked to his window. He stared toward the river. *Celebration of life, Cassie called it … pictures to look at. They must've let me out – maybe day parole. I didn't know she was sick. The girls didn't say anything. Karen must've thought I couldn't understand. I understand lots. I don't say much sometimes. Like always. Didn't say anything when I had nothing to say. Shelagh understood.*

Jack didn't know how Cassie came up with Shelagh's photo spread of the Burning of the Clavie to display at her celebration of life. But now, he remembered how pleased he'd been with Shelagh's enthusiasm to photograph it. She'd opted to use the Speed Graphic camera she'd borrowed from her base at RAF Lossiemouth. How she'd hugged and kissed Jack when he was able to obtain a 4x5 Kodachrome film pack from a contact at *The Scotsman* in Edinburgh.

Now still at the window, Jack shifted his view to cars coming and going in the parking lot. He thought more about Shelagh's first commercial success, couldn't quite come up with the 1947 date. He could see her standing back from the crowd surrounding the burning clavie, her large press camera at the ready, held securely with one hand on the flash gun bracket and the other on the base, release cable between her index and middle fingers, shutter cocked ready to fire, framing her perfect shot. *That's the camera I used at the Peterborough Examiner*, he thought.

They called her Daisy May on her station. Everybody had a nickname. I could've just been Iain. But, no, my whole life I've been Jack. And now when they try to call me Iain, I don't know who they're talking about. Then they think I'm stupid. That's the name on the chart, they tell me. Shelagh and Karen don't like me to cause trouble. But not Cassie. No … Cassie wasn't even there. She was always working somewhere …

Planning, planning. Shelagh did that. I was flying every day. Still training. How we wanted to get into battle. To get at those Germans.

I had German friends at Orenda. Engineers. During the war, they built V-2 rockets for Hitler. Then they built the Avro Arrow for us. For the good guys. But they were really okay. Nice people. We were good friends. Good thing I didn't bomb them or they wouldn't have built the cottage.

▪ ▪ ▪

"What was your job at Orenda Engines, Dad?" Karen interrupted his thoughts about Shelagh.

"Engineering." Jack answered abruptly, his mind still on Scotland.

"But you weren't an engineer."

"I worked on important plans."

Karen nodded to Jack and raised her eyebrows questioningly in an effort to encourage her father to be more expansive but when he didn't pick up on her prompt she realized he didn't remember anything more. She also recognized how much improved he seemed so she decided not to push him. *The answers are just for my satisfaction, anyway*, she thought.

▪ ▪ ▪

Do ye ken John Peel? Been thinking about it ever since, just spinning through my mind. I can't get the tune out of my head. Can't get my mind offa you. You're too good to be true. I prefer the old big band tunes. Cassandra says that's an earworm. John Peel's coat was it grey or gay? Gay would be a whole different meaning today. Like that Christmas song about gay apparel. Makes no difference to me. Two of my friends were gay. Both dead now. Better relationship than most couples I knew. Don't know if we had gays in the air force. Never thought about it. We were so young, we might have been an intolerant lot. I don't know what would've happened. It was wartime. I wish I could remember my friends' names. The old alphabet search – all the names starting with "A", then "B", then "C". Todd Buchan. That was a day or two ago. Right there in the "B" section. Buchan, Todd. Or was it Buchans. But his nickname? Something funny. Can't think of it.

24

APRIL 1944 – KNARESBOROUGH, YORKSHIRE, ENGLAND

The six women strolled slowly through the peaceful town pausing occasionally to admire flower gardens in full summer splendour. *It's only April,* Shelagh thought. *Vancouver might have a display of blooms this month but only Victoria would have plots looking this wonderful this early.* She looked at the practical interplanting of vegetables among the flowers but quickly realized it was probably just the reverse – a few showy flowers planted amongst the vegetables.

At Margo's suggestion, they went into the Elephant and Castle Hotel for high tea. Margo, their self-appointed leader, sat at the head of the table and accepted her natural role as tea-pourer. The women ate a variety of salads – ham, potato, beet – followed by canned plums with whipped cream for dessert. After tea, Margo read their teacups.

"Look at this, Pearson," she began. "These hills mean many journeys ahead. You're thinking of an overnight to see Jack again, aren't you?"

Although she knew it was all in good fun, Shelagh was embarrassed to be singled out. This was just what her sisters at home would do when she'd imparted too much information about her private life to them. *I'm blushing,* she thought. *My cheeks feel so hot. It must be so obvious.* Shelagh knew Margo wasn't malicious but nonetheless was relieved when Mac became the next tealeaf target.

After tea, they walked down to the river and hired a rowboat. It only held five.

"I'll wait here," Shelagh said. "I really don't mind."

Tammy was also happy to stay behind. "I'm not much for water," she confided as the two of them watched the others depart, content to sit on the bench and wait.

Shelagh crossed her ankles and swung her feet under the bench. "I'm okay with water but we have much nicer boats in Stanley Park."

"This water looks so dirty."

"So, the next bus is at 10:10?"

"Yeah ..."

"That's soon enough. We all need our beauty sleep though, else we'll turn into crows."

Tammy laughed with Shelagh.

After the others returned, they wandered around town looking for a place for a snack. One place they looked at was so crowded they decided not to go in.

A man on the street seemed to sense their hesitation and approached Margo. "If you're looking for a nice cuppa," he said, "my wife has a tearoom around the alleyway. She'll be glad to make you something. We're so pleased you Canadian girls have come to help us."

25

JULY 2006 – *LA MAISON ENSOLEILLÉE*

"Where was Mom stationed?" Karen asked her father.

"Allerton ... they called it Allerton Hall or maybe ... Allerton Castle." Jack looked toward the window. "No. 6 Group Headquarters, Bomber Command."

"I wonder what those places are like now."

"We only went back when your mother was stationed at Lossiemouth. She never wanted to return after that. Not after Cassandra was born."

"Mom often mentioned her aunt –"

"That'd be Aunt Margaret – her mother's sister. When Shelagh visited her, Margaret hadn't seen her own sister for over thirty years. And now she was seeing your mother, her sister's youngest daughter. Even now, you would still have relatives around Edinburgh – your grandmother's family. And your grandfather's family near Newcastle. They'd all be your relatives. I'm sure they would love you to see you if you went."

"Would you like to go?" Karen asked.

"I've got old-timer's, you know. Al's hammer disease. I can't go."

"Alzheimer's."

"I know what I've got."

"You don't have Alzheimer's, Dad. Just some memory loss. You seem much more interested in things now. Maybe you had Jack's boredom disease."

Jack looked at Karen and smiled. "Maybe ..." He paused. "Sometime can you show me how to use the Internet? I want to write letters."

"Sure. I could do that."

"It's because my handwriting is no good. Even I can't read it. That's why I don't write anything. I've got lots of ideas."

...

Technical writer. Karen was right, I wasn't an engineer. Part of the engineering team. They needed someone to put procedure manuals into plain English so the assemblers and other trades could follow instructions. Rob Davies showed me the job ad. Said it would pay better than newspapers. I worked on every detail. Sometimes it seemed I knew more than the engineers. I needed to describe the whole jigsaw puzzle not just individual segments – the specs for the complete aircraft. Should tell Karen. She must wonder about me. But engineering was right. Just didn't remember what I did there. It's been a long time.

Todd the Bucket. Todd Buchans. Gotta be a story there. Could make one up. Shelagh always said I made up words. Specially in French she said.

No, not the complete aircraft. It was the engine. The Iroquois engine. I knew it inside and out. It should still be flying. The old DC-3 is probably still flying. Those De Havilland animals too. Beaver and ...

26

FEBRUARY 20 1959 – NOBEL, ONTARIO

Shelagh leaned across the kitchen table and placed her hand on top of Jack's. "What story are you working on?"

A year or so after he'd started with the Avro Canada subsidiary Orenda Engines, Jack had been approached by the *Sudbury Star* to work as a stringer and occasional reporter for the Parry Sound area. He knew they really only wanted someone they could telephone whenever stories of interest popped up, however infrequently. They offered a small retainer and the promise to pay appropriately for articles that made it to print. Jack began to set a pattern of attending town and township council meetings primarily to acquaint himself with the inner workings of the community and citizens of local import. Before he'd agreed to any of this he approached both the plant manager, Major Woolner, and Hans Stein, senior engineer.

"Any story that even mentions Avro or Orenda must be passed by me and headquarters," Woolner had said. "Two issues here. Industrial security. This is the most sophisticated aircraft in the world. We need to keep our guard up. And national security of course."

"Maybe, I won't bother. Sounds too complicated."

"No, no. I wouldn't say that. Besides, you know –"

Jack frowned. *I'm an Orenda employee but I'm not in PR.*

Woolner didn't finish his thought. Instead he shook his head and said, "If you keep those limits in mind, I don't see a conflict of interest."

. . .

Now Shelagh asked what he was working on. He was about to tell her about the request from Sudbury to interview the family of an eleven-year-old hockey player. To get a photo of him with his family. Some kid named Orr. But before he could complain about being asked to write stories about children, the telephone rang a distinctive two longs and a short. It was for them. Probably the school – a request to drive a forgotten lunch for Karen or Cassandra, most likely Cassandra.

Jack answered since most phone calls were for him – the *Sudbury Star* or even one of the girls who seemed to prefer to make their requests of their father rather than Shelagh.

"Mr. Borden, Jack …" The major's familiar voice. "I can't talk on a party line. We need you at work."

Jack started to object that it was a scheduled day off but stopped when he detected an urgency in Woolner's voice.

. . .

Jack glanced into the engineering department before heading to the plant manager's office. He was startled by the silence and inactivity. Hans Stein was standing with two of the other German engineers. Others sat at their desks either staring at the ceiling or with their heads in their hands. Two were in tears.

"Jack," Woolner said. "I need you to contact your paper to see what they know."

"About what?"

Woolner looked surprised but quickly realised Jack had been at home all morning. "Diefenbaker pulled the plug. Shut down the Arrow program."

Jack's shoulders slumped. "When?"

"Eleven this morning. Effective immediately. We're finished. There's no more work."

Jack looked bewildered. "But it's the best …" He shook his head, sat on the visitor chair, opened and clenched his fists, repeatedly. "What about the offshoot programs?"

"Everything. Everything's finished."

"Did Malton have advanced warning?" Jack was asking about the head offices of Orenda and Avro. He'd switched to reporter mode. He wanted to know who knew.

"Nobody knows anything. It's politics."

. . .

"We want a statement, Jack. Nobody's been answering the phone at Orenda. I finally got through." Jack was speaking with Jerry Ryder, his editor-in-chief, who was calling from Sudbury. "We're getting info from CBC Radio," Ryder said. "Nobody's answering our phone calls. We need a statement from Orenda."

"I'm an Orenda employee, Jerry. I need to avoid a conflict of interest."

"Conflict of interest? Damn it, Jack, you might not even have a job anymore. What's to protect? This is no small town local story. It's a black Friday. It's full-blown national. You're an insider, Jack. We can scoop everybody."

"What did you just say? Black Friday? There's the headline, Jerry – Black Friday."

. . .

"Sheils, I'm out of work." Jack finally said, trying unsuccessfully to keep his exasperation out of his voice. "I've been offered a newspaper job. In Sudbury. The *Star* wants me."

"I won't go, Jackie. I've worked too hard on my Georgian Bay photo exhibit to leave now."

"Sudbury's just an hour and a half up the road. It's all new highway, for goodness sake."

"I don't want to drive."

"Damn it, Sheils, you can come back down here whenever you want. Otherwise, I'm out of work. Can't support our family."

"The studio wants more." Shelagh spread her arms in hopeless appeal. "I need to support my exhibit."

"There is nothing for me here. No job. Nothing. Nothing for me. There's more than two hundred of us out of work."

"Then you go."

"Do you know what you're saying?"

"I like it here. I'm finally working in my own medium. Photo opportunities are endless."

"You don't seem to understand." Jack was immediately annoyed with himself for using the *you don't understand* words.

"Just go ahead and do it if that's what you're going to do." Shelagh remained oddly calm.

"What about the girls?"

27

JULY 2006 - *LA MAISON ENSOLEILLÉE*

Subject: Re: HI!!!
Date: Fri, 26 Jan 2007 03:48 EST
From: cassandra.borden@symplicity.com
To: kg1@softmail.com

Hi K-G. How good to hear your "voice"! Thanks for the update on Dad. I'm glad to hear he's interested in life again. Do these progressive diseases remit? Let me know if Dad ever responds to wanting to visit the UK. Tom and I could fly from Prishtinë to join you. It'd be neat to be with Dad revisiting places like his old airbases. All the best, Sis. Love, Cassie

...

"Your mother liked Wally," Jack said. "She even found him a girlfriend. I don't know why she didn't want him at the wedding. He was my best friend."

"Maybe, she just wanted to keep things simple, Dad. So after the ceremony you wouldn't need to worry about Wally getting back to base," Karen suggested.

"You coulda dropped Wally anywhere in England and he woulda found his way back to base."

Karen didn't say anything.

"Shelagh was looking forward to it. She did all the arrangements. She arranged our whole life."

"What about ..."

"I didn't really mind. Did I tell you this before? I always liked to work. That was a problem sometimes. Originally your mother did more socializing and travelling in the RCAF than I did. After, we went underground like an old married couple."

"I'm surprised you were able to receive letters from Canada by air mail during the war."

"That's what I said in my letter. I wouldn't lie."

"Of course not, Dad. Your letter was written in 1944. You wouldn't be making anything up."

"What about the computer?"

"I have one for you. I've asked Jeremy to teach you to use e-mail."

"Cassie's Jeremy?"

"The same. If you let him show you some things, he'll make it easy for you."

Jack very quickly retorted, "It's okay. We're buddies. Me and Germy."

28

APRIL 1944 – YORKSHIRE

Shelagh displayed a gold wedding band in her palm. "Elspeth sent me the ring. Do you like it?"

"It's great!" Jack reached to pick it up with two fingers.

"You should take it with you. Just don't lose it before the wedding."

"And I'll try not to lose it after the wedding either, Sheils." Jack laughed.

Shelagh scowled at him. "I mean it."

"So do I. You can count on me."

"Sure. I'm glad Elspeth bought it for us. It's just impossible to find good jewellery around here."

"It was very considerate of her. Especially when she hasn't even met me."

"I gave you a good reference."

"Thanks."

Shelagh nodded in reply. "The other night three of us went for a bike ride. The moon was just so great."

"Who went?"

"Hey, it's my story." She punched Jack's shoulder lightly. "Anyway, I wished I was with my man not a bunch of silly girls."

Jack leaned in to kiss her but Shelagh pulled back. "We've got things to talk about. I think I can get enough time off for a proper honeymoon. But if I can't, there are some lovely places around here. I know I can at least get overnight passes easily."

"My C/O gave me a week's leave. I don't see what the problem is with Allerton."

"Things are hopping here." She looked directly at Jack. "I didn't say I couldn't get the time."

"Have you applied for leave?"

"Not yet. But, I still don't think Wally should be your best man. All we need is two witnesses – I could ask a couple of girls from my base."

"Wally's my best friend."

"Then Jackie, if you think he'd be disappointed, by all means, ask him. He'll just be in the way. We'd have to worry about entertaining him."

"My goodness, Shelagh. Wally's a grown man. He can entertain himself. Besides, I want him at our wedding."

"Well. You don't need to get huffy. Just bring him!"

"I will. And you make sure you bring Mac. Then there'll be no need to entertain Wally."

29

JULY 2006 – *LA MAISON ENSOLEILLÉE*

Don't lose the wedding ring before the ceremony. She was like that. I should have seen the signs. Air Force had to decide if we could get married. In the end, it wasn't that hard to get permission. But they wouldn't let us get married in the base chapel at Allerton.

They know what I had for breakfast. Maybe they want to slip me the same breakfast tomorrow. Fine by me. I ate the same breakfast most of my life – toast and peanut butter and coffee. Now they don't want me to have coffee. Guess they don't want me to stay awake. Mind you, I enjoy a good nap. But not as much as I enjoyed a nap with Shelagh. We were such good friends. Just a bit bossy.

I'd like to write something. Maybe I've got nothing to write but I'd like to try. Like when I wrote for the newspaper. Needed two new stories a week.

Otter! That's the other plane. Beaver and Otter!

▪ ▪ ▪

"Look what I found." Karen offered a piece of paper to Jack. "A poem, Dad. But both our names are on it."

Jack examined the handwriting on the piece of lined foolscap. He smiled. "I'd forgotten …" he laughed. *Forgotten indeed. Along with just about everything else.* He looked again at the paper as if feeling its texture. "So, your mother kept it after all."

Karen hesitated before she lied. "Yes," she said.

30

APRIL 1944 – YORKSHIRE

Jack grabbed Shelagh's hand. "There's something important we need to talk about."

Shelagh looked at him quizzically.

"I'm an optimist," he continued, "but, I think you realize, once I'm posted to operations, my name could show up on an official list." *Dying. I'm talking about dying. Just don't want to say the word.*

"You're not trying to back out, are you?"

"No, no, Sheils. Nothing like that. I want to get married straight away, but maybe that's selfish of me. I'm so conflicted."

"I've never seen you this serious. What brought this on?"

"Nothing. I just thought it's something we should be aware of. That's all."

31

AUGUST 2006 – *LA MAISON ENSOLEILLÉE*

I don't remember having that serious talk. About dying. I kind of remember something about official list. Doesn't Cassie call that a euphemism or euthanasia or something?

I was too busy flying to help with wedding plans. Training to fly. Training to fight. Training to move over to heavy bombers. Me, twenty-one years old, pilot. Me, in command.

We didn't have to get married or anything. We worried a couple of times. The padres didn't like Canadian lads having to marry Brit women. They tried to sell you a lot of chatter about different cultures, how tough it was to uproot a woman to live in Canada. They assumed Shelagh was Brit. Surprised them she was Canadian. They always found problems. They caused problems. If there wasn't a problem, they made one up. Always, always.

Shelagh put me in this place. No … not Shelagh, my daughters. After Shelagh died. They call it a home. I want to leave and go back to my real home. No wonder they worry about my memory. Nice kids though, Karen and Cassandra. The doctor and the scientist.

Do I want to go to England, Karen wonders. Maybe, maybe not. It scares the crap out of me. Funny about old people's language. What I hear around here. Shit, piss, fuck. Oh, I know those words. We've had a relationship, me and them. But we never went steady.

Maybe I didn't want to get married. But we did it. I don't remember half the stuff. The letters are real. The letters are proof. Could be I'm just a forgetful old fart. Karen says I don't have Al Heimer's revenge. But I had measles. There was an outbreak. The base was contaminated. Not that … quarantined, that's the word! Cancelled our leaves. Cancelled our training flights. Took longer to qualify for combat. The real war. I thought we'd have to cancel the wedding. Then the outbreak was over and we did it.

▪ ▪ ▪

"Mom often teased you were never sure you were legally married," Karen said.

"I hope so for your sakes. Though it doesn't seem to matter for Jeremy's generation. Jeremy's twenty-four. He's going to teach me e-mail. My grandson. I like the little rat. I flew Lancaster bombers over Germany and was back home again working, long before I was twenty-four."

"So, you couldn't get married on base."

"We found a small chapel in Green Hammerton, a nearby village. Shelagh and Mac walked from Allerton. About five miles, I think. The old minister rode a bike from about twenty miles away. He was bushed by the time he got to the church. He kept losing his place in the ceremony. He stopped and started again so many times. You can imagine us kneeling on those, I don't know, benches. Your mother's knees were trembling anyway. And she was shaking and giggling each time the minister lost his place in the book. That's what she meant about not really being married. We were never sure he actually finished the ceremony."

"That must have been distressing, Dad."

"Not so much. Somebody from the back of the church walked up to the front and said in a loud whisper, 'Consider yourself married.' We accepted that, signed the papers and took off."

Karen stayed with the marriage theme. She was curious why neither of her parents had spoken of that period of their lives.

"Yeah, we got married. Managed a week's leave. Went to Edinburgh for a few days."

"Edinburgh? Why not London?"

"London was more dangerous. Edinburgh was different somehow. Different attitude. Lots of uniforms. Still the war. But different. A more positive feeling."

"Maybe, you were going home again, Dad."

"Scotland?"

"We're of Scottish heritage, aren't we?"

"Our family left the place over a hundred and fifty years ago."

"Maybe you felt more positive because you just got married. Maybe you were thinking of having children."

"That, young lady, is none of your business." Jack straightened the cushion behind his back. He laughed. "And yet, here you are."

32

OCTOBER 1960 – NOBEL, ONTARIO

"I'm doing this for me. It's not about you or your job," Shelagh said. "I want to take portraits. I'm tired of landscapes. I'm going to Ottawa to work with Mr. Karsh."

"Yousuf Karsh?"

"The man himself."

Jack didn't know how to respond. He knew Shelagh was lonely when he spent three days a week in Sudbury. He felt lucky he'd been able to negotiate covering the Parry Sound area for the *Sudbury Star* rather than have them hire a new stringer. That way he was often only away for one night, occasionally two. "Have you been in touch with Mr. Karsh?"

"No, not yet. When I get to Ottawa I'll make an appointment to see him. Or maybe his brother."

"Why do you think either will take you on? Do they take students?"

"I'm hardly a student, Jackie. I'm a professional photographer. I've had shows and sold photographs."

"Locally." Jack stopped there with his comments. He didn't want to provoke an argument but he wished Shelagh would come back to reality. She seemed so enthusiastic, so high on this idea. As far as Jack knew it was out of the blue, completely without foundation. *This will pass,* he thought.

"If Mr. Karsh isn't able to take me on there's always his brother. But surely Mr. Karsh needs an assistant. He's so busy."

"What about the girls?"

"Oh they'll stay with you until I'm established."

"I work in Sudbury." Jack calculated the logistics of continuing to live in Nobel while working in Sudbury, ninety minutes away by car in good weather. Karen and Cassie were both in high school in Parry Sound. Their school bus left just before 8:00 a.m. He could set out for Sudbury once they'd left the house. Their return bus got them home sometime after 4:30 p.m. He knew they were capable of entertaining themselves. They often went to friends' places after school anyway. *It's just,* he thought, *emergencies I need to worry about. The neighbours are good. Like in Burghead.*

...

About a week later, Shelagh asked Jack to drive her to Peterborough. "I can take the train to Ottawa from there."

"When were you thinking?"

"Tomorrow."

"Can't it wait until the weekend when I'm off work?"

"Oh Jackie, time is of the essence. And I already phoned Elspeth to tell her I'd be staying with her. You can visit your mother and the old hometown."

"I'm working. The girls are in school."

"They'd love a day off school. They don't get to see their grandmother very often."

...

Jack took advantage of his few days in Peterborough to drop in on Rob Davies. He asked about contacts at the *Ottawa Citizen.*

"Tired of Sudbury?"

"It's a long story." Jack told Davies about Shelagh's quest to become a portrait photographer. Davies seemed impressed.

"Ottawa's a good town for a woman. My sources tell me Charlotte Whitton is likely to win the next election and become mayor again. If it doesn't work out with the Karshes, there are several woman photographers in Ottawa. Can't think of their names right now but give me a little time."

▪ ▪ ▪

"I miss the girls." Shelagh phoned Jack for the first time after she'd been away three weeks.

"Are you ready to come home?" Jack knew by the excited tone of Shelagh's voice it was probably a stupid question.

"No, oh no. Jackie, I've got a job."

"Yousuf Karsh hired you?"

"I've got a job with the NFB. Oh sorry, we talk initials in Ottawa, National Film Board."

"I know what the NFB is."

"Jackie, I got the job because of my landscape portfolio and because I'm an RCAF veteran. It's so exciting."

"Well yes, Sheils, that is good news." *What'll we do now?* Jack thought. *I didn't realize she'd taken a portfolio with her. She went prepared. The NFB makes sense. That's a good job.*

33

NOVEMBER 1946 – BURGHEAD, SCOTLAND

"What did you two do today?" Shelagh had asked. "It sure wasn't nice enough for your usual jaunts."

Jack grinned. "Karen and I wrote a poem."

"Get out!"

"Yep, a poem. Didn't we Karen?"

Ten-month old Karen sat on the floor playing with her Rosebud doll.

"Here, look at this." Jack offered Shelagh a piece of lined foolscap.

Scones and Such

You may say that's a *lorry*,
Karen thinks it's a truck.

You may call them *tyres*,
They're smooth and round as mine.

You may drive on the left,
We have adapted to that.

And you may call them *scones*
No argument there, if there's jam.

Jack Borden
Karen Gabriella Borden
November 17, 1946

Shelagh asked, "Have you finished the piece for *The Scotsman*?"

"No, but I'll get to it. Maybe as early as tomorrow."

"But you have time for this nonsense." She frowned at the poem in her hand.

"You know, Shelagh, writing is writing."

34

SEPTEMBER 2006 – CASSIE'S HOUSE, CHURCH HILL, ONTARIO

Roberto stared at the modern post-and-beam and log building as Jeremy drove up the laneway. "When you said your mom lived in a log cabin, I guess I pictured something else."

Jeremy shrugged.

"I know about modern log structures, especially in Yellowknife. But I had another image altogether," Roberto said.

Jeremy opened the driver's door, got out, stretched, then leaned back into the car. "Come see the place. Like I said, I check on it when my mother's away."

"Why don't you live here? It looks great and it would be cheap too."

"I don't want an hour's commute. And I prefer my own space. Come on in." Jeremy led Roberto into the house through the back entrance.

"Wow. I love the open concept. So roomy."

"The main floor's about two thousand square feet. Then there's the loft." Jeremy pointed to the balcony above. "Three bedrooms up there."

"Now you've completely destroyed what was left of my notion of a log cabin."

Jeremy laughed. "Sorry about that."

Roberto smiled. "It's wonderful."

They walked through the house, up to the loft, down to the basement, Jeremy pointing out the low energy lighting, the dovetailing of post-and-beam and log construction techniques. "At Christmas time, we usually have a full house," he said. "My Grannie used to come. And, of course,

Aunt Karen and Marianne, my sister. Mom and Tom always come home for about two months around Christmas."

Roberto looked closely at the bookshelves in both corners of the loft balcony. "Lot of books."

"Yeah. Hundreds."

Roberto picked up a few titles. "You didn't mention your grandfather when you were talking about Christmas. He ever come?"

"He's never come to this house. He and my grandma weren't living together. Marianne and I would go see him at his place occasionally."

"Just occasionally? You have a close relationship at *La Maison*."

"He's had … I guess … dementia for a while. He was hard to get along with."

"That's not the Jack I know."

Jeremy suggested they continue the tour outside. Roberto marvelled that the gardens could look so good without regular maintenance.

"Oh, they're hardly untended. A local landscaper looks after things. My mom's big on horticulture. It's mostly perennials. Less continuous care, I guess. And there's an automatic sprinkler system." Jeremy turned a check-valve to ensure the system was operating properly then walked to a small, almost insignificant wooden cover. "Emergency generator." Jeremy pulled the start rope. The motor roared, then quickly settled into four-stroke smoothness. "It starts automatically if the electricity goes out. You probably know all this stuff."

"Like I told you, I'm a townie." He smiled and shook his head. "What would I know of generators?"

"Let's go back inside. There's not much in the way of food but there's a good supply of beer and wine. Tom always buys the best."

▪ ▪ ▪

As Jeremy retrieved frosted beer mugs from the freezer, he found a frozen shepherd's pie they could reheat in the oven for later. They settled into the leather easy-chairs adjacent to the fieldstone fireplace in the well-windowed living room. He suggested they could stay the night if they happened to have more than a couple of beers. Roberto agreed that sounded like a good plan. There were things on Jeremy's mind, including a conversation he wanted to have. Roberto had pushed him to purify the curcumin quickly. He wanted to know why.

"I'm always impressed by the books people choose to display," Roberto said still focussed on the library he'd come across in the loft. "That's quite an eclectic collection. Is that what you grew up with?"

"That's my mom and Tom. My dad tends more toward conspiracy theory. Weird stuff."

35

MAY 1944 – EDINBURGH, SCOTLAND

Shelagh picked her way cautiously along the rocky shore, across and through the large boulders, rounded smooth by centuries of tidal action. She signalled to Jack. "More over here." She bent to pick up one of the seashell souvenirs she sought. So far, her collection consisted mainly of cockle and mussels shells. Although the song was going through her head, she resisted voicing *Molly Malone*. Her prized shell so far was an intact brownish orange scallop shell with hints of red.

Jack made his way slowly to her side. He didn't have the same seashore agility she'd acquired growing up in Vancouver. "You've got a nice collection," he said as he reached for her hand and pulled her around into a hug.

Shelagh laughed and slapped his shoulder softly. "Not here," she said as she looked to see who might be observing. "You're a married man. Behave yourself."

"I was thinking we should find a place for lunch. Then maybe go back for a nap."

"You can spend the rest of your life sleeping. Right now, I want to have fun."

"Maybe I wasn't thinking of an actual sleep nap."

"But –"

"But me no buts whilst I wander the firth. Which firth you may ask. Why milady 'tis the Forth firth, the Firth of Forth."

"Silly man." She put her arms around him.

"Look across the water to the opposite shore, Sheils. That's the Kingdom of Fife on that side. Do you see the shore?"

"Yes."

"Then it's going to rain."

"What?" Shelagh stared across the channel toward the far shore at the base of the Forth Bridge.

"If you can see the shore, it's going to rain."

"And if I can't see the shore?"

"In that case, it's already raining."

Shelagh swiped at Jack open-palmed. He ducked away to slip the slap. Shelagh stumbled but Jack caught hers before she fell. This time she relaxed into his arms. Her lips trembled as she responded to his kisses.

. . .

Jack stood, stretched and brushed his hands over his uniform. Sitting on the rocks holding Shelagh had been enthralling at first but had eventually become uncomfortable. He was constantly aware they were both in uniform and was determined not to appear unkempt whenever they decided to walk back to their guest house in nearby Queensferry. "It'll soon be dusk," he said. "Maybe we should head back now."

Jack offered two hands to help Shelagh up from her seated position. He looked further down the Firth toward the North Sea.

"Look, Sheils." He pointed to a formation of ten aircraft flying south inland from the coast. "That'll be me soon." He straightened proudly. "They'll be headed to the rendezvous point. They'll form up to head over to bomb Germany."

Shelagh looked where Jack pointed then glanced around once again as if to see whether they were being observed. "You can't talk like that," she said.

"Whadda you mean?"

"You know."

"For goodness sake, Shelagh. Is it rocks have ears now?"

Shelagh laughed nervously. "I'm serious," she said. "Loose lips and all."

"You work at Bomber Command. You hear things like *rendezvous point* all the time. Besides you're my wife. We should have no secrets."

"Jackie, let's just be careful."

Jack just pulled her into a hug and laughed.

36

OCTOBER 2006 – *LA MAISON ENSOLEILLÉE*

Assigned to new bases. For different training. Specialized. Headed for bomber training. We hoped that was what this was leading to. Especially Wally and me. We wanted to fly the heavy stuff. That's why we enlisted. And Bill. Billy Walker, yeah, Walker. When Karen asked his name, I did well – didn't answer, didn't say I don't know. Now I can just slip it into the conversation one day. She'll never know. No … I told her Burgess. Who the hell was Burgess?

We knew nothing of D-Day. June sixth, about three weeks from that point. Sheils knew something was happening because she worked at headquarters. It was suddenly hard to get leave. They'd only allow a day pass to go to town. No overnights.

■ ■ ■

May 13/44

My darling Shelagh, I think we're going to be posted up to [redacted] tomorrow. Yesterday was absolutely beautiful. For PT we went for a run of about four miles. Part of the route was [redacted]. The ground was absolutely covered with a carpet of bluebells. It was so nice I kept wishing you and I could be there alone, wandering about.

I got another parcel. Another pair of pyjamas, a shirt and peanut butter. And a registered letter from Toronto with a cheque for £5 with congratulations and best wishes. Also a card from an artist friend in Peterborough. She is giving us a picture when we get back. That will be nice.

All my love, darling, Jack

▪ ▪ ▪

Parcels from home. I had so many pairs of pyjamas I could have opened a store. Peanut butter, though. The Brits thought we were crazy until we shared with them. We converted them into believers pretty fast. Funny, something so common at home yet little known elsewhere.

I wrote letters. Lots of them. To Shelagh, of course. Then to my mother, Sheils' mom and sisters, my cousin, my aunts. And got lots of replies. Even friends from school. The officers always pushed us to write letters home. To keep us busy, I suppose, so there was no trouble during off hours. We could be a randy lot. They said things like you gotta write 'em to get 'em. And everybody liked to get letters. Funny though, you couldn't write about what you were doing. Everything censored. Why did they want us to write? Sounds like a make-work project to keep the censors so busy they couldn't cause trouble.

▪ ▪ ▪

"What's a W/OP?" Karen showed Jack the letter she was looking at.

Jack looked at the letter. "Wireless operator." He rubbed his chin. "Funny," he said. "Johnny we called Johnny. Nicknames. I was just thinking. William Shipton we coulda called Bill, Billy, Will, Willy but no, we called him Mother. You know Mother Shipton, the witch, the prophet. She was from Knaresborough, the closest town to your mother's base at Allerton."

"And you spent time around Knaresborough."

"Not really that much. Your mother could get time off easier than I could. So usually she would come to my station."

"I see. Before I forget, Cassandra sends her love. I got an e-mail from her yesterday. She and Tom are doing fine."

"When's Jeremy going to show me the e-mail business?"

"I thought you already started learning."

"Right – I'm waiting for him to show me more." *Maybe we started. Maybe we didn't. I'll just agree with Karen. Right now, things are foggy. Knaresborough this, Knaresborough that.*

"I have a surprise for you, Dad," Karen said.

"What is it? Is the dog okay?"

"What do you mean? You haven't had a dog for years."

Jack hesitated. "You said surprise."

Karen pulled a pile of envelopes and airmail forms from her purse. "Look what I found. Letters from Mom. You saved her letters."

"Where'd they come from?"

"Your old flip-top writing desk. Now you've got both sides of the conversation." Karen handed them to Jack. He seemed reluctant to accept them.

"Look at this one." Karen pointed to the topmost piece of paper. "It matches the letter on the top of your pile. See?"

> May 14/44 (9, 12, 25)
>
> My dear sweet and wonderful husband, I feel rather proud of myself. I have written enough letters to keep everyone at home satisfied. Jack, I think I will come Friday. Monday seems too long to wait. I'm planning to come at least once a week. So find someplace nearby for me to stay. Maybe the village. I think the two fifty-one train suits me best. I leave work at noon, eat, catch the bus, arrive in York at two-ten, get my ticket, have a cup of tea. With no rush at all I can get to the proper platform and be on my

way. It all really sounds too perfect to be true. So long my darling husband.

All my love, Mrs. Iain E. Borden

. . .

Nine, twelve, twenty-five? What's that? It's on several letters. Probably code. Can't be a date but maybe something about our first kiss. Halifax. First kiss on Citadel Hill.

The trains were good. Especially when we were both stationed in Yorkshire. Sheils often had weekends off and she would come to a guest house near the base and I would join her when I was off duty. We got to be quite friendly with the owners.

. . .

May 15/44

My darling (9, 12, 25). Boy it was good to hear from you today. It looks as though I'm going to be terribly busy here so I won't be able to tell you whether I'll be off Monday night or not. Tonight I had to go to a lecture at six o'clock after tea. The course lasts approximately [redacted] and then we go to [redacted] for about [redacted]. I got my Flight Engineer today, [redacted]. English chap. He seems like a decent type. I took my battle-dress in to quarter-master stores tonight and had no trouble getting new stuff. It's RAF issue of course. I cut my old wings, hooks and Canada badges off the old one so I wouldn't look like a sprog in the new outfit. Well, my dear, I'll be signing off. Love & kisses, Jack

■ ■ ■

"Hey, Gramps!" Jeremy poked his head into the open doorway of Jack's room.

"Hey, Germy!" Jack motioned him to come into the room.

Jeremy picked up one of Jack's letters. "Are these your letters? This thin blue paper?"

"Questions, questions! First answer, yes. Second, those are airmail forms. You write on the inside and on half the outside. They already had stamps on them. They don't weigh much. How do you know about my letters?"

"Aunt Karen told me," Jeremy said.

Jack thought about the propriety of Karen discussing his letters with Jeremy and decided there was no reason why he shouldn't know.

"I guess you couldn't just go on-line." Jeremy laughed at his own joke. "Boy, the censors really went to town on these."

"Yeah. You'd think we gave away secrets. So we're sending a message to your mother."

"Yup, today's the day. Let me boot up the old laptop. Aunt Karen says you can keep it if you like."

"Thanks, Germy boy."

"I've been meaning to mention the Germy thing. It's okay with me but not in front of people."

"That's what your sister calls you." Jack frowned.

"I guess. It's not like you're dissing me."

"Hey, I may be old and I may forget. But I don't need to make my buddy uncomfortable."

■ ■ ■

Subject: HI!!!
Date: Fri, 02 Feb 2007 17:53 EST
From: germy@softmail.com
To: cassandra.borden@symplicity.com

Hi Mom. How RU? Grandpa's here and I'm going to let him talk.

. . .

Hi Cassie. I am so excited to write to you I can barely think of what I wanted to say. I haven't really written anything in years. But I'm eager to use this computer.

Much love to you and your new husband. Dad

. . .

"His name is Tom." Jeremy looked at his grandfather. "You know that."

"I just forgot. But I know. Do you like him?"

"Yeah, he's fine. He's different from my dad but he's fine. They've been married three years. He's not so new."

He's new to me. Sheils said he was better than the last one. Doug, Doug Goode. We knew him a lot of years. I never liked him much. Never thought he was good enough for Cassie. That's funny, Doug Goode not good enough. Used to call him Doug B. Goode. I wonder if his middle initial was actually B. Maybe we did have some fun with him after all. Funny growing old.

37

OCTOBER 2006 – CASSIE'S HOUSE

Jeremy headed to the refrigerator for more beer. This time he brought four back in an ice bucket.

"My dad insisted we read as kids," Roberto said. "He always said you can learn a lot from a good novel."

"What'd your dad do?"

"He worked at The Ledge since it opened."

"The what?"

"Legislative Assembly. Head of housekeeping. He finally had a good job. With benefits. But he died after only three years."

"I'm sorry."

"Thanks." Roberto paused. "It's funny. He always had a book with him. His co-workers used to tease him but he was the one they came to when they wanted to know how to do something. Wasn't just the housekeeping people either. He always seemed to be the go-to expert on things mechanical."

What about curcumin, Jeremy thought. *We need to talk.* He had left the package of capsules in Roberto's office at the university when Roberto wasn't there. He recognized Denis Carroll, Roberto's office mate from one of his undergraduate courses. After some friendly chatter about what each was doing, Jeremy asked, "Can I put this package in your fridge for Roberto?"

"He's not in today. Just make sure it's well labelled. Everything's secure as long as it doesn't look like food. Nothing consumable lasts long in this department."

They shared a laugh.

Now, Roberto eventually asked, "How tough was it to prepare the stuff?"

"Wasn't easy. What you supplied was adulterated with fillers."

"Yeah, that's over-the-counter pills for you. Active ingredients but lots of fillers."

"It took me several runs to get a good concentrate. Then I converted the extracted material to ultrafine particles. Probably some single molecules but I think most would be what we term nanoclusters – small agglomerates."

They continued to discuss scientific protocol over beer – potency measurement, safety data, testing models.

"We know the content of each capsule," Jeremy said. "Now we need to establish how to determine uptake. Then we can move on to animal testing."

"I want to talk with you about that. I'd like to start immediately with human testing," Roberto said.

Jeremy shook his head. "You're kidding of course. We can't do that before we have safety data!"

"Let's just move quickly."

38

OCTOBER 2006 – *LA MAISON ENSOLEILLÉE*

"Hey, Gramps, how are ya?"

"It's the Germ man."

"Aw, Grandpa. Don't make me pay for my comments. Germy is fine with me."

"Good joke, eh? Germ man?"

"Maybe if I read your letters, I'd be able to respond to your war references."

"Read them if you want. They mean a lot to me but maybe just an old man's remembrances. Nothing too personal … no, they're all personal. Nothing too intimate. We were young – wouldn't want you to have the wrong impression of your grandmother."

Jeremy looked up.

"Ah, you'd find it boring." Jack shook his head. "I think your Aunt Karen is coming this weekend. It's been so long since I saw her."

"She was here a couple of days ago."

Jack looked blank. "Oh yes, of course."

"Aunt Karen visits you most weekends, Gramps."

"I know. What about you? You seem too busy to see me."

"I'm here now, Gramps. I come whenever I can. It's my course work."

"So, what's that about?"

"Being busy?"

"No, your thesis, wise guy."

"Oh that! I'm just starting the research. Genomic changes in the Montreal strain of *Clostridium difficile* that facilitate toxin elucidation."

"*Merci beaucoup*!" Don't understand but thanks for telling me.

"*De rien*!"

. . .

"I was surprised to realize you weren't part of D-Day. Why weren't you part of it, Gramps?"

"D-Day. June 6. Boy, the base was buzzing. Everyone trying to find out what was happening."

"But you weren't part of it," Jeremy said.

"We weren't quite ready." Jack looked up to retrieve more memory. "That's right. We still needed to do more simulated bombing runs before we were … um … certified. We were almost ready."

"That must have been tough. To miss the turning point of the war."

"So close but …" Jack said. "We weren't on an operational base yet. We didn't even know the crews that flew that day."

"Still, it must have been hard."

"Well, we were your age. We could swagger into the pub in Doncaster as if we were part of it all. We were aircrew. We were cool!"

Yeah, cool, scared, but ready to go. Ready and willing, impatient to join 12 Squadron at Wickenby.

. . .

June 11/44

Darling Shelagh. I'm sorry getting together just didn't work out. Flying wasn't scrubbed even in that weather. That was our last trip, by the way, and now training is finished. It went quite well although the oxygen failed and we had to come down below ten thousand feet. But from that low I saw plenty I haven't seen before from the air. Part of an island over on the west coast, then we got up to Scotland

and passed between Edinburgh and Glasgow. I could see the Forth Bridge plainly and also the Clyde River at Glasgow. As far as I know we're off to Lincolnshire as early as Tuesday. Well, my dearest, I'll sign off now. All my love, Jack

PS I always wear the sweater you knitted for me when I fly.

...

This letter wasn't censored. I shoulda been more careful. That's a lotta detail. Maybe because I wasn't operational, still training. Maybe because it was mail between bases. Maybe the censors were overwhelmed with work.

39

JUNE 6, 1944 – D-DAY

"No listen, Bordsie, we're hammering Italy. We're bombing the hell out of France and Germany. We've got to send ground troops across the Channel. That's the next step. It just makes sense." Wally, avid reader that he was, continually fashioned theoretical schemes to run the war better than high command was doing. Earlier that week in the cinema in York, they had watched newsreel footage of the Allied advance on Rome.

Jack listened to Wally's expounding and speculation almost every time they got together. Always a better plan. Now, he shook his head, knowing that constant repetition did not make Wally right. But something about today was different – training flights inexplicably cancelled, personnel restricted to base until 1600 hours, no alternate activities. When he'd tried to phone Shelagh, hoping she might know what was happening, he couldn't get through. He felt tense, his shoulders tight. He needed to get out of the barracks. Wally's suggestion of the pub in York sounded good to him.

"Why are we grounded?" Jack finally asked Wally as they walked toward the bus stop. "We haven't flown for two days."

"Don't worry, Bordsie, Squad says we'll be back in the air tomorrow." Wally slapped Jack on the shoulder. "You old married guys just don't like sitting around, do ya. Is the wifey off today too?"

"I tried to phone Shelagh this morning. Operator says she was told the lines will be tied up all day."

"Nixon knows something. He had this little smirk when I complained about not flying on such a beautiful day."

"Aw, Nixon always smirks. That how he smiles."

"No, Bordsie, I'm serious. There's something going on today. You wouldn't know. You and the new missus have only got eyes for each other. My eyes and ears are open. Mark my words and remember I told you first."

When they arrived in York they disembarked from the bus in Saint Helen's Square. Wally nodded toward Bettys Café Tea Room. "Let's go over to Bettys Bar. There'll be aircrew there." He was talking about the bar in the basement of the café.

Wally was right – the place was packed, buzzing with excitement. They looked around to see if there was anyone they knew from one of the nearby operational bases.

Jack squeezed his way to the bar for two pints. All the while he listened, hearing snatches of conversation – *never seen so many boats … even fishing boats … hit the beach hard … took out the ack-ack.* He saw Wally across the room and chose as direct a route as possible, jostled all the way, managing not to spill either beer.

"Bordsie." Wally motioned him over as he stood with a group of six airmen. "These blokes are from Marston Moor. You know Alden Brooks."

"Jack Borden. Haven't seen you since Victoriaville." Brooks extended his hand. "I've seen lots of Wally." He laughed. "Mostly here."

Brooks introduced his mates then said, "Wasn't that something today? You Lanc boys must have seen everything, flying so high."

Jack was about to explain they weren't there, were still training, when Wally jabbed him in the ribs with his elbow.

"Yeah right," Jack said. "Exciting."

"Carlyle …" Brooks pointed to the bar. "Carlyle's going to nick the diamond pen. We're starting a new section on the mirror for June 6."

Jack looked at the engraved signatures on Bettys Mirror and decided he would continue to perpetrate his fraudulent presence in the bar today by signing the mirror with the others.

Jack and Wally stayed for about two hours. As they headed to the bus stop Wally cupped his ear and grinned at Jack. "Now you see walls really do have ears."

"Yeah and we didn't need to wait for the newsreel."

40

FEBRUARY 2007 – *LA MAISON ENSOLEILLÉE*

Subject: DAD
Date: Wed, 31 Jan 2007 15:45 EST
From: kg1@softmail.com
To: cassandra.borden@symplicity.com

Hey Cassie. I've just had the most wonderful conversation with Dad. You know how it's been so hard to find an open-ended question he couldn't just single word answer. Today, he talked about their wedding. He knew details. It was vivid to him. Sometimes he doesn't know what happened yesterday. Today his sentences were imaginative and complete. I'm so glad I gave him the letters, after all the agonizing you and I did about upsetting him.

I think we're seeing depression and not Alzheimer's after all. I could accept even a bipolar diagnosis if it meant he didn't have dementia. He's lucid. Jeremy is teaching him how to use e-mail. He wants to write!

Love, K-G

...

Subject: re: DAD
Date: Thu, 01 Feb 2007 01:23 EST
From: cassandra.borden@symplicity.com
To: kg1@softmail.com

Such great news, K-G! I'm astounded! I know you were always leery of an Alzheimer's diagnosis but I thought you were mainly worried about the genetics, about our futures. He's had good medical care. It's great Suzanne Best has so much interest in him. Just a thought, not Dr. Better, not Dr. Worst but Dr. Best. When Jeremy e-mails that his grandpa's fine, I figure he's being naïve. Thanks. Such good news for an early morning. Love you, Cassie

...

Subject: WE ARE OKAY
Date: Sat, 10 Feb 2007 10:24 EST
From: cassandra.borden@symplicity.com
To: kg1@softmail.com

Hey sis, just a quickie to let you know Tom and I are fine. If you watch the news tonight you'll see a demonstration turned violent in front of the government building today. That's just around the corner from where we live. We didn't witness it ourselves but we heard several demonstrators were killed. It's scary but we're okay.

Please tell Dad we're fine. However much autonomy they may gain if the report on Kosova independence is accepted, the ethnic Albanian population will not be satisfied to be forced to maintain ties with Serbia. They don't wish to seek Belgrade's permission for anything. And that is the worry.

Love, Cass

. . .

June 7 1944

My darling man. Gee whiz the week has nearly gone and we haven't made any plans for meeting. Please tell the guest house I'll be coming Saturday. After pay parade tomorrow I plan go to town. I hope my watch is ready. I presume you got the latest news. Irene and I went to the movies last night. It was *Lifeboat* – very good. In the middle they stopped it so we could listen to the King's speech. It was rather peculiar to see all the Canadians listening so intently to something we knew our parents would be hearing also. Well darling I must go. So long now. All my love, Shelagh

. . .

Subject: WE ARE STILL OKAY
Date: Tue, 13 Feb 2007 14:46 EST
From: cassandra.borden@symplicity.com
To: kg1@softmail.com

Hey K-G. Things have settled down. Prishtina feels normal today. Over the weekend, police responded with rubber bullets and tear gas as thousands marched on the government buildings. Even rubber bullets can kill if they're taken in the head. Two demonstrators were killed. I will update you when we have more info. I can tell you we are pretty shaken up. I've been keeping Jeremy updated. So not to worry.

Much love, Cassie

. . .

Jack stared through the solarium window hoping to distinguish the aircraft at the head of the high contrail. *Can't hear it,* he thought. *We didn't fly that high. Lincoln ... Lincolnshire ... Wickenby. Bombing raids over Europe. Training and practice. Two years training to spend four months operational.*

Good God, the house. I almost burned it down. Why'd I remember that? Kitchen fire. But it turned out okay. Old Franz next door called the Fire Department. He was Luftwaffe. Used to have a beer or two in the backyard. Swapped flying stories. Same as me. Just wanted to fly. Left school to join up. Didn't want to wait to end up infantry. Good friend.

They asked me to report on the German engineers at Nobel ...

41

DECEMBER 1957 – ORENDA ENGINES LTD TEST SITE, NOBEL, ONTARIO

Jack watched George Woolner, the works manager, walk through the engineering office, past the drafting tables. Direct path toward his work area. The boss, he thought. *The two men with him. Close-cropped hair. RCMP. Want to talk to me again.* During his almost ten years as a reporter Jack had cultivated an ability to intuitively evaluate people. He hadn't liked the previous two visitors. Too clean-cut an image, he'd judged, as if he knew what it meant to cut an image too clean. But first impressions – policemen, not real folks. Not that he disrespected authority.

"Good morning, Mr. Borden." Woolner, ex-military himself, maintained an unstated barrier between himself and his staff. Not a large man but ramrod posture. Always nattily dressed. Today a pin-striped dark blue suit. Served as a major, preferred to continue to be addressed that way on the job.

"Good morning, Major."

"These two officers have requested permission to meet with you." Woolner gestured with his head to the accompanying two men. Then he looked around the active department – the ordered work tables – the men casually looking their way, measuring the interaction of the other three with Jack. "Let's see if we can't find someplace more private."

Jack glanced at the dozen or so engineers and draughtsmen. Hans Stein caught his eye and nodded almost imperceptibly. He and the other German engineers knew what this meeting was about. Meanwhile, Major

Woolner led them down the hallway to a small vacant office. To this point neither police officer had spoken.

"Thank you, Major Woolner. We'll take it from here." The shorter of the two seemed to be in charge. Shorter but older. Jack made him to be mid-forties.

"Well, Flight Lieutenant …"

Jack shook his head. "I'm not military."

"Sorry. I'm Sergeant Knudsen, Mr. Borden. This is my colleague, Corporal Schmidt." Each man extended a hand in formal greeting. "You met previously with Constables Kraus and Winkler," Knudsen continued.

Jack nodded. He hadn't particularly liked Kraus and Winkler. Found them officious and self-important. And almost indistinguishable. In fact, he couldn't remember who was whom. Neither seemed to be in charge. *Young and inexperienced,* Jack thought. *Too young to have served during the war.*

"What have you observed?" Schmidt said.

"Observed?" Jack was startled by the directness of the question.

"The German engineers."

"I haven't agreed to do anything."

Schmidt smiled. "I'm simply asking what you've observed."

"Two of them are friends of mine …"

"So much the better. You can keep tabs on them more easily," Knudsen said.

Jack sensed a rehearsed, well-practiced interrogation style. He knew he wasn't the subject of interest but suspected these two would be effective. *They'd make good reporters,* he thought. "Look, I haven't agreed to spy on these people." Jack looked directly at Knudsen.

"Iain, Iain …"

"It's Jack. I go by Jack." *They don't know everything.*

Knudsen made a quick notation. "We need to know what these former Nazis are up to. Designed buzz bombs. V-2 rocket bombs. Sent them to destroy London. Now we trust them to design our interceptor bomber? I don't think so. Not without surveillance."

Defeat the enemy then find a new one – *Soviets, North Korea,* Jack thought. *Or at least discover a paradox, real or imagined. Shelagh would understand. She'd love to do this. This would be her element – she'd observe, take secret pictures. A little spy camera. These are her people. But mum's the word. I won't mention anything. We don't need anything more to argue about.*

▪ ▪ ▪

"How can you work with them?" Shelagh had asked.

They had just left a Sunday afternoon engineering department gathering hosted by Hans and Greta Stein. They'd been celebrating Hans' appointment as senior engineer.

Jack didn't reply but looked at Shelagh disdainfully. He'd heard this before. He'd tried to explain they were no different from us.

"They were fighting for their country," he always responded to Shelagh's variously repeated *They're the enemy* comments. "The war's over."

"And now they're designing our aircraft?" Shelagh had sounded just like Knudsen did now.

▪ ▪ ▪

"Just to reiterate what our colleagues told you last meeting, this is top secret. Not a word to anyone. Nada." It appeared Schmidt had interpreted Jack's silence.

Reiterate, Jack thought. *Sure. Try to sound intelligent. But parade conspicuously through the department. So identifiably cops. So RCMP.*

"What exactly do you want from me?" Jack asked.

42

LATE JUNE 1944 – OVER THE ENGLISH CHANNEL

"Cut the chatter." Jack could hear Squadron Leader Nixon in his earphones. They had maintained radio silence the whole mission except when the Wing Commander identified the railroad bridge as the intended target in France. Once they were back over the English coastline, normal radio operation was resumed. Their Squadron Leader, however, had told them before they took off he discouraged chatter, once again invoking the *loose lips* propaganda slogan.

"Wally, you still with us?" Jack had radioed.

"Just off your wing, Bordsie. One down, eh? Twenty-nine to go."

It was the return flight from their first night sortie. They both knew Nixon was right to cut off the small talk. There was no point letting the enemy know both squadrons had returned unscathed. The pilots would wait for the debriefing before they knew whether the mission was considered successful.

43

MARCH 2007 - *LA MAISON ENSOLEILLÉE*

Subject: WE ARE STILL OKAY 2
Date: Sat, 10 Mar 2007 04:47 EST
From: cassandra.borden@symplicity.com
To: kg1@softmail.com

Hey K-G. Nothing new to report. Prishtina is a city of demonstrations, mostly officially sanctioned with parade permits and all the same bureaucracy we would go through at home. There is at least one demonstration a week. Partly, I think, because of their newfound freedom to demonstrate.

How's the kid? His e-mails are infrequent. Quite a camaraderie he has with Dad. I am glad to see that relationship continue. It must be easier now that Dad is more lucid.

Love you, Cassie

▪ ▪ ▪

June 13 1944

Dearest Shelagh. It was like a family reunion coming here. Wally, Jingle, Spankie, Link & myself all together again. We're good friends with most other crews, too. So Wally and I decided to explore the black market. We set out on a couple of bikes, touring the neighbouring farms for eggs. On our second call, we were lucky and managed to buy a dozen and a half. So I have just finished a lovely fried egg on toast, some sardines, cheese, jam. Bang on, eh? We borrowed an electric hot-plate from some Aussies and cooked our eggs in a …

Jack sorted the loose pages in his hand, turned them over to check the reverse. *There's a page missing. Ink's smeared. Must have got wet.*

… still being unable to fly, we volunteered to go to Grimsby to do some wet dinghy drills in the public baths. This was over about four-thirty meaning we had the rest of the evening until ten-thirty. Link and I went to see your old friend Frank Sinatra in *Higher and Higher*. He sang some good stuff. I don't see why you don't like him, he certainly isn't bad looking and he has a nice personality and sure can sing. After the show, we were looking for something to eat, as usual, and found another American Red Cross café. We barged right in this time and we made ourselves at home. They were serving some swell sardine and tomato sandwiches and Cokes. We got talking to an American merchant seaman who gave me a package of "Luckies". I received your letter with the pictures and the forwarded letters yesterday just before I left for Grimsby. Those are darned good pictures of your mom and pop. I'm keeping one as you suggested and sending the rest back to you.

Gosh this is unusually long for me. I'd better quit or you will expect this length all the time. All my love, Jack

Most of the letters are in good shape. This one's not too bad. Water stains. Some ink smudges. Sheils did a good job keeping them. Never said anything. More than sixty years. That's a day or two she kept them. I'm surprised.

I don't think we were stationed at Wickenby yet. Letter says Grimsby, Lancaster finishing school. Converting to the big Lancs from the Halifaxes. RAF Waltham. Whew. Pulled that name out of the air. Most of the Lancs were in service. They couldn't spare many aircraft for conversion training.

I don't know how to answer Karen. Would I like to go to England? Would I like to go to England one last time? Before I die. That's the problem, death. Gave up my driver's licence. Medical problem. Dementia, impaired mental function. Can't let me drive! Oh no! Not like the other idiots out there. They're legally demented.

Quite a concept – one last time. Sheils always said death was part of life. I can't quite get my head around that. Oh, I know what she meant. I'm not stupid. At least, not that stupid, just demented. Maybe that's the answer – if I could just accept death, they'd think I was okay again.

Do I want to go to England? Jeremy showed me photos of Wickenby airfield from the Internet. It's all changed. Nothing there that we knew. Just the old control tower. Now it's a private airfield. How would I feel seeing that? Nothing familiar. I just don't know.

One last time. Read the Ottawa Citizen or Globe and Mail one last time. Watch a hockey game one last time. Then it'd better be the Senators and the Leafs. A ride in the car one last time. Why?

44

MARCH 2007 – *LA MAISON ENSOLEILLÉE*

"You mentioned a mascot, Dad." Karen stopped reading the letter in her hand. "What was it?"

"Oh, the mascot … we settled on a cat. That's what it was … Blackie. You can guess why. We really wanted a goat but none of the crew knew how to take care of a goat."

"I'm looking through the next few letters. Looks like big gaps in the dates," Karen said.

Jack raised his shoulders to loosen his stiff neck muscles. He hoped Karen couldn't hear the cracking. "It was harder to have time to write when we were operational. Censors were tougher than on a training base."

"That restricted your writing?"

"It wasn't as much fun," Jack said. "Your mother showed me some of my letters with whole sentences blacked out. It took the fun out of writing."

"Giving away official secrets to the enemy?"

"Of course not, Karen!"

"That was a joke, Dad. I know you wouldn't do that."

"I'm sorry … We all were very careful writing home. We were convinced the Germans were reading our mail. Sorry I over-reacted."

Karen nodded her head and smiled at Jack. "Cassie says she and Tom are fine. She sends her love."

"Where's Jeremy?"

"He's pretty busy with school. He should be finished most of his course work this spring. That'll leave more time for his research."

"Can you show me the computer stuff again?"

"Sure, Dad. Not a problem."

"I think it was just the new guys."

"Sorry?"

"That the censors paid so much attention to. Scared the crap out of them. Showed them they're outta school and in the real war now."

...

Later that day, Jeremy arrived.

"Mom asked whether you're receiving her e-mails okay." Jeremy leaned against his grandfather's bed while Jack sat in one of his occasional chairs. Jeremy inclined his head toward the laptop on Jack's writing desk. "Do you mind if I look?"

"It's yours," Jack said. "Or maybe Karen's ..."

"No, Grandpa. It's yours. It's personal, like a diary or notebook. I'm asking permission."

Jack was surprised. "I ... go ahead. I didn't think of it that way."

Jeremy sat at the desk and booted the computer. "You haven't downloaded messages in a while. Since Monday by the look of it."

"I don't know how."

"Of course, you know how. Just click Send/Receive."

"I forgot."

"We can't remember everything, Gramps. I'm making you a sticky note with instructions."

We never had sticky notes, Jack thought but he said, "Does it help?"

"You don't need to remember. It'll be right here on the note. Stuck to the laptop."

"I hope you write another note to remind me to read that note."

Jeremy laughed. "Don't be hard on yourself. Me, I've got sticky notes all over. You know, like put the garbage out on Mondays. Heck, I almost need one to remind me to get up in the morning. We can't expect to remember everything."

"I can't remember how to do all this stuff."

"Hey, I'm impressed you're even interested in learning."

"Thanks for not saying it." Jack looked toward the computer but remained in his chair, crossed his legs and folded his arms across his chest.

"Not saying what?"

"Not saying at your age."

"Aw, Gramps, learning new tasks is never easy."

"Okay. Let's write your mother."

"First, let's make a deal. Don't tell me you don't know how." Jeremy leaned close and spoke in a loud conspiratorial whisper. "But it's okay to say you don't remember the steps. This is complex stuff we're doing."

"Right."

"Let's start by reading Mom's message."

▪ ▪ ▪

Subject: HEY REXY!
Date: Sat, 7 Mar 2007 13:09 EST
From: cassandra.borden@symplicity.com
To: grampasaurus@softmail.com

Hey Grampasaurus! How are you, Rex? A beautiful March day here! About fifteen degrees! I know I shouldn't be bragging after Jeremy told me you've still got lots of snow. We ate breakfast on the patio. Lots of *café au lait*. Just like a spring Saturday at home. I know we're pushing the season because it wasn't that warm. Funny, three months from now fifteen degrees will be positively frigid.

We're planning to travel to the UK in a couple of months for a microbiology conference. I know

Karen's been talking to you about meeting us in England. That would be great!

I love you, Dad, Cassie

. . .

"Grampasaurus Rex," said Jack. "Might as well call me a dinosaur to my face."

"You chose that name."

"Must have seemed funny at the time."

"Okay the easiest way is to reply is to simply answer her e-mail." Jeremy showed Jack the Reply symbol. "Now just write. You're on your own."

. . .

Subject: re: HEY REXY!
Date: Sun, 8 Mar 2007 15:29 EDT
From: grampasaurus@softmail.com
To: cassandra.borden@symplicity.com

Hey yourself, Cassandra! Your boy is here helping me master this electronic stuff. I can't always remember what to do.

They tell me daylight savings time started today. But it's still dark when I wake up. So not much difference. Just got breakfast a little earlier this morning.

Computer is neat. It knew the time changed, just like that. Should put a computer part in this old brain. Germy says it's called a chip.

Maybe I would like to go to England if Karen would take me and we could meet you there. I am just a little afraid though. I'm having good days now. But I remember the terrifying days, Cassie, when I didn't know where I was or who people were. I'm leaning toward saying yes but I need to think more about it.

Love, Dad

45

SEPTEMBER 1944 – YORKSHIRE, ENGLAND.

September 5 1944

Hello my man. The weather has been absolutely wonderful. I hope it's the same for you. Fergie, Margo and I went cycling to Halfway House for ham and eggs last night …

■ ■ ■

"I didn't think the restaurant would be closed." Margo squinted at the sign in the window. "I was sure they'd be open on a Tuesday. What do you think we should do?"

"Let's keep going," Shelagh said. "Maybe there'll be something open in Boroughbridge."

Each restaurant they encountered was closed so they turned around and headed back to Allerton.

"It's not so bad," Fergie said. "I've squirreled away a few supplies. We'll need to be quiet though because I don't have enough to feed the whole barracks."

Fergie opened a tin of salmon and the three women had toasted salmon sandwiches. She also offered a tin of milk, coffee and sugar, all from packages sent from home.

Shelagh was secretly glad it was just she, Fergie and Margo that evening, that Mac was on shift.

"How was your weekend with Jack?" Fergie asked.

"Good, but he brought his friend, Wally, along."

. . .

Shelagh waited until Jack had left the sitting area at the guest house to retrieve his wallet from their room. Mac had gone to the washroom to straighten her makeup. They were going out for dinner. Shelagh stood. "Come here, Wally."

Shelagh kissed Wally on the cheek shifting her lips to be sure to implant lipstick. She was surprised when Wally responded with unexpected passion and turned his head to kiss her lips. She reacted stiffly at first but relaxed into his embrace, her breathing becoming rapid and shallow. She enjoyed the feeling of urgency, the softness of his lips. She heard footsteps in the hallway. She quickly tried to recover her composure. Stood away from Wally, straightened her uniform jacket and skirt. *Just a joke,* she reminded herself. Her lustful response was unintended. Her mind racing, she willed her heart rate to slow.

Jack was back first. As Mac re-entered the room, he tapped Wally's cheek. "There's lipstick all over your face. What've you been up to?"

Shelagh laughed uneasily.

Jack looked from Shelagh to Mac.

Mac blushed. Shelagh pointed at her and laughed.

Next day, Mac told Shelagh, "You shouldn't have embarrassed me like you did."

"If the shoe fits …"

"Dammit Pearson." Mac's face was flushed. "You … you really have to have it all, don't you."

46

MARCH 2007 – *LA MAISON ENSOLEILLÉE*

September 13 1944

Dear Jack, I haven't accomplished anything since you left except writing a letter to my mother. It took ages and ages to write. We have a stove in the hut. Everyone sits around it eating toast and drinking cocoa. Darling, I just can't think in this hubbub. It gives me a headache. So that's all I'm going to write.

I love you, Shelagh

...

"Mom was never good in group situations," Karen said.

She liked her own space, Jack thought. *Sometimes she didn't even want me in it.*

"In her other letters, she seemed to enjoy the girls. In this one she says it's a hubbub." Karen looked at the pages in her hand.

"That wouldn't fly now, would it? Couldn't say that," Jack said.

"Couldn't say hubbub?"

"No, girls." *It all changes so fast, say this thing, don't say that thing.*

"Depends on who's saying it. We can call ourselves girls if we want. But if it comes from a man it's sexist and demeaning," Karen said.

"You believe that?"

"Actually, yes. It's always important to know how groups in society wish to be described. What does it take to conform with the new normal?"

"But you said women call themselves girls."

"Yeah, you can't win."

Certainly not us old guys.

47

MARCH 2007 – CASSIE'S HOUSE, CHURCH HILL

Once he and Roberto were out of the car and headed toward the house, Jeremy picked up on the conversation they'd been having on the drive from Ottawa. "If you give me more of those capsules," he said. "I'll process more material."

"Well, obviously, I don't carry them with me. I'll get the vial to you but I've used a couple. Human trial."

"What!" Jeremy exclaimed. "What'd you do, take them yourself?"

Roberto regarded Jeremy dismissively with an almost aggressive shrug. "Why can't we use dogs as test animals?" he asked.

"Dogs would never pass the ethics committee."

"You people and your dogs. Your precious pets."

"You people?" said Jeremy. "What do you mean? Non-native people?"

"C'mon, it's not racial. I just mean southerners. In the north, dogs work. They need to be productive."

"Dogs give no testing advantage over mice."

"Sure they do. We can induce arthritis in dogs."

"What advantage is that? We can do that in genetically engineered mice."

"Dogs mimic human genetic diseases like leukemia. Or diabetes. You think Banting and Best approached an ethics committee?"

"This is now," Jeremy replied. "Things have changed. We're more humane."

"Oh, for Christ's sake, Jeremy, grow up! Each dog year is seven human years. They provide the advantage of faster aging."

Jesus, he's obviously not a scientist. "The clearance time of curcumin is going to be more than twelve hours whether it's in humans or dogs, not seven times faster. I can't see …"

"You're willing to let people like your grandpa wait decades for something that could help them now?"

"My grandpa?"

"Yeah. And every other resident of *La Maison*."

"He doesn't have arthritis." Jeremy scowled at Roberto.

"Give me a break. You know there are many applications for curcumin."

"The university no longer uses dogs or non-human primates. We have technology to extrapolate data from experiments with mice and rats."

"I'm not talking monkeys. Just dogs. Dogs who mimic human aging with the same chronic conditions."

"Mice are readily available," Jeremy said.

"Why don't you listen?"

"Why don't you? You're careless – taking the stuff yourself," Jeremy said. *I can't go along with this,* he thought. *He's so cavalier.* "This isn't going anywhere."

Just then, a female voice called from the back door. "Hello … Jeremy?"

My God, my sister.

▪ ▪ ▪

Jeremy and Roberto stood as Marianne walked into the living room.

"Hey bro," she said. "I didn't realize you'd be here. I needed a weekend away so here I am."

Jeremy introduced Roberto. Marianne smiled. "Hello, Roberto. It's good to finally meet you."

"Hello, Marianne," Roberto replied stiffly.

This feels awkward, Marianne thought. *As if I've interrupted something. Almost like walking in on a lover's quarrel.* "Hey, I didn't come to cramp your style."

Jeremy made a face at her.

She threw her jacket onto a chair. "How long you been here?"

"Not long. Just time for a couple of beers." Jeremy tried to smile. "You want one?"

"Is there any red wine?"

"I'll check," Jeremy said. "Tom usually keeps a decent supply." Jeremy opened the clock cabinet in the corner of the room. "There's a Petite Sirah from California. What do you think?"

"Fine." Marianne frowned at him. *He seemed nervous, jittery.*

"You staying the night?" Jeremy asked.

"I brought my bag."

"Well in that case, I'll decant the whole bottle." Jeremy grabbed a glass decanter from the cabinet and proceeded to pour wine into it. "I remember it having a bit of sediment." After a moment, he handed Marianne a large wine glass with two fingers of deep ruby-coloured wine in the bottom. "It hasn't breathed yet but try this."

Marianne swirled the wine, judged its legs and clarity, then sipped. She nodded sagely then laughed. "Did you like that? That's the sum total of my wine expertise," she said. "It's delicious."

She sat on the leather loveseat and the two men returned to their chairs. Neither spoke but stared at the beer mugs in their hands.

"I don't need to stay," she said.

"No, no, you came for the weekend." Jeremy raised his hands as if to motion her to stay in her seat. "There's lots of room."

"Okay."

The silence continued until Marianne said, "I spent a couple of hours with Gramps earlier. He was really talkative. We discussed his letters and he was quite expansive about his war experiences. Mom always said he and Grandma never talked much about war time."

"That's like my grandfather," Roberto said. "He was a medical corpsman in Italy and Holland. It's like he wanted to forget."

"Interesting, isn't it?" Marianne said.

Roberto and Jeremy nodded. Then there was silence. Marianne's discomfort increased.

"You know, Roberto," she said. "You've done a lot for my granddad. He really looks forward to your visits."

"It's been my pleasure. Jack's a remarkable gentleman."

"And since Aunt Karen brought him the letters, he seems to have regained his interest in life."

"Yes," Roberto said.

For goodness sake. Am I that much of a wet blanket? Even Jeremy's silent. Then she said, "He attributes so many actions to you. Robbie this, Robbie that. It's funny in a way. You know how he is."

Roberto met Marianne's eyes for an instant then looked away. Jeremy looked at Roberto quizzically.

"Is there a problem?" Marianne finally asked. "You two are acting oddly."

Jeremy looked at Roberto and raised his eyebrows in a 'you answer' expression.

Roberto spoke abruptly, "We're working on a project together. We were discussing our progress."

"We're looking at preparations of curcumin. It's …" Jeremy said.

"Whoa! Don't go all science on me," Marianne said. "Remember, I'm an accountant,"

"I'm making ultrapure solutions so we can inject mice to truly measure treatment efficacy."

Roberto looked toward Jeremy. "We're looking at things like relieving arthritis. Assessing some of the old wives' tales about healing properties."

"How do you test that?"

"Jeremy and I have some disagreement there. I'd like to skip animal testing and go right to human trials."

"Isn't that dangerous?"

"Curcumin is available over-the-counter in health food stores. I don't see a problem."

"There are Swedish studies where they induced rheumatoid arthritis in mice. I prefer that model," Jeremy said.

Roberto looked away.

Marianne wasn't sure why she was feeling uncomfortable.

Jeremy said, "I don't think we'll find the solution tonight." He turned to his sister. "We were going to heat some frozen shepherd's pie. How's that sound?"

"Sounds good."

48

MARCH 2007 – *LA MAISON ENSOLEILLÉE*

RAF Station Wickenby
Nr. Lincoln
Lincolnshire

September 23 1944

My darling, it hasn't been long since my last leave but gosh it will be swell to see you again next week. The score stands at nineteen. Things have been [redacted] so I've been to [redacted] a couple of times. This week I saw *Road to Zanzibar* and *Road to Singapore* – Hope & Crosby. They're still good.

There are a few streetlights in [redacted] now and it certainly makes a difference. Well I've got a [redacted] to do so I must go.

I know you want to enjoy yourself but why don't you wait until I'm around to get drunk? Be seeing you soon, darling.

All my love, Jack

. . .

"How old was Grandma when this was taken?" Jeremy picked up Jack and Shelagh's wedding portrait from the desk.

"Well, she was your age when we got married. She didn't drink but, as you can tell from the letter, she wasn't enjoying going to the pub with her mates and drinking ginger ale. She wanted to have fun, too."

"You watched a hell … a heck of a pile of movies. I'll bet most of them are still available. Remastered, so in good shape."

"I used to tape old movies from the TV. Didn't always turn out. Sometimes missed the ending."

"Why? Not too good with that technology either?"

"Oh, sometimes the tape ran out. But I think I set the clock wrong lots."

"Tape." Jeremy smiled. "I kinda remember those VHS frustrations. You'd love watching DVDs. So simple. Just a few buttons on the remote."

"Whoa, Nelly! Sometimes I can't even turn on the TV. Can't find the clicker or else the damn thing doesn't work."

"You know what, Gramps? I'm going to look up some of your old movies. I'll bring you a DVD player. I'd like to watch with you, especially some of the ones you mention in your letters."

. . .

Sept 24 1944

Hi Jack, here are a couple of letters I received today. Letters are zooming back and forth from Canada so fast now that we can almost hold an argument.

Gee my Dad's a swell guy. So is your Mom. I read these letters several times today. They're grand! Well darling, time to say g'night, sleep tight and all that stuff.

Love you, Shelagh

. . .

Timing is funny. Shelagh saying how fast the mail was. Today, they expect e-mail replies in minutes. Else they're telephoning walking down the street. Shouting into their phones.

It's all relative. Cassie can't even phone home from Kosova but she can e-mail. Unless the power's out. Then she can't do anything. When we got back from overseas, we would plan to call Shelagh's folks in Vancouver or my aunt in Toronto. Usually Sheils would write a letter to her parents so they'd be expecting the call. Now Jeremy pulls his phone out of his pocket and calls anyone, anywhere, all around the world.

Letters. I took my rotation in charge of mail-call. I still see the disappointed expressions of the men who received no mail. Others quickly secreted what they received to savour in private. Still others ripped their envelopes open on the spot, responding with either a big smile or a look of total dejection at the news.

It was like summer camp at first. New friends, camaraderie, not living with your parents. So busy training. In between, though, a lot of hurry up and waiting.

I don't know if I can travel. What if my symptoms get worse? Karen doesn't know I have bad days. It's different now. I know when I'm having a bad day. I know I can't remember names or what I had for breakfast. Maybe I don't want to be in England when that happens.

. . .

"Iain, it's time for your meds."

"Jack, it's Jack." A new one. She's going to ignore me. Pretending to look at the chart.

"Iain Borden?"

She's trying to assess my dementia. She thinks I'm raving mad.

"They call me Jack. Have all my life. Nickname, you know."

"Right."

"I'm not making this up."

"I know. I was just thinking there should be a note on your chart for those of us who don't usually work this section."

"You can call it a ward with me. I know where I am. But don't ask me about breakfast. Where's Marlene?"

"She needed today off. Her son's birthday. But I'm here. I'm Terry. Teresa actually, on the nametag, but Terry works just fine."

▪ ▪ ▪

"I can't travel." Jack looked around the solarium. He'd always kept his words private. Disliked loud restaurant conversations where everyone around could overhear. Health concerns are private. He turned back to Karen. "What happens if I have trouble?"

"I'll be there with you. I am a doctor, you know. You'd be travelling with your personal physician like presidents and royalty."

"Are they demented, too?"

"I'll pretend that's a rhetorical question. Don't get me going!"

One of the staff wheeled another resident into the far corner and left him in a pool of sunshine. *Cal Mason,* Jack thought. *He'll be caterwauling in a minute or two. Too hot. Too cold. That's the problem with this place, everybody complaining about everything. No, maybe the real problem is the smell. Even I would complain about that. And I'm not a complainer.*

"Karen, you know I would love to see Cassie as much as anything. There's nothing much left of those aerodromes anyway. I'm afraid it'll disappoint you girls, I mean, women."

"*Girls* is fine, Dad. We're still your girls." Karen leaned forward to pat Jack's hand. "You don't get to see Cassie very often with her being away so much. And it would be good to spend some time with Tom."

"What would I say to the new husband? I liked the old one better."

"Doug? You hated Doug. You've barely met Tom."

Used to stay married in the old days. Not like today. Shelagh and me. She was always my friend.

"Well, I'm not going to push you to travel. I'll find out from Cassie when she needs to be in the UK. We can discuss it again. Maybe she could come home awhile instead."

49

MARCH 2007 – *LA MAISON ENSOLEILLÉE*

"We traded, scrounged, bartered." Jack walked with Jeremy along the corridor from his room toward the conservatory.

They paused where they usually did to admire *The West Wind*, one of the Tom Thomson and Group of Seven prints hanging throughout *La Maison*. Jack admired Thomson's interpretation of Georgian Bay.

"Some of your grandmother's photographs were like that," Jack said. "Black and white, though. Her specialty."

Jeremy didn't reply because they had similar conversations each time they strolled along this hallway.

"The same thing happened at home."

"What thing was that?" Jeremy asked.

"Bartering. Like we were talking about."

"Yeah, okay."

"My father was a lawyer. Even before the war, he willingly accepted chickens as payment for drawing up a will."

"Chickens?"

"From country folks. Maybe two chickens. Something like that. City people paid with money."

Since nobody was in the solarium, they chose two armchairs in the brightest corner, in a stream of morning sunshine. Jeremy made sure Jack was seated securely, then took the adjacent chair. Jack continued to talk about parcels from Canada arriving on base. "Sweaters, scarves, other clothing – the air force issued uniforms and flight gear, air force stuff, no comfort things."

Jeremy waggled the papers he held in his hand. "Grandma mentioned something called a Kirby grip in this letter."

"Show me." Jack took the proffered page. "I keep forgetting … there's an understatement … I guess we would call them bobby pins."

"So, why would you have them?"

Jack smiled. He shrugged impishly. "Maybe your grandmother left them behind when she visited me." *I don't really want to discuss air force sex life with my grandson,* he thought. *Let's deflect this conversation.* "What do you think of Tom?"

"Tom? Tom's great. He's good for Mom. I love my dad, but he can be such a pain in the arse."

There, now we're on another tack. Not that our life was much different from any other eighteen or twenty-year-old lads living away from home. We always look at each current crop of kids as worse than ever.

"Tom pulled strings to get me the advisor I wanted for my Masters."

"How'd he do that? I thought he'd been away from Canada for years."

"I don't ask. Willie thinks the world of Tom. And of Mom, too."

"Willie?"

"Willem vander Kolk. He's at the University of Ottawa now but it was when he was still at McGill that Tom knew him. He worked with Mom and Tom on a project in Kosova. That's where they met. Willie's an expert on nosocomial transfer."

"Sure, pull more jargon on the old guy."

"Let me explain …"

"It's okay, Germy. I get it. You've already explained about infectious diarrhoea in extended care facilities."

"Oh … you remember all that."

"Memory's no longer my strong suit. But I'm not stupid, you know."

"I didn't mean anything … I wasn't implying …"

"It's okay."

The two looked away from each other and sat several minutes in silence.

"I brought you some articles Tom wrote about Kosova for *The Magazine*. I think you'll find them interesting." Someone was coming into the solarium. Jeremy looked. "Aunt Karen's here," he said.

Karen came in carrying a cardboard drink tray with three cups of coffee and a small bag of goodies. "Hi, Dad. Hi, Jeremy. I hoped I'd find you here. Double-double?"

Jeremy accepted his. "Thanks."

"I brought coffee, Dad." Karen moved toward Jack's chair, placed a take-out cup on his side table then leaned into him with a hug and a kiss. Turning back to Jeremy, she asked, "Can I stay at your place tonight?"

"Sure. Be a change from going out to Mom's."

Jack examined Tom's articles, flipping through pages, pausing to read short passages, only half listening to Karen and Jeremy.

"I've only got overnight," Karen said. "Clinic's short-staffed because of March break. So, I'm back to Kingston in the morning. I want to do some shopping at the Rideau Centre while I'm here."

"Well, I'm sure glad to see you." Jack said. "These articles look interesting. Can I keep them a while?"

"Of course. As long as you want." Jeremy bent to give his grandfather a hug but backed away when Jack stiffened. "Anyway, I need to get on with things. I'll be back in a couple days, Gramps. See you later Aunt Karen. I brought a DVD player. Maybe you can show Grandpa how to use it?"

"Well … yeah, I'm sure I can do that."

Jeremy waved as he left.

"I'll phone to let you know when I'm on my way." Karen called after him. "See you later."

Jack and Karen sat peacefully for a moment until Karen broke the quiet. "I'm glad you two are getting along so well now, Dad. It must feel good."

"Okay."

"I'm not criticising the past."

"Okay."

"Don't do this to me, Dad. Don't pull away into your head."

"I'm sorry."

Karen tapped her fingers on the arm of the chair. "Let's talk about your new favourite subject. Mom always mentions the number of missions you flew in her letters. What's the difference between missions and sorties?"

"Sorties ... we always saw them as short flights like across the Channel and back. We flew into Germany with lots of other aircraft. That was definitely a mission."

"As I see it, Mom wanted you out."

"Well ... we ... uh ... we agreed I wouldn't sign up again. We were closing in on thirty missions. One tour – the magic number. It was becoming more dangerous, more night raids."

"Why'd you let ..." Karen hesitated to criticize her mother. *He must have felt bad. Maybe even guilty, agreeing with Mom about limiting his service. After all, they were both in the Air Force.*

"It was time. Most of my crew was going to do whatever I did. We became such good friends, all of us. We talked about it. But, you know, by then I'd been at it more than two years."

"Okay, I understand." *Not really though,* Karen thought. *Taking a whole crew out of service.*

"I didn't know if I'd be allowed to leave. They didn't publish statistics but we all knew crews that didn't come back from a mission. None of us knew whether we were still needed. It wasn't like now where you can just watch the news."

"I guess not."

"The Air Force spent so much time training me. I'm flying combat missions since middle of July and this is October. And I'm thinking of flying only six or so more missions?"

"I guess today we worry about cost-benefit analysis. Doesn't look like a benefit realized," Karen said.

"But my life had changed. Now I had a wife. And we were starting to suspect that you were on the way."

"Me, but ..."

"No ... That can't be right. I'm compressing my memories again." *As if life weren't short enough, I recall the* Reader's Digest *condensed version.*

"It's okay, Dad."

50

APRIL 2007 – CHURCH HILL, ONTARIO

"Tell me how you picture delivering curcumin," Jeremy said. "I know you don't think much of eating it. And capsules liberate less than thirty per cent of the stated herb content into the bloodstream. The rest is digested or excreted."

"Oral is not reliable enough. I guess I'd want to inject the purified stuff." Roberto poured two glasses of a Cabernet-Merlot blend.

"Thanks." Jeremy sat back on the lawn chair. "Every day?" he asked. "Like insulin?"

"I would hope it would become a once-a-week or maybe twice-a-month dose. We really don't know anything, do we?" Roberto sighed, sipped his wine, looked around the garden. "Who did you say looks after your mother's place?"

"A local. He does the gardening, lawn cutting. His wife cleans inside. Aunt Karen and I do a bit, kinda keep an eye on the place."

"What about your sister?"

"Marianne only comes up occasionally but she's not the cooking, cleaning type. Are you interested in her?"

Roberto pretended to be startled. Eventually he said, "Sorry man, she's not exactly my type."

Jeremy shrugged. "Okay. What about an inhaler?"

"Like for asthma?"

"Those work with powder. I'm thinking of a nebuliser to deliver nasally. Then you're rapidly into the bloodstream."

"So, this nebuliser … Is it something easily available?"

"Yeah, we use a modified one in the lab for rats with COPD."

"Pardon," Roberto said.

"Sorry. Chronic Obstructive …"

"Yeah, yeah. Pulmonary Disease. It was the rats I was questioning."

"We create the condition. Well, it's not my area, so royal we." Jeremy took a sip of his wine. "But why I suggested a nebuliser – we can deliver liquid finely atomized. Small, small particles."

"Okay."

"Going back to when you first tried to charm me with talk of pizza delivering herbs …"

"Oh that," Roberto said. "And nasal delivery using your mesmeriser is better than pizza?"

"Nebuliser. But then we can use rats as a test subject because we've already developed a rat nebuliser."

"Royally, of course."

"Yes, royal we." Jeremy laughed.

"Okay, Jeremy, sounds good but why up the nose instead of injection?"

"The nose is so well vascularised with a large surface area of capillaries. It's like injecting our nanoparticles right into the blood stream. Why do you think cocaine is snorted? But the real speculation is whether our nanoparticles are small enough to cross the blood-brain barrier."

"Is that possible?"

"The nasal veins have direct, circulatory communication to the cavernous sinus. I don't know enough about the physiology. Maybe I shouldn't even have said anything but wouldn't you rather breathe something in than undergo regular injections?"

Roberto lifted his wine glass to toast. "Now you're talking, science man."

51

DECEMBER 1944 – PETERBOROUGH

Jack wasn't sure what to tell Shelagh about the voyage from England back to Halifax – very different from going over.

> My dearest Shelagh
>
> It feels strange to be writing you from Canada. I've been home three days now. This is the second time I've sailed away and left you behind. But I didn't have that same sinking feeling as when I stepped aboard ship to leave Halifax. That time I expected I might never see you again. We had a quiet Christmas Day, just me and Momma. Very different without Poppa …

He sat in his mother's parlour in a chair he'd seldom occupied. This La-Z-Boy recliner had been his father's. Not that either his father or mother ever said anything but it seemed to be part of an assumed collective wisdom that declared his father's sole proprietorship. He knew he'd sat there before. He suddenly envisioned a small boy, about seven or eight years old, sitting beside his father in the large leather chair, studying *The Globe and Mail. Yes*, he thought, *chair occupied with permission.*

I was only in England a year and a half. It just seems like it was forever. The shipboard meals were swell. Three a day was such a bonus. Bacon and eggs, chicken, pork chops sort of broke us in for Canadian food. I had to be careful not to mention food to Shelagh but getting away from the taste and smell of mutton was such a blessing. Even our sweat smelled of it. And to think lamb chops were such a special meal when I was a kid.

Jack knew he still needed to worry about censors. He was still in uniform, on three weeks leave before he was expected to report for RCAF reassignment. His combat days were over – he would not be sent back overseas. He would be designated to a training base as a flight instructor.

His father's chair. His father. Wally had asked him whether he'd been close to his dad. He hadn't known then how to answer – it hadn't been the hunting and fishing closeness his buddies talked of fondly when describing relationships with their fathers. His, he realized now, had been a cultured household with trips to a bookstore, library or art gallery – important outings.

▪ ▪ ▪

Almost two years earlier, Jack paced back and forth in the Halifax barracks after talking with his mother on the telephone. He would have liked to have gone back home, even just for the funeral. But he knew their contingent would be leaving for England any day. His contemplation was interrupted when Wally came into the room.

"Very sorry about your dad, Bordsie." Wally walked over to shake Jack's hand. "Squadron Leader just told me. Are you taking the train home?"

"No, I'm not going."

Wally frowned.

"My mother and I talked. She suggested I not go home for the funeral."

"And you're okay with that?"

"Well, yes and no. It's not like there's anything I can do."

"You could support your mother," Wally said.

"Sure and turn right around to get back here so I don't miss the ship."

"Yes, but …"

"Don't worry. She has two sisters and my dad has … had … two sisters also. She'll have plenty of support. There's not much more I could offer."

"Haverhill could probably get you a seat on the mail flight to Ottawa." Wally was referring to the Squadron Leader. "It leaves at 1350 hours."

Jack shrugged. "He told me he didn't know when we're scheduled to ship out. Then he said even if he did know when, he couldn't tell me."

Bill Walker quietly joined them. "So sorry, Bordsie," he said.

"The chaplain spoke to me about applying for a hardship discharge since I'm an only child," Jack said.

"How will your mother cope?"

"Well, we're not a farm family. She doesn't need someone to look after things. And it's not like she will need to take in laundry." Jack allowed himself to smile. "My mother will be quite all right, guys. Thanks. Besides I don't want out. I want to fly. I volunteered for this."

▪ ▪ ▪

Jack reclined slightly in the La-Z-Boy, raised his feet from the floor to the matching footstool. He thought about how much life he'd experienced in such a short time.

The first two days of the voyage back to Canada aboard the *Queen Mary*, Jack did little other than read. First the two books he'd purchased – *Epitaph for a Spy* and *A Tree Grows in Brooklyn*. The Eric Ambler was a quick read. The other required more time. Wally had also given him *Razor's Edge*.

"Try this one, Bordsie." Wally handed the book to Jack. "I'm not so big on it. It's about a flier, so I thought I'd like it. But his life after the Great War is so dark."

Jack always enjoyed reading Somerset Maugham. "Thanks, Wally. I'm amazed, it's new and you not only already have it, you've had time to read it." Jack held the book open to the publication information on the back of the title page. "Just published this year."

Wally shrugged. "Another thing I didn't like. Maugham appears in the story as himself. Seems more than a little self-serving."

"Where'd you get it?"

"You know, from home."

Wally often received books in his parcels, although Jack couldn't imagine when he managed to read. Jack didn't find time himself with nightly blackouts. Even his shipboard reading was all daytime because the *Queen Mary* was also blacked-out at night. They sailed alone, not in convoy.

Wally was not part of the draw to go home this time. "I think I may stay on for another tour," he told Jack. "They tell me I could be promoted to Squadron Leader almost immediately. Maybe even Wing Commander if the war lasts long enough."

"I'm ready for home," Jack said.

"You just want to get all the babes before the rest of us are back."

"I'm married."

"Oh, don't I know that. So what is it? You're a top pilot. The wifey wants you home out of danger?"

Jack tried to laugh. *He's so right. It is Shelagh. It's only fair to her to take myself out of danger. I can't imagine not being part of it. Going to miss these guys. Their easy camaraderie kept me going.* When he was learning to fly, he had envisioned a career in the RCAF. Now, he simply answered, "Maybe."

. . .

Jack reclined further in the La-Z-Boy. *All I did was read when I first got on the ship. The only ones I knew on board were my own crew. Then suddenly there was the English petty officer and the American army doctor who just wanted to play bridge.*

52

APRIL 2007 – *LA MAISON ENSOLEILLÉE*

"I'm surprised you kept your letters." Jeremy picked up the pitcher from the table and carefully poured two glasses of water, deliberately holding back the ice and lemon slices from Jack's glass.

"When I first got back, they were all I had to show for those years of my life. Them and my pilot's logbook. Once the war ended, re-reading them kept me … I don't know … I think you say grounded now."

"I hear you."

"I used them with other source material when I wrote about the war years."

"I gather you were well received coming home," Jeremy said. "Better than the troops coming back from Afghanistan."

"We were treated like heroes." Jack stood, walked back to his bed and began to sort through the papers on the night table. "Look at this letter."

Peterborough, Ontario
December 28 1944

My darling, I'm out of official stationery. Now that I'm home I have switched over to civvy paper. I have so much to tell you. You didn't know your husband was a very important man around this burg – being stopped on the street to shake hands every five steps …

. . .

"The *Peterborough Examiner* asked me for an interview. Then the *Toronto Telegram* wanted a picture for a story they ran." Jack raised his eyebrows and smiled at Jeremy. "I wish I'd kept a copy."

"I bet it felt good to be recognized."

"It was … I don't know the words …" Jack said.

"You looking for something like exhilarating?"

"Mmm, maybe just surprised. I wished your grandma could have been part of the moment." *Hero. Never really felt right about that. Me the hero, at home, Shelagh over there, my mates still flying missions.*

Jeremy looked at Jack. He recognized that something about this discussion bothered him. He was home before Grandma. He looked back to the letter.

"The war was almost over when your grandma got back. Everybody was coming home then. It wasn't a big deal anymore."

"You came back on the *Queen Mary*."

"Same ship both ways," Jack said. "It wasn't luxury, if that's what you're thinking."

"No. I read on the Internet how crowded it was. Twelve thousand transported on a single crossing. Normal capacity something around a thousand."

"Not luxury for sure," Jack said. "This was December. We weren't sunning ourselves on the decks enjoying the pleasures of the North Atlantic." He paused. "I don't remember now. It took five or six days, maybe seven. We were running fast. It's vivid but it's a blur. It's been more than sixty years."

"Yeah, I guess."

"You know, the first couple days I found myself a corner to sit in and read two or three books. The first time in years I had a chance for uninterrupted reading. I always had a book on the go but I only ever managed to snatch five, ten minutes at a stretch."

"Even as a kid I always noticed how much you read," Jeremy said.

"I liked war stories, spy thrillers, crime – Neville Shute, John D. MacDonald."

"Ian Fleming?"

"No," Jack said. "That James Bond stuff isn't my style. I never did cotton on to gadget stuff. I like realism. Realism, escapism. It has to be possible.

Don't think I ever read anything better than *Most Secret, No Highway, A Town Like Alice.*"

"What about history?"

"I've always preferred fiction. Facts I dealt with for work. I wanted escape at home." Jack gestured, palms up. "You're the scientist, the detail man. Between you, your mother and your aunt, you study enough data the rest of us don't need to."

Jeremy walked to the window and adjusted the vertical blinds until the sun no longer shone in Jack's eyes.

"Then this English petty officer and an American army doctor wanted to play bridge so this other Canadian and I took them on. Funny, I don't remember their names. We never kept in touch. The English chap was a master. He gave us a crash course. He itched for decent competition so badly he taught us to play properly."

"That must have been good."

"Well, we asked lots of questions the first few hours or so. It made a big difference to really understand the game. I'd played the odd time but never competently. After that we spent about six or eight hours a day for the rest of the voyage. Time just flew."

"Grandma used to play a lot of bridge when she was looking after me when Mom was travelling to Kosova."

"That's how I met your grandmother – playing bridge in Halifax. Yeah, she was a good player. When she was around …"

▪ ▪ ▪

January 23, 1945
Peterborough, Ontario

Dear Sheils

Despite being in my hometown and meeting so many people, I am very lonely for one person. Last night I dragged out my skis, walked about two blocks to Victoria

Park, to do or die. That I hadn't skied for such a long time didn't make so much difference after all. Only once did I go down on my face. Today it was Jackson Park. But first, so I could have the car, I drove my mother over to Wartime Housing where she volunteers. Right now I am writing this in the Shaw's living room (across the street). Momma and I have been over for the evening. The Harringtons (next door) are here also. They are both young couples. You'll like them very much. Well, sweetheart, I plan to write you as often as I can. I know how I would feel over there if you had sailed away.

I love you very much.

Lots of hugs and squeezes, Jack

...

Date: Fri, 20 Mar 2007 09:06 EDT
From: cassandra.borden@symplicity.com
To: kg1@softmail.com

Hey K-G, thanks for the update on Dad. It would be great if he could travel. Tom and I plan to be in Manchester June sixth for our conference. We could be in the UK before that or we could stay on for a week or two. We haven't taken a break since Christmas.

Things here are anxious – we briefly met UN special envoy Ahtisaari when he visited the hospital complex. He's looking for a long-term solution. Tommy says this could herald the first real peace for the region in about six hundred years. Keep your fingers crossed for us.

I'll keep you posted, Cassie

. . .

"Hey, Dad."

"Hey yourself, Karen. I didn't expect you today."

"It's supposed to rain tomorrow. I thought I might as well travel in comfort. Jeremy's in Montreal, so I'm staying at Cassie's. I know Jeremy checks the place but I like to do it myself. Kids. And I'm looking forward to spending time with you." Karen passed a piece of paper to Jack. "Maybe we should try to call Cassie. We could e-mail her to see if she can arrange a phone connection."

"I haven't been using it … the computer." Jack glanced down at his hands, folded in his lap.

"Why's that?"

"I don't remember what to do. I don't want to break anything."

"Ah, Dad. You can't really break anything. Just turn it on and play around until you figure it out. Most of us don't remember from time to time."

"Why does Cassie have to go to such a place? That's why your mother and I went to war. To end it all." *But it didn't work.*

"I suspect we'll always have wars," Karen said. "It's different for Cassie and Tom – humanitarian work. Helping to rebuild."

"Yeah. There I was back in Peterborough, your mother still in England. She didn't like that. I was still in uniform but in my hometown, reconnecting. She thought I was having such a great time. Newspapers running stories about me as if I had done great things."

"It must have been hard to be apart. You hadn't even really lived together yet."

"I guess." Jack gestured dismissively.

"Don't clam up, Dad. Sorry if I touched a nerve."

"Okay."

"I'm just going to get us more tea."

"Okay." *It wasn't easy living together. Shelagh hated Peterborough. She wanted to live in Vancouver. She wondered what she had signed on for. I felt she had regrets.* Feel, felt, found. *Wasn't that some management technique I learned? Some kind of brainwashing to get someone to do things the approved way.*

53

APRIL 2007 – *LA MAISON ENSOLEILLÉE*

Karen dropped into the nursing home on her way back to Kingston. Once again she found Jack in the solarium. He was poring over the articles Jeremy had left with him. "I'm on my way home, Dad. Just wanted to see how you're doing."

"I'm fine, Karen. Thanks for coming."

Karen bent to hug Jack.

"This guy's a spy."

"Who?"

"Tom."

"He's an investigative reporter, a features writer."

"Yeah." He shrugged. "Sometimes there's not much difference. Just a feeling, you understand."

Karen nodded. "Gotta go, Dad." She hugged him. As she left the solarium she turned to wave but Jack was once again captured by the articles Jeremy had left.

...

Subject: YOUR E-MAIL
Date: Mon, 16 Mar 2007 06:41 EST
From: cassandra.borden@symplicity.com
To: kg1@softmail.com

Hey K-G, thanks for the news on Dad. I'm pleased he and Jeremy are hitting it off so well. I always felt Jeremy missed the opportunity for a good relationship with his grandfather. What a blessing to get a reprise! Of course, Jeremy and Mom were always close. You and I missed out, not having living grandparents.

I may seem to be rambling but there is something more. What Dad said about Tom. Please delete your outgoing message. I can't say more.

Talk with you later, Cassie

. . .

Jack picked up his water glass. As he sipped his mind was on Shelagh. *Poor lass. Never good in crowds. Or maybe just boisterous gatherings. She resented someone else being the centre of attention. Of course, it is hard to concentrate in the midst of laughter and frivolity. Like Karen said, she was constantly obsessed with my number of completed trips. Kind of like a teacher or boss looking over your shoulder, keeping track of every aspect of your current assignment.*

He lifted the letter he'd been reading.

October 28 1944
My dear Jack

Much to my surprise I enjoyed my trip to Alston. My relatives are such nice people. I would love to take you there. The leaves were turning colour. It was beautiful. The moors are very interesting ...

. . .

Shelagh was so concerned her English father's people wouldn't like her. But they were so accepting, no so, so … accommodating … welcoming, that's it. Thrilled to meet a Canadian niece … or maybe, cousin. I'm not sure which. I met some of the Pearsons later, too. Great group. Shame we never got back to visit. Only Christmas cards and letters.

▪ ▪ ▪

Then we were finished! Finished! This tour of duty. I immediately wrote Shelagh. I knew she would be pleased. I'm glad I still have this letter.

November 3 1944

Hello dear! Hi-de-hi & hi-de-ho! We're off to Warrington tomorrow morning bright and early at eight. Today I have been madly packing. Yesterday we all turned in our flying kit. It's going to be nice to have one less kit-bag to drag. I'll write when I get there and tell you about it.

Love & kisses, Jack

▪ ▪ ▪

I'd been excited to be going to Warrington, to RAF Burtonwood, for reassignment. Part of Burtonwood was the huge USAF base where Humphrey Bogart and Bob Hope entertained the troops. We'd heard about these shows the whole time we were in England. Never able to get there – all the way up in Cheshire, nowhere near any of our assigned bases. It was a good chance to see some of the North West. But only for a few days. We were just near enough to Liverpool so they could assemble us in safety and then send us home.

Shelagh was delighted the flights over Europe were ended for me. I was probably happy too. This had been my life for so long, I didn't know what I felt. Besides, I wasn't sure the RCAF would let me go home just because I wanted to. They trained me to perform. And I trained with crews that … heck, I flew with them over Germany … that wouldn't ever be going home. I hoped there was enough chivalry left between armies that the fallen would be given decent burials. I know that's what I would have wanted for myself.

54

AUGUST 1975 – BATH, MAINE

Jack, Karen and Cassie walked into The Gull, a bar and grill just off Centre Street. They had wandered around downtown Bath earlier in the afternoon then made their way to the waterfront along the Kennebec River. When they found themselves along Washington Street in the industrial section near the navy yards, they decided against looking for a seaman's pub there. They walked back to Centre Street and on a side street found The Gull.

Jack was tempted to sit at the bar. The leather-backed swivel bar stools looked comfortable. There were only a few customers. But there was something that suggested regular seats, almost as if they had a name on them. Reserved for … It had never been how Jack wanted to spend an afternoon. He certainly enjoyed a beer but as a reward after work, after accomplishing the tasks of the day. He was enamoured with the marine accoutrements, though – large wooden ship's wheel hanging on the wall behind the bar, porthole windows on the swinging doors he presumed went to the kitchen, nautical-themed paintings and large maps displayed throughout the room. His story instinct kicked in. Other than those who worked the shipyards what did people do in this ten thousand population town? Some obviously drank but that hadn't been his impression as they wandered around. A couple of small art galleries, pottery shops. An amazing bookstore.

"Let's grab a table." Jack steered Karen and Cassie toward a small round wooden table with four chairs in a corner, mid-way between the entrance door and the bar. As the waiter approached, Jack ordered three beers.

"No, just two, Dad," Cassie said. "I'll have a Coke."

"All right then, two it is and a large Coke, lots of ice." Jack nodded toward Cassie. She smiled back, pleased he remembered her preference. Then Jack said, "I'm really glad we were able to get away. During the night, I had the sudden realization this could be one of our last family times together." He paused when he saw their puzzled looks. "No, no … nothing wrong. I just meant you're headed off into your own careers."

After a moment both women began to speak at the same time until Cassie laughed and let Karen take over. "I know I'm talking for both of us, Dad. We wouldn't trade this for anything."

"Nor would I. I wasn't being maudlin, just facing facts."

"Too bad Mom isn't here," Cassie said. Neither Jack nor Karen responded. The three of them sat quietly, waiting for drinks, studying the menu. Walking about four miles had made them hungry.

Jack pointed out the map hanging on the wall. "Look at that," he said. "See how Maine's nestled between New Brunswick and Quebec with Nova Scotia just across the water. Maine should be part of Canada. Wonder how that happened."

The waiter returned with his tray of drinks – two Samuel Adams Boston Lager and Cassie's Coke.

Jack pointed to the menu. "Are your lobster rolls good?"

"Some of my friends say there's no such thing as a bad lobster roll." The waiter looked around, then bent toward Jack. "We've got a good seafood menu. But you're not from these parts."

"No."

"If you're staying in the area a few days, go on up to Wiscasset. Red's Eats. Right on Main Street. Route 1. Can't miss it. Best lobster rolls in New England."

"Thanks, maybe we'll do that tomorrow."

"What I can recommend is today's catch – grilled halibut steak, served with boiled potatoes and mixed veggies."

Jack looked at the other two. "Sounds a little heavy for me."

"Our fish and chips are great. That's halibut also."

While they sipped their drinks, Cassie asked, "Can you get to Nova Scotia without driving up through New Brunswick?"

"There's regular ferry service. There's a car ferry that leaves from Portland."

Karen looked at Cassie – saw where she was headed. "Portland's about an hour from here, eh Dad."

"About that."

"Have you been back to Halifax since the war?"

"Halifax?"

"Cassie and I have never been. We're in the neighbourhood. We could just slip across."

"Well, I …"

55

APRIL 1946 – PETERBOROUGH

Shelagh handed Karen to Jack soon after he came through the apartment door. “We’ve had a good day, haven’t we, Kari?”

Jack held the three-month old away from him with his arms extended, making faces, trying to get her to smile.

“Your daddy’s such a silly man, isn’t he?” Shelagh pressed her face into Karen’s.

Jack pulled the baby back in to his shoulder and rubbed her back. Shelagh smiled at Jack and placed her hand atop his. “I’m due back at the armoury next week.”

Jack looked bewildered. “What do you mean?”

“My maternity time is running out.”

“But you’re just reserve status …”

“But nothing. It’s a paid job.”

“What about Karen? What about feeding her?” Jack held the baby closer.

“I’m switching her to infant formula anyway. Dr Burgess says it’s much more nutritious.”

“But she’s too young for a babysitter.”

“Maybe your mother …”

Jack shook his head. “Oh yes. After we just moved out.”

■ ■ ■

"We've found ourselves an apartment, Mother," Jack had told Rose.

"But Jackie, that's so unnecessary." Rose looked pained. "I have more than enough room here. You're certainly no trouble for me. And having my granddaughter, having Karen here …"

"We'll just be down on Park Street – not that far away."

"It's too bad you feel the need to move. Privacy, I guess."

"Now, Mother, you've been very kind and hospitable to us."

"I'm so sorry Shelagh and I seem to clash – my son, her husband – maybe we can't share."

"It's not that at all, Mother."

"Oh, my son, of course it is."

▪ ▪ ▪

Karen was napping when Jack arrived home from work. Shelagh had prepared tea in anticipation of the two of them sitting on their small second floor balcony on either side of their newly-acquired terrace table. They had bought the table downtown at Cherney's – it could be folded away when not in use. Now, the teapot sat on its surface with two china cups and saucers.

Jack rested comfortably against the back of one of the red metal lawn chairs appreciating the afternoon sun. He was telling Shelagh he'd felt cooped up indoors today working the city desk while George Park spent most of the day in conference with Rob Davies and others.

"Most days at least some of my time is outside," he said. "Sometimes only travelling between interviews but outside nonetheless. How was your day?"

Shelagh appeared to be agitated, not able to get seated comfortably, fidgeting in her chair. She looked at Jack and smiled nervously. "I think I hear Karen whimpering." She stood to leave. "I'll just check." She returned a few minutes later. "I must have been imagining things. She's fast asleep. Brenda said she put her down just before I got home."

"I hope Brenda works out. She's not much older than we are. But Mother says she's very experienced looking after babies."

"I think she'll be fine for the short while we need her."

Jack cocked his head toward Shelagh. He'd no expectation that Shelagh would quit the reserves now that she'd started managing the office.

"Wing Officer Morrison dropped by today …" Shelagh paused.

"Your CO from Allerton?"

"Yes, yes … but she's posted to Toronto now … Avenue Road Detachment."

"Boy, that's taking a chance, eh. With the armoury only open a couple days a week."

"Oh, she knew I'd be there. She checked first."

"What –?"

"I'm going to tell you about it."

56

FEBRUARY 1945 – PETERBOROUGH

Jack gravitated toward the Shaws, the young married couple in the big house across the street. He spent several evenings a week with them rekindling old friendships. He'd known Randall since childhood and had gone to school with both of them. This was the house Randall grew up in. It was now shared with his parents, Rand and Florence, with a separate flat. Jack understood he was doing the same thing – living in his mother's home. He knew he and Shelagh would continue to do that once Shelagh was home and they were finally living together. He hoped that would be soon. He listened to war correspondent Matthew Halton's reports on CBC radio. Jack could tell from Halton's thinly disguised excitement the war was winding down.

"What are your plans, Jack?" Florence Shaw interrupted his thoughts. "Will you go back to school?"

"Oh, my school days are over," Jack said. "I got my higher education in the Air Force. I'm ready to work for a living."

"I'm sure your time overseas was no picnic."

Jack explained that contrary to what he'd first thought, he was not about to be reassigned. Instead, he was going to be discharged. Recruitment numbers were being reduced, fewer new pilots were needed, the Commonwealth Air Training program had been disbanded – available trained aircrews were surplus to continuing war needs – the war itself appeared to be in its final stretch.

"What kind of work interests you?" Randall asked.

Since he'd been home Jack wondered why Rand hadn't served. "It seems so long ago now but I used to work at the Roy Studio after school and weekends."

"I remember that," said Florence. "And you ran the photo club at school."

"Well, Mr. Smith ran it. I was only the student chairman. All the while I was away, I wished I had a camera. I remember things so much better when I have pictures."

"You used to write well," Randall said. "Am I right ,Flo? Remember sitting in English class mesmerized by Jack's stories."

"Mesmerized. So you say now! The teasing I endured whenever Mr. Wells complimented me. You especially, Rand. I can still hear you parroting him." Jack mimicked Mr. Wells' affected voice. "Class, Borden's descriptive passages are so evocative, you would do well to emulate his style in your writing."

Florence laughed.

"Sorry, man. I don't remember that." Randall looked sincere.

"What about this, take both those skills, writing and photography ..." Florence hesitated. "I don't want to interfere. What I mean is Rand's mother knows Senator Davies quite well. The family owns newspapers and their son, Rob, is editor of the *Examiner*. I don't want to embarrass you or anything ..."

"Flo's right, Jack. It might take a bit of help to land a job, what with so many coming home. My mom could arrange for you to speak with Rob Davies, if you like."

...

Two weeks later, Jack entered the *Peterborough Examiner* offices for an interview with the editor.

After they talked for about ten minutes, Robertson Davies said, "Well, Mr. Borden, I'm satisfied. You will start as reporter/photographer. Most likely the county beat. When I introduce you to the city editor, George will try to offer you fifteen dollars a week but hold out for twenty-five."

"Thank you, sir."

"I know it's a holdover from the Air Force but relax with the *sirs* around the office. Mr. Davies will do."

"Yes, sir … Mr. Davies."

Davies threw his head back and laughed. "We will expect you Monday," he said. "Welcome to the *Peterborough Examiner*. And, Jack, once you've become well acquainted with the people on staff, I expect you'll come to call me Rob."

▪ ▪ ▪

During his first month at the paper, Jack saw Davies infrequently but when he did the editor took time to offer encouraging words about the articles Jack had written. One day in mid-March, Robertson Davies called across the reporter pool area and motioned Jack to come to his office.

"I feel I should commend you on the photos accompanying your house fire story. The Norwood one. You really captured the nitty-gritty. Well done. But let's talk about something else. Have you written anything about your war experiences?"

"No."

"Did you keep notes?"

"Some. My pilot's log and my notebooks."

"You should plan to write something. You have the experience and background material."

"I would love to except I signed an oath of secrecy," Jack said.

"Sure, of course you did. I suppose everyone did."

"It may have been different for us officers."

"How long is the oath in effect?"

"Forty years," Jack replied.

"You were willing to sign that? How can those bureaucrats expect you not to say anything until you're an old man?"

Jack shrugged his shoulders. "I wasn't presented a choice."

57

APRIL 2007 – *LA MAISON ENSOLEILLÉE*

Jeremy was about to knock when he heard Jack speaking with someone in his room. He glanced around the corner of the door and realized Roberto was there. He was about to enter when he thought he saw Roberto lay a syringe down on the bedside table. Jeremy slipped back into the hallway to collect himself, aghast at what he thought he'd just seen. From the room, he heard Jack laugh at something Roberto said. Then he heard their goodbyes.

Jeremy continued to stand in the middle of the hallway in front of the door to Jack's room when Roberto emerged carrying a small case in his hand.

"Jeremy, how long you been standing there?"

Jeremy could detect anxiety. "What did you do to my grandfather?" he whispered coarsely. "Was that the turmeric?" He was speaking more loudly now.

"Wait. Not here. We'll talk later. When I'm off work."

"You're not a doctor. Or a nurse. You can't …"

"We'll talk later. Please calm down."

"Calm down!"

"Family members who are disruptive or upsetting to our clients will be removed by security,' Roberto said in an affected voice. "And barred from visiting."

"And what about volunteers who give unauthorized injections?" In other circumstances Jeremy would probably have laughed at Roberto. Instead they stared at each other. Then they agreed to meet later. Roberto walked away leaving Jeremy standing in the hallway. He wasn't certain he felt like visiting Jack now. He wondered whether he should just take off on the bike trail along the river so he could clear his head. *He must be injecting my curcumin preparation. Testing it on my grandfather. Does Grandpa know?* After a further moment of reflection, Jeremy entered Jack's room.

. . .

"What the hell were you doing?" Jeremy had agreed to meet in the graduate students' lounge. He knew it would be deserted. He didn't think a restaurant or bar was appropriate. Certainly, didn't want to meet at his or Roberto's apartment. Wanted the ability to escape quickly if the situation deteriorated.

Roberto sat calmly, lips clamped together.

"You injected Grandpa with something. My grandpa!"

Roberto raised both his hands in an effort to calm Jeremy. "Let me explain."

"Explain what? That you're doing something illegal to my grandfather?"

"How was Jack when you saw him?"

"He was fine. But –"

Again, Roberto raised his palms toward Jeremy. "Pretty lucid, was he?"

"Yeah, but –"

"Carries on a decent conversation, doesn't he?"

"Where are you going with this?"

Roberto shifted in his seat. "Ready to talk now?"

Jeremy simply nodded, his need to vent exhausted by Roberto's calm refusal to react.

"It's easy to assess an eighty-four-year-old as demented. Something not remembered. Doesn't know what day it is. Nurses and other staff see him every day, report things. Imagine if we young whippersnappers were subject to the same attention. Did you remember to pick up milk and butter on the way home? Dementia? Of course not."

"I still don't see where you're going with this."

"Right. Let's talk curcumin. Before I even met you, I was giving Jack turmeric capsules because I noticed something. It's not the same but it reminded me of an autistic man who stayed a few weeks at a shelter where I was working in Yellowknife. Everybody there thought he was aphasic ..."

Roberto had Jeremy's attention.

"Anyway, this man, Aaron, well ... there was something between us. I didn't accept aphasia. I thought maybe he was simply not interested. But, as I said, there was something between us. We were both Métis. That's not a big deal in Yellowknife but we were both urban creatures, knew nothing of life on the land. It's a long story and it doesn't really matter how we clicked but we did. He wasn't aphasic, in fact his language skills were very good. He just had never felt like engaging in idle conversation."

"That's what you think about Grandpa?"

"No, not really. It's just I found the same sort of connection with Jack. Not terribly responsive, but totally mobile, then every once in a while, we engaged in a bit of banter."

"Okay, skip to injection. That's what I saw you doing."

"Your aunt thinks Jack became more interested in life because of things like the letters she brought. Don't get me wrong. I think that new interest and focus is important." Roberto paused. "I'd been giving him pills for at least a month by then."

Jeremy uncrossed and recrossed his legs then uncrossed them altogether and sat with his feet flat on the floor. "Let's cut to the chase. You injected what I purified."

"Right."

"That's illegal, unethical and just criminal. Not to mention potentially harmful!"

"Well, Jeremy, what did you say when I asked how your grandfather was when you visited?"

Jeremy hesitated, caught off-guard by the question. "He's fine, just fine."

. . .

Roberto fumbled in the dark to locate his ringing mobile phone.

"Nobody can know," a voice said when he answered.

"What … Jeremy … what time is it?"

"Nobody can know about Grandpa. Not now. Not ever."

"For Christ's sake, it's three a.m."

"Do you understand?"

"Yeah, yeah, I got it."

58

EARLY MAY 1945

Shelagh walked quickly to the end of the train platform in Union Station. She was sure this was what the ticket agent meant when he told her today's train was extra-long. It was coming directly from Halifax, filled with armed services personnel. Go to the far end, he'd said. Those cars are going all the way to Vancouver. Other cars will be dropped off in Winnipeg.

She didn't really understand how that was done, dropping off train cars. She appreciated his assistance. She knew it was his job to help travellers but he was probably the most helpful person she'd met since she'd come home. Nevertheless, she checked her ticket for the third time to ensure she was on the right platform. As she expected, the train arrived late for its 6:00 p.m. departure. Not like England. She was already tired of travelling, tired of nothing being on time.

Here she was, on the move again, barely recovered from crossing the Atlantic, then train travel from Halifax to Toronto, all in the last three weeks. At least Jack had met her in Toronto, driven her to Peterborough in his mother's car. Not like this morning when she walked in her RCAF uniform the mile from the house to meet the 7:00 a.m. train, hefting her suitcase all the way. She refused to allow Jack to drive her or call a taxi. She'd had enough. *Peterborough's so provincial. Toronto's no Vancouver, either. Everything about Ontario is cold. The weather, the people. Now this train station is frigid and damp.* She hugged herself involuntarily. *It's May for pity's sake.* She knew it was heartless, leaving that way.

"I don't want to live with your mother," she'd said. "I've been living with strangers for three years now. That's enough."

"I know you want to see your family." Jack was unsure what to say. He'd been so happy when Shelagh telephoned from Halifax. Her ship had arrived in port. He felt his ship had come in, too – a new job he loved, his new wife to bring home to his mother, a comfortable place to live while they decided their future together. "I understand." He hesitated. "Can you wait a couple of weeks until I can get the time off to go with you?"

"No, you don't understand. I don't want to live with your mother. Not now, not ever."

"Just 'til we get started."

"I thought I knew what I was marrying. I didn't realize I married apron strings." She held back from mentioning his hoity-toity friends who they seemed to be spending an inordinate amount of time with.

"Wait a minute, Sheils. Mother would do anything for us. She's trying so hard to make you comfortable."

"Well, she should stop trying. Why don't we have our own place?"

"I'm making good money – twenty-five dollars a week. But I just started. The first thing I need is a car, so I can stop borrowing Mother's."

"It's always what you need –"

"The car's necessary for work. The paper pays mileage."

"I'm not staying. There's a train in the morning. I'll be on it."

"Don't do this Shelagh –"

Shelagh turned on her heel and left the room.

. . .

"Shelagh." A man in uniform stood in the middle of aisle of the train car looking at her. "Is that really you?"

She couldn't see. She felt like she was fumbling around, trying to find her assigned seat. Wally – she knew his voice. *That's all I need. One of Jack's friends. Oh well, at least I like Wally, which is more than I can say for Jack right now.* She took Wally's proffered hand in hers.

"It's so good to see you. How are you? Is Bordsie with you?"

"Whoa there, Wally. One question at a time."

"I'm sorry. I never expected to see someone I know. Are you off to see your folks?"

"It's only my mom."

"That's right. I remember."

"Let me just find my seat." Shelagh looked to her ticket to confirm her seat number.

"You're on this car. I'm on the next – the sleeping car. You're not planning to sit the whole way to Vancouver, are you?"

Shelagh was so desperate to leave she hadn't considered anything about the trip. She just wanted to get away. Not even certain she wanted to face her family. She simply wanted to leave. Coach was all she had money for. She couldn't ask Jack to bankroll her escape. "That's all that was available," she said.

"I didn't realize. How is Bordsie, anyway?"

"He has a job – with the local newspaper." She wasn't ready to give voice to what she was thinking – she had left Jack. It was over.

"That's good. Reporter. That'd suit him, always scribbling in that notebook of his."

"What about you? You look pretty good as Squadron Leader."

Wally was pleased Shelagh mentioned his new rank. He wore both the sleeve stripes and shoulder boards he'd earned. He was travelling directly from disembarking in Halifax. He had no other decent clothing. Unlike Jack, who'd been discharged, Wally and Shelagh were both still on active duty. Shelagh wore her sergeant's uniform because she thought it would get her respect and maybe travel perks. She knew it would have been simpler had she told Jack she needed to report to Vancouver to be discharged from the base where she'd enlisted. She almost missed that Wally was answering her question.

"I haven't had time to think about it. Once the war's over I'd like to stay in as a test pilot. The next thing's going to be jet engines. Test pilot – that'd be right down Bordsie's alley."

"I don't know …" *No, I don't know. Married for a year. We talked about getting home – not about what we would do at home.*

59

AUGUST 1975 – ON GEORGETOWN ISLAND, MAINE

Jack, Cassandra and Karen sat on the cottage deck, overlooking Sheepscot Bay. They'd seen a lone whale that morning. The sea was calm, without waves. The whale breached, jumping about half its length out of the water.

"Cassie, would that be a Humpback?" Jack asked.

"I don't know, Dad. I'm a microbiologist, you know. Micro. Small."

"Yeah, yeah, I know." Jack laughed. "I just for a moment thought you might have absorbed some general biology along the way."

"Nothing about whales, I'm afraid. How about you, K-G?"

"Whoa! I may look after bigger animals but I'm not a veterinarian."

They consulted a *National Geographic* children's book on whales they found in the cottage and settled on a consensus finding of Humpback whale.

Later, walking on the beach, they amused themselves watching piping plovers scurry after the leavings of the retreating rollers. Even with calm seas, the surf still broke over the sand. The birds appeared to be playing – darting to follow the receding water and scurrying the other way to avoid having their feet wetted by the next advancing swell. In unison. Choreographed.

Now the three vacationers sat on the deck watching fishing trawlers returning home with the day's catch.

"What's Uncle Wally's surname?" Karen asked. Jack's friend Wally had rented them this cottage, his summer place, for two weeks.

"Oh, let me tell you, he's no sir." Jack used what had become a family standing joke from when Karen was small.

"C'mon you two." Cassie feigned disgust. "Time for some new humour."

"Well, then give us some fresh jokes, Sis. Eh, Dad?"

"Obviously we've been in isolation too long. We need to revisit the outside world. What say tomorrow we go check out Bath? Maybe find a real seaman's pub."

"Do you think it would be a tough part of town?" Cassandra asked.

Jack promised they'd be careful. "Bath looks like a nice town – it's not that big. I wouldn't take my daughters anywhere dangerous."

"Of course you wouldn't, Dad." Karen smirked at Cassandra. "Sounds like a good time to me."

Karen always seemed to have been Wally's favourite. Sometimes Jack thought he barely acknowledged Cassie. Wally had made Jack a standing offer of the use of the cottage. This was the first time he'd taken him up on it. Shelagh always vetoed going when the topic of a trip to Maine arose. So, they'd never gone. This time Jack wanted to do something special with his daughters whether or not Shelagh accompanied them. Karen was about to join a general practice in Kingston having completed her internship. Cassie defended her PhD thesis in the spring. His two doctors. Their special trip.

60

MAY 1945 – PETERBOROUGH

"Reading, my friend, is the best way to learn to write. I'm not talking about news writing," Davies said. "You seem to have that down pat."

"I still don't know if I'm ready or, for that matter, how I can write about the war. Not until it's over anyway."

"Well, from what I hear, it's only a matter of days now."

Jack looked around Davies' office. He didn't know how he expected an editor's office to look but he was surprised how utilitarian – *yes, that's the word,* he thought – how utilitarian it was.

"Fiction," Davies was saying. "That's how you'll do it. I'm writing a novel myself."

"I thought plays were your thing."

"Of course, and I'm working on two plays right now. Theatre is my passion, you probably realize. In the future though I picture myself a novelist."

"Your writing is so …" Jack paused.

"Highfalutin?"

"Well … I guess."

"You weren't going to say pompous, were you?"

"No, no. I was searching for a word. Maybe erudite."

"Why, thank you, sir." Davies laughed. "Perhaps you'd like to write a column like Samuel Marchbanks writes. Is it something you'd like to try?"

"Of course, if you think the paper has room for two humorous columnists."

Davies laughed again.

. . .

"Mr. Davies says you might be interested in writing Samuel Marchbanks' column next week." George Park stood beside the desk where Jack was working.

"You mean Mr. Marchbanks wouldn't mind?"

"When was the last time you saw Marchbanks around the office?"

Jack paused. "I … I don't know."

"Have you ever seen him?"

Jack didn't know what to say. He'd met so many people since he started, in and out of the office. He often couldn't put faces to names.

George looked around the room then leaned in. "Jack, my boy, I need to swear you to secrecy."

"Of course."

"Rob is Samuel Marchbanks."

61

MAY 8, 1945

Shelagh awoke to commotion in the corridor. Shouting, the sounds of running. And laughter, lots of laughter. Singing. Although she was initially disoriented, she soon remembered she was in Wally's berth.

The previous evening, Wally invited her to join him in the dining car.

"I don't have any money," Shelagh said. "I spent everything I had for my ticket."

Wally frowned. To him, that didn't sound like Bordsie. "Come with me. We're both in uniform. Maybe we can work a deal."

During dinner, he said, "You can't possibly sit and sleep in your seat the whole trip."

"I'm fine. I can do it."

"Take my berth. I'll take your seat."

Shelagh looked at Wally as if he'd suggested the moon was green.

"You need at least one good night's sleep before you see your family. You want to be in good shape for them. Just so they're not worried about you."

"I can't take your bed."

"Well, young lady, you're going to. Nobody has the lower berth so you'll be safe. It isn't even made up. I'll check on you."

"Thank you, Wally. That's so kind."

Now, shouting, merriment. Wally poked his head through the heavy drapes separating the berth from the corridor. "Shelagh, you decent? I'm coming in. War's over, kid."

Wally stood with his toes on the bottom berth. Shelagh opened her arms to celebrate. They hugged. Then she kissed him and, once again, he didn't resist.

"You must be tired." Shelagh pulled him onto the berth.

Wally lay beside her. She began to unbutton his shirt.

"No, Shelagh. Bordsie –"

▪ ▪ ▪

NAZIS QUIT.

Bold three-inch headlines from the special edition *Peterborough Examiner* were taped to the inside of each of the Water Street windows of the Examiner Building. Men and women on their way to work and others who had just heard rumours crowded around on the sidewalk waiting for more information. Passing cars slowed and honked horns. Two men were trying to start an impromptu parade.

The editorial staff had been called into work early after CBC Radio had initially reported the unconditional surrender in Rheims, France. Rob Davies reminded them it was only the European section of the war that was over – a big deal but the war in the Pacific was ongoing.

Jack thought of Shelagh and realized she would still be on the train. *They probably have the news. She should be here.* Then he remembered as a child standing with his father at the railway station watching a station agent use a long wooden looped message pole. Something was fastened around the loop – a message or route instructions, presumably – the agent stood at the edge of the platform holding the stick high so as the oncoming train approached, the engineer on the train offered his forearm to catch the loop of the pole. Jack wasn't certain exactly but that was what was imprinted on his memory. That, he thought, would be how the news would be shared with the train. He was certain everyone would consider this news important enough to pass on.

62

JUNE 2007 – WICKENBY AIRFIELD, LINCOLNSHIRE

"Look out to the horizon." Jack pointed across the flatland toward the horizon. Jeremy and Marianne followed his direction. "Out as far as you can see. That shape in the mist."

This is exactly where I stood with Shelagh. Me pointing the same direction.

If you are free the afternoon of the 24th, she had written, don't go into town, stay around the base. I have a surprise for you.

As it turned out, he had little choice. Wing Commander Macbeth put Jack and the other pilots on standby duty in case, as he said, the visiting muckety-mucks from Bomber Command Headquarters felt they needed information from squadron pilots.

Six of the young pilots stood lounging against the wall of the control tower, most smoking, their wedge caps set jauntily on their heads. They watched three jeeps speed up Watery Lane and stop on the road. Macbeth hurried to meet the senior officers as they stepped from their vehicles, doors held open by their drivers. Female drivers, all wearing uniform trousers. The interest of the waiting pilots was piqued. Almost as one, they stomped out their cigarettes, straightened their ties, repositioned their hats. They identified an Air Vice-Marshal and two Group Captains by their shoulder decoration.

"Who's the brass?"

"That, my friends, is Bomber Harris." Squadron Leader Hillman emerged from the control tower building in time to answer the question. "Look alive, boys. They'll be coming this way." The pilots snapped to attention.

At that point Jack noticed the lone female, other than the drivers, attached to the party. Her uniform included a skirt and sergeant's stripes. Jack remained at attention but managed to wink at Shelagh as she passed.

"Flying Officer Borden," Hillman said. "A wink is not appropriate." He paused, levelling Jack with his gaze. "However, if you'd like to accompany me, I might be able to arrange an opportunity for you to speak with your wife."

"Thank you, sir."

Harris spoke briefly with each man and eventually asked Jack about his thoughts about the rumoured lack of fire-power of the cannons aboard the Lancaster bomber. As they discussed the issue, Shelagh was close at hand.

He's doing this on purpose, Jack thought. *I'm sweating. He has to have noticed.*

Once the official party had passed, some of the other pilots laughed and slapped Jack on the back.

Jack tried to avoid looking directly at Shelagh. Certainly he hadn't been able to come close to her. She smiled whenever they made eye contact but Jack realized she seemed to be assigned to Harris. *Perhaps,* he thought, *as an aide.*

As the tour wrapped up Harris spoke quietly with Macbeth who in turn spoke with Hillman.

"Jack, my boy." Hillman approached. "The Air Vice-Marshal's party is about to leave. He suggested he would wait fifteen minutes if you wish to speak with your wife."

Jack and Shelagh walked along the edge of the tarmac.

"It's so good to see you, Sheils." Jack resisted the impulse to grab her hand. This was the first time they'd met while on duty with that added awkwardness.

"Oh, Jackie. I'm so sorry I can't just stay. The whole time inside I could only think of sneaking away to the guest house in the village."

"I'm so glad to see you but I don't understand why you're here."

"In case the Air Vice-Marshal needs –"

"What? A weather report?"

"Don't be so silly. I… I really don't know why."

63

JULY 1945 – VANCOUVER

Betty Pearson came out of the house to the front porch to meet her daughter. She'd been watching from the livingroom window. Alternately sitting and standing, trying not to pace. Now she came out when she saw Shelagh get off the bus. Betty sat in the wicker chair. She stood again, swayed side to side, as she watched Shelagh cross the road – shoulders stooped, her service raincoat done up full length, almost like a shield against the warm day. Betty worried about Shelagh. She'd been in Vancouver more than two months. She gave no indication she was going to rejoin her husband.

"Momma." Shelagh steadied herself with her hand on the handrail as she reached the top step. Her voice trembled. "Momma, I'm pregnant."

Betty stepped toward Shelagh, a smile developing from the corners of her mouth. She'd known it wasn't stomach flu. "Well that's great news, lass."

Shelagh tried to smile. Her chest felt tight. She hugged herself as if cold. Her mother thought this was good – Shelagh wasn't convinced. She tried to steady her hand as she accepted a cup of tea from her mother but the cup still rattled on the saucer. A nice July day, she removed her coat but kept her sweater on. She sat with her mother on the porch but she felt drained. She didn't feel like talking. Eventually, she excused herself.

"I'm just going up to my room, Momma. I'm a little tired." She climbed the stairs to her room, shut the door and sat on the bed. She stood again, restless. *What do I do now?* she thought.

▪ ▪ ▪

Two days later when Shelagh returned from her shift at the base, her mother and her sister were sitting on the front porch waiting for her.

This looks like trouble, Shelagh thought. *Wonder what they'll be on about. As if I don't know.* She smiled at her sister. "Irene, you're off work early."

"A little early, I guess. I thought we should talk."

"So you think you need to bring in reinforcements, Mother."

"It's not like that, Shelagh. You make everything sound like a military exercise." Betty twisted in her chair to position herself more comfortably. "Shall I bring the tea out here? It's such a beautiful afternoon. I bet you'd like some tea."

Shelagh saw the other two already had cups and saucers on the small table. "Sure, Momma."

When Betty was in the house, Irene cleared her throat and placed her hands in her lap. "You know, Shelagh," she said, "I believe what happens between a husband and wife is no one else's business. So please don't think I'm prying. You get letters from Jack almost every day."

Shelagh looked surprised. "Momma can't ever just stick to her own business, can she?"

"Wait a minute. She's concerned about you."

"So?"

"Shelagh, we've both enjoyed you being in Vancouver these last few weeks –"

"But?"

"But it's time to go back to your husband. You have a child on the way."

"Jack lives with his mother. And I'm in the Air Force."

"That's just a part-time job."

"Maybe Jack should come here." Shelagh focussed her gaze on Irene.

Irene looked sternly back at her sister. "Give up his job? And what, live with *your* mother? You're kidding, right?"

64

AUGUST 1975 – BATH, MAINE

Jack hadn't really wanted to go to Halifax but Karen and Cassie were enthused by the prospect of visiting the place their parents had met thirty-some years before. *I'd rather go there with Shelagh. Especially if we're going to drag up old memories. Maybe to do that would be good – rekindle something, remind us how we started, maybe even why we started. We've never gone back but it seems important to the kids. Kids! Karen's almost thirty and Cassie's right on her heels. Maybe they helped smooth the rough spots – two daughters barely thirteen months apart. Poor Sheils, two quick pregnancies. I wish she'd come with us.*

They crossed the mouth of the Bay of Fundy on the M/V *Bluenose*. When Cassie looked at the map of the routes, she suggested Bar Harbor so they wouldn't need to cross the greater expanse of the Gulf of Maine.

"I've never been to sea. I don't want to spoil our trip by being sick. My tummy's already a little unsettled. Besides," Cassie continued, "this route passes through Acadia National Park. Champlain was there."

"Champlain! Where do you get this stuff?" Typical Karen.

"And if we go through Wiscasset, we can check out Red's Eats. "

Jack doubted Cassie's estimate of two hours driving but he said nothing about it. As a kid Cassie was his navigator – always happy to pore over maps. She planned their canoe routes and camping trips. Jack, of course, studied navigation when he learned to fly. It was just something he preferred not to do – pore over maps and charts. "That's why I'm a pilot, not a navigator," he used to tell his buddies. In the end, the trip required four hours including a stop at Red's Eats for the freshest, most generous-portioned lobster rolls Jack had ever eaten.

"We could wait until we get to Bar Harbor, Cass, but we should find a drugstore to buy you some Dramamine."

"Some what, K-G?"

"For your motion sickness," Karen said. "You know, Gravol." *I almost said morning sickness. Cass would never forgive me if I let that cat out of the bag. Dad hasn't seemed to notice she isn't drinking alcohol. Or maybe he just hasn't said anything.* "Just a precaution."

"I love this highway." Jack drove along two-lane US Route 1. After they left the relative inland and got to Rockland, they understood why this section of Route 1 was called the Atlantic Highway. They skirted the shoreline of Penobscot Bay and further north, Belfast Bay. Whenever the road came close to the sea, the shore wasn't as rocky as it was at the cottage they'd left. Pleasure boats scooted about, mostly motor but a few under sail. Others were anchored in the smaller coves, out of the weather.

"I could live here forever," Cassie said.

Karen turned her body to look directly at her sister in the backseat. "It's quaint all right but I don't see jobs for PhDs. The economy can't be all that strong."

"They say the recession's over," Jack said. "Can't tell in these small towns, though. Nobody's on the road. I'd guess people are still stung by high gas prices."

"You squares! Okay, you've changed my mind. I'll just live here every August. You know Dad, Maine reminds me of Georgian Bay. Just a grander scale."

When they reached the Eden Street ferry terminal in Bar Harbor, the M/V *Bluenose* was already in port. Jack was surprised but relieved to see only two of the five vehicle boarding traffic lanes were in use. They had not pre-booked their passage so he knew it would be luck of the draw. As they took their place in the queue, memories of another line-up, uniformed men not cars, flashed. Could be Halifax outbound. Could be Liverpool returning. Waiting to board the *Queen Mary*. Now, the assembled cars and trucks started to roll slowly toward the ship's gaping maw and onto the vehicle deck.

Once aboard, he joined Karen and Cassie on the upper outer deck to watch the *Bluenose* pull away from the wharf and travel into Frenchman's Bay. The three of them marvelled at the precise manoeuvrings through the narrow passage.

▪ ▪ ▪

Driving to Halifax from Yarmouth should have taken about three hours but when Karen noticed the highway signs for Peggy's Cove, she asked if they could take that detour. Cassie immediately pulled out her Nova Scotia road map.

"We can leave 103 at Peggy's Cove Road. After we stop there we don't need to backtrack. We can carry on to Halifax following Prospect Road. It's inland and looks narrow on the map but better than backtracking."

"I'd like to get to Halifax by about seven o'clock so we still have some daylight," Jack said.

They did the highlights of Peggy's Cove – took photographs along the waterfront of the quintessential east coast fishing village, then walked out to the lighthouse on Peggy's Point. The terrain was rough and rocky, difficult footing off the beaten path. But the breeze was slight, the day gorgeous, sunny.

"Look at these orphan rocks." Karen pointed to the large round, water smoothed boulders lying on granite outcroppings that formed the basis of the point extending out into St. Margaret's Bay.

"They're glacial erratics. Dropped there during the ice age."

Karen looked at her sister in mock disgust. "Aren't you just a fount of knowledge today?"

Of course, they photographed the famous white with red top structure from all angles. Jack was amused watching the two girls compete to outdo each other bending, kneeling, crawling to create a new unusual perspective to capture the most famous photographed structure of the east coast. *So like their mother,* he thought. Both of them. *They're just having fun. They're not foolhardy.* Jack looked at the sign:

WARNING
INJURY AND DEATH
HAVE REWARDED CARELESS
SIGHT-SEERS HERE
THE OCEAN AND ROCKS ARE TREACHEROUS
SAVOUR THE SEA FROM A DISTANCE

65

EARLY FEBRUARY 1946 – PETERBOROUGH

Jack scrambled to answer the telephone before it disturbed his mother. She'd waited up for him the night before until he was back from the Civic Hospital.

"Well, young man." It was Dr. Burgess. "I hope you're ready to be a father. Your daughter's been born. Now get yourself over here to the Civic and meet her and welcome her into the world."

"Is she okay? Is Shelagh okay?" Jack asked. "I thought you said it wouldn't happen until later."

"One thing at a time, my boy. Everything's fine. Tell Rose she's got a fine granddaughter."

"Thank you, Dr. Burgess," Jack said. "Thank you very much."

"My pleasure, Jack. She's a beautiful baby."

66

SEPTEMBER 1946 – RAF LOSSIEMOUTH, SCOTLAND

Shelagh sagged as she walked from sick bay toward the photo recon hut. She'd debated going to a doctor off-base. Ultimately, she simply couldn't see dealing with a country physician in one of the villages. Maybe Elgin would be better but that didn't seem convenient. Any medical care she'd needed had been handled by military doctors or medics. Prior to enlisting, her infrequent medical necessities had been provided in the sophistication of Vancouver. No, a country doctor just wouldn't do. So she'd opted for sick bay. Better the devil you know.

Now she struggled to maintain her usually erect military bearing. When she was home, even her mother had commented on what good posture she'd developed. She just didn't feel like it today. She changed her route and headed instead toward the mess. She was early for her shift. *I need to figure this out,* she thought. *Clear my head.* She squared her shoulders. Wished she had a cigarette. Not that she smoked. But she had taken the odd puff from Jack's and inhaled deeply. It seemed to calm her. She actually wished Jack wouldn't smoke, at least not in their flat. He was good at emptying ashtrays, though. It didn't seem the dirty habit it had at home when her father was still alive.

"Shelagh. Wait up."

Shelagh turned to see Katy Burns wave as she hurried toward her from the meteorology hut. Katy smiled as she caught up. "Well, sergeant," Katy said. "Permission to join you for a cuppa joe, ma'am?"

Shelagh couldn't help smiling at the mock formality. Just the person she needed to see. Katy she could talk to. "Certainly corporal," she replied. "I have half an hour before I'm on duty."

"You'd think they could at least paint the cinder block – brighten the place up a bit." Katy reiterated a pet peeve as she guided Shelagh to a small table. "Look at this." She frowned as she wobbled the table. "It's like I need to carry shims around with me." She laughed. "Haven't seen you around this week. How ya doin'?"

Katy, Shelagh thought. *You've always been able to lift my spirits.* "I'm fine, Katy. Just fine."

"You don't seem it."

Shelagh sipped her coffee. *I need to organize my thoughts. Talk to someone before I go home to Jack.* "I just came from sick bay."

Shelagh knew Katy was a talker but always a good listener too. She could always be relied on not only to do the right thing but to know what the right thing was. Shelagh remembered being miffed at her when she didn't share her opinion on what happened to Jim Tanaka. That whole enlistment schmozzle had left them estranged. But there she was suddenly, after no contact since Katy's mother had brushed Shelagh off at the door. There she was at Lossie.

"Shelagh Pearson, as I live and breathe," she had said. "Oh, sorry. Good afternoon, Sergeant Pearson."

They were in this same enlisted mess that lunchtime, the day Shelagh reported for duty. Katy eased the tension that time by commenting on the decorating or lack thereof. "Men don't care," she'd said. "And there's more of them than us."

Since then they'd had coffee together at least once a week. Hadn't done anything socially. Just coffee. Shelagh arrived on base for her shifts and left for Burghead immediately after. But they'd managed to revive their Vancouver friendship – to relive and laugh about their teenage escapades. Laughter, empathy – that was important to Shelagh.

Now she looked directly at Katy.

Katy's face showed anxiety.

"I'm pregnant."

Katy's smile was immediate, natural. She reached for Shelagh. Hugging didn't seem appropriate for uniformed air force personnel. "Congrats, my friend."

Shelagh forced back her tears.

"You're not happy about this?"

"I don't know. I just don't know."

"What's your husband think? Jack, isn't it?"

"I haven't told him. Anybody."

"How far on?"

"Oh, about two months." Shelagh waved her hand dismissively. "It's hard to get any time off, Katy, let alone to have a baby. We're so busy."

"I don't even know what photo recon does."

"Sometimes we interpret pictures for your section – clouds, storm damage, stuff like that."

"There's more, isn't there? Something this summer about photographs of a sunken German ocean liner."

"Yeah, we did that." Shelagh paused. Not top secret. It'd been leaked to the newspapers. "Nine thousand dead yet nobody knew. The *Wilhelm Gustloff*. Sunk in the Baltic by a Soviet submarine about a year-and-a-half ago."

"Who was on board?"

"German refugees from Poland. Mostly civilians. Half the passengers were children. They tried to get them away from the Eastern Front to safety in Germany."

"I've never heard that. Only something about pictures."

"This summer," Shelagh continued. "Our converted Mosquito bomber slipped in and out without detection. It was fairly shallow water so the photos were superb."

"We sunk the ship?"

"No, not us. The Soviets."

The two women looked away from each other. *Children,* Shelagh thought.

"So that's the sort of thing you do."

Shelagh was startled by Katy's voice. "That and other things," she said. *And I'm good at it.* She'd been congratulated the previous day.

"Pearson," Pamela had said. "You identified those structures as missile silos. Believe me, high command is impressed. We're going in for a closer look. Who knows what the Soviets are up to?" Shelagh smiled as she accepted Pamela's congratulatory handshake.

I'm proud of what I do. I don't want to take time off. We'll be shipped home soon enough. RAF won't need us here much longer. They're ready to take over.

"It's important work you do, Shelagh," Katy said reassuringly. "If you decide to continue the pregnancy –"

Continue? Shelagh was shocked. She hadn't even thought of that. "No," she said slowly. "I want to have this baby."

"Then you need to decide to be happy about it. For your sake. For the sake of the baby. And Jack, of course. What will Jack think about it?"

"Oh, Jack'll be thrilled. He's a wonderful father. You should see him with Karen. They're off on adventures every day." Shelagh smiled, nodded her head.

"Then be happy for Jack's sake. And, if you can't be genuinely happy, pretend to be happy."

67

AUGUST 1975 - ON THE ROAD

"The Wright Clinic," Karen said. "And before you say it, no I won't be working in the wrong clinic. It's right …" Karen looked at Jack. "Right in downtown Kingston. Five-minute walk from the university." She adjusted the rear-view mirror to check the backseat. Cassie was still asleep.

"And your friend Suzanne?"

"She's doing a geriatrics residency at the Ottawa General."

"She's from Ottawa isn't she?"

"That's right. I'm surprised you remember. You haven't met her that many times."

"I remember she impressed me. Actually, most of your friends impressed me. Right back to high school."

"Always a great bunch. Even now, most of us have kept in contact."

"You'll miss Suzanne."

"Yeah. I won't see her very often. But we'll have an interesting connection. Our clinic sees more elderly patients than most general practices. Brian and Arnie – the Wright brothers …"

"I always thought it was Orville and Wilbur."

"Hey, this is my story."

Jack grinned. "So sorry, Karen."

They both laughed.

"Anyway, my Wright Brothers are both faculty members at Queen's. Family medicine is slowly gaining acceptance as its own specialty. Brian had me help him prepare a lecture on getting ready for an aging population.

He's looking at my generation, mine and Cassie's – proportionally, we're going to form the largest geriatric population ever seen. According to Brian, we need to plan now or we won't be ready."

"A study in demographics."

"Demographics?" Karen glanced at her father as if she was trying to figure out the punchline.

"A story I wrote for the *Toronto Star*. I interviewed a PhD student at McGill last year. I can't think of her name right now."

"Hmm, memory loss. That must be a sign …"

"Anyway, Karen." Jack smiled. "The gist of the article was exactly what you were saying about your Orville –"

"Brian."

"… about what Brian talked about. We have a different population profile. Something never seen in the past."

"Brian also said we've defeated infectious disease. We've had over thirty years of penicillin."

"Yeah, as the song says the times they are a-changin'."

"I didn't know you were a Dylan fan."

"I keep my ear to the ground."

"You don't really like rock music."

"No," Jack said. "It's the minor keys. Give me big band any day."

"Anyway, back to Suzanne Best …"

"Who?" Jack feigned a puzzled look.

"Exactly – cognitive impairment. Suzanne's rotation starts with studying memory loss related to aging. She thinks it may not be that long before we can delay dementia, or even cure it. It could be caused by something as simple as thyroid dysfunction or Vitamin B deficiency."

▪ ▪ ▪

Cassandra was awake and listening to as much of the discussion as she could hear from the back seat. She was glad they were using her mother's car. *Air conditioning – this is the way to travel. Not like our other family trips – windows wide open, air rushing in, Mom and Dad yelling at each other to make themselves heard. It felt like they were always yelling at each other, even at the end of the journey.*

She began to think about her job offer at the forensics laboratory. And the people she'd be working with, some of whom she'd already met during her brief time there on her post-doc appointment. She was pleased a permanent position had been offered so quickly. *I'm not going to say anything, but I'm not so confident about infectious disease being defeated. Thirty years of penicillin. They sentenced me to thirty years of penicillin. Sorry, Leonard Cohen. First, we take something or other … infection, gonorrhoea … Then we take penicillin. Stop, stop – I'll be thinking of that all day.*

Dirk O'Reilly – always helpful. Tom Stephenson convinced me to take a new direction with my research. He knew how it felt to be a newbie. And Doug. Dear Doug.

Cassie took over driving again after they had stopped in Kingston for dinner and left Karen at her apartment. They were now headed to Toronto.

"You can stay with me tonight, if you like, Dad."

"I think I'll just head home, thanks," Jack said. "Got to get your mom's car back."

"Oh. I'm sure she's had a great time with the Healey."

"Yeah, on some backwoods photo shoot."

"That's silly, Dad. You know Mom would take care of your baby."

"Yeah, Cass. I know."

Cassie shifted in the driver's seat. "There's something I need to tell you, Dad."

"I'm all ears." Jack turned his head to her and grabbed his ears to pull them toward his face.

Cassie laughed. She mocked Shelagh's voice. "Don't pull your ears or they'll stay that way." She paused then said, "I didn't renew the lease on my apartment … I … I'm moving in with Doug."

"Oh." A pause. "That would be Doug Goode, I presume, who you talk about all the time."

"Yes, Dad. That's the one – the only Doug."

"I see."

"And … I think I may be pregnant."

Jack sat in silence. He pulled his shoulders up toward his ears to release tension, held that position, then dropped them down past normal posture, then relaxed. He wanted to measure his response. He didn't want Cassie to feel she was being interrogated. He decided to let her tell him in her own way.

"Probably a little more than two months," she said. "So a February baby. Around Valentine's Day."

"That's nice. Did you –"

"No, Dad. It wasn't planned and before you ask, Doug and I were talking about getting married. Maybe just sooner now."

"What's Doug think?"

"I haven't told him yet. You're the first … well, maybe K-G –"

"Your new job …"

"I've already checked. I can claim a maternity leave benefit after I've been employed six months. It'll be touch-and-go. Hopefully the baby won't be born too early. I really don't want to have to quit my job."

Jack looked out the side window. Layered limestone rock cuts, poplar trees starting to turn yellow. *Early. Must be dry. Cassie, Cassie, Cassie. That Doug's an arrogant son-of-a-bitch.* He looked back to Cassie, willing her to say more. But she had nothing more to add.

68

APRIL 1946 – PETERBOROUGH

The conversation with Wing Officer Morrison had begun at the armoury.

"Pearson. Good to see you again."

"Yes, ma'am. Thank you, ma'am."

"Relax, Pearson. I've come to talk about your letter about re-enlisting. There's something I'm working on. Maybe I'll pose an offer."

"An offer, ma'am."

"For goodness sake, Shelagh, relax. Stop repeating everything."

"Okay, boss."

Morrison fixed Shelagh with her famous killer stare, wagged her head in feigned disgust, then grinned. "Maybe that was a bit too relaxed. I'm glad to see you haven't changed, Pearson."

"Perhaps I have changed. I'm a mother now. Sweet little girl."

Morrison's face fell. She looked around the dark, grey office then stepped toward Shelagh's desk and stooped to examine the small framed photograph of Karen. "Oh, she's cute. Congratulations." She stepped back, nodded her head, tightened her lips. "This puts a crimp in what I wanted to discuss."

"Why is that?"

"It's a situation we're not used to in the WD – mothers. Look Pearson, I need to get my CO's advice back at Avenue Road. I'll come here again day after tomorrow."

. . .

Then two days later Wing Officer Morrison was back.

"Welcome back, ma'am."

"Thank you, Pearson. Can we talk where we won't be interrupted?" The office area was busier than on her previous visit when Shelagh was the only one there.

The armoury commander appeared at his office door. Shelagh stepped toward him. "Wing Officer Morrison is here to see me, sir. Everything's under control."

Captain Elliott looked relieved not needing to deal with a high-ranking female officer. "Right, Pearson. You can brief me later."

Shelagh escorted Morrison to the canteen, empty at 11:00 a.m. "Coffee, ma'am?"

"Thanks. Cream and sugar."

They sat at a rickety table on temporary, quick set-up, armoury chairs.

"I'm so pleased to taste real coffee again. Even if it is military issue. Pearson, yours is something we have little experience with – women in a regular, not auxiliary, role. A whole new set of problems – women get pregnant, raise families. When we were overseas, we just shipped them home. Now, suddenly, it's a problem."

"A problem?" Confused.

"Now, keep this under your hat. What I'm going to tell you is top secret."

"Yes, ma'am."

"Understand me. I don't want your automatic response. I need to know I can continue to rely on you."

"Yes, ma'am. I understand what you are about to tell me is top secret."

"Right. We're pulling together as much of the Allerton crew as we can," Morrison said. "The photo intelligence section is needed at RAF Lossiemouth."

"In Scotland?"

"Indeed. If you're willing to be included we can reactivate you from the reserves."

Shelagh said nothing for a moment, letting Morrison's offer sink in.

"It's not like re-enlisting. You'd still be a reservist."

Shelagh gripped the edge of the table. *Jack won't be happy. But I'm doing this for me.* She smiled at Wing Officer Morrison. "Count me in," she said.

. . .

Jack stared at Shelagh, his mouth open in disbelief. He asked her to repeat what she'd just told him but still didn't understand. "The war's over," he said. "Why would they need Canadian Met Service personnel in Scotland?"

"Because we weren't really Met Service."

"I don't know what you're saying, Sheils." Jack continued to look bewildered, puzzled by what Shelagh was disclosing, unsure what to ask or say.

"Jackie, I can't say more –"

"But –"

"No. Hear me out. I'm sorry I've never told you … When we met in Halifax I was assigned to the Met Service, just as I told you."

"But … I –"

"Except … I was a cypher clerk."

Where is this coming from? Who is this woman? He didn't interrupt, still didn't know what question to ask.

"Then I was posted to Allerton. We had such a good time, didn't we?" Shelagh looked directly at Jack. "But really, didn't you ever wonder how I became sergeant so quickly as a teletype clerk?"

Jack looked down at his hands. *Why would it ever have occurred to me she wasn't exactly who she appeared to be?*

Shelagh lifted her shoulders. "I'm sorry, Jackie. I truly am."

Jack snorted. "You didn't trust me." He didn't look up.

"That's rich coming from you. You never discussed mission details. Even minor ones. I never pressed you. I understood. We were under oaths of secrecy."

He looked up now. "I was your husband."

"And you still are. You know we're still not supposed to discuss our air force experience."

"Even together?"

"Even together. You're a journalist. You talk about writing a novel."

Jack smirked. "You're jealous. That's what this is about."

"Wing Officer Morrison assured me you and Karen can join me once I'm posted. And we won't have to live on base."

"But you're reserve." *What's she expect from me? Is she leaving me again? What about my job?*

"I'll be reactivated. Could be for as short as six months."

Jack reached for her, moved his hands up to her shoulders. "Sheils, I'm less than a year into a job I love. We have a family. You have a part-time job."

"We're still in Peterborough, Jack. It's not enough."

"You've already agreed to this, haven't you?"

Shelagh compressed her lips and nodded yes.

. . .

Morrison had explained the mission to Shelagh. "It's a continuation of the photo intelligence we did for Bomber Command. We did the bulk of the work. We have the experience. We will assist the RAF until they have sufficient personnel trained to assume those functions."

"Why continued surveillance? We defeated the enemy."

"There's a different enemy now. We don't trust the Soviet Union – we don't know what they're up to in Eastern Europe or if there's a threat to us." Morrison further explained that Shelagh would be posted to RAF Lossiemouth on Scotland's Moray Firth. "You'll be properly briefed before you leave. It's important work. Look at the map on the wall."

They moved to view the World War II map of Europe, one of the few decorative enhancements in Shelagh's small office. Morrison pointed to the Moray Firth. "Imagine sending a high-flying aircraft with sophisticated photographic equipment over Germany, Poland, maybe as far as Ukraine. I'm not saying anything you couldn't deduce simply looking at this map each day you're in the office."

Shelagh wished she'd been able to explain more to Jack before he got his back up. Instead the conversation ended with Jack leaving the apartment. Something about garbage day, she thought he said. *Garbage day!*

When this is important. He doesn't even know I was in photo intelligence. He'd be so surprised if he knew.

▪ ▪ ▪

Jack slept fitfully that night. Thoughts cycling through his head. He didn't think there was any point in getting up. There was nowhere to go in the apartment unlike in his mother's house. He eventually tried to concentrate on what it could mean for him if he didn't go with Shelagh. If she insisted on taking Karen with her. How could she raise Karen without her father? My mother, not being able to know her granddaughter. Taking her only grandchild away. And Shelagh's mother hasn't even seen Karen.

He eventually got up when he could no longer find a comfortable position. He folded himself into their small chesterfield. He began to think about the trouble the delivery men had moving that piece of furniture up the stairs, around the corner of the landing, angling it through the apartment door. *I need to sleep. I need to be able to function at work tomorrow. Rob will know what to do.*

▪ ▪ ▪

"If you could live nearer Edinburgh, it would be easier," Rob Davies said. "If that were the case, I have contacts at *The Scotsman*."

Jack nodded nervously. "The largest centre near the base is Elgin. Do you know of anything there?"

"Only if you're ready to work for a tabloid. Come to think of it, you did well with the Samuel Marchbanks pieces. It could be an adventure."

"You really think so?"

"Actually, you're too serious a writer. But remember, writing is writing. Anything can be written well." Davies paused. "By the way, I don't want to forget to say you'd be welcome to return to the *Examiner*."

■ ■ ■

"Sheils, I'm sorry I reacted the way I did. You took me by surprise. Coming out of the blue like that."

"It was like you didn't think my skills could be in demand. That your career was the only important one."

"No, Sheils. I must admit I was suspicious such a high-ranking officer would come to Peterborough twice to visit a teletype clerk."

Shelagh tightened her jaw. She was determined not to let this escalate into an argument again. She didn't respond immediately.

Jack raised his palms. "Karen's not quite four months old. It's one thing for you to work part-time at the armouries and quite another to be in the air force full-time. We would need a nanny or something."

"You could look after Karen if you're that concerned."

"Wait a minute. How would that look?"

"Jackie, I'm sorry I said that." Shelagh opened her arms inviting him into a hug. Jack was slow to respond but eventually did.

"Actually, Sheils, it could be quite the adventure. Rob Davies was showing me the map of the Moray Firth area today. He told me there are good newspapers in Inverness and Aberdeen but they look too far away from the base for my liking. It'd be a long bus ride to either city."

"I told you we can live off-base."

"Somewhere nearby – Elgin's about five miles away. There's Hopeman, Burghead. Lossiemouth village might make the most sense, right near the base."

"Why does Rob Davies hold such sway with you?"

"He's my boss, Sheils. He gave me a proposal today to write a series – former Canadian airman revisits Britain in peacetime."

"You've researched the whole thing. When were you going to tell me this stuff?" Shelagh squinted at Jack. "You actually like this idea, don't you?"

"You just had to give me time, Sheils. All I needed was a chance to think about it. Get used to the idea."

"Yeah. Give you enough time until it seems like it was your plan from the start."

"That's not what I meant. That's unfair. Just so you don't think I'm holding out on you, Rob Davies says my articles will be published in the *Examiner* and *The Scotsman* in Edinburgh."

"Well, well. You've got yourself looked after."

"He says I can have my job back when we return."

Shelagh shook her head. *He still doesn't understand. I don't want to be in Peterborough when we return.*

69

AUGUST 2005 – CASSANDRA'S HOUSE, CHURCH HILL, ONTARIO

"I'm going out to the osprey nest," Shelagh called to Cassandra. She'd spent the morning sipping tea and reading the weekend newspapers. She didn't understand why Tom needed to pick up three newspapers from the corner store in the village. *Jack all over again. Why do they need so many points of view?* She was here to visit for a few days because Cassie and Tom were home in Church Hill on a two-month sabbatical from their jobs in Kosova.

"What's that, Mom? I didn't hear what you said."

"I'm going to see what's happening at the osprey nest."

"If you'll wait 'til tomorrow, I'd go with you."

"It's okay Cassie. You have your work and I have mine."

"But –"

"I've been sitting around since I got here. I need to move a bit before I solidify." Shelagh moved to the front entrance to change into her hiking boots.

"Well, offer still stands, Mom. But if you're determined to go, I'll see you when you come back." Cassie hugged her mother and kissed her cheek. She was used to her mother's photographic impulses.

...

Shelagh drove to the place Jeremy had shown her to park when they went out together about four years before. *That was fun,* she thought. *Who knew my own grandson would be interested in my kind of photography?* Once she parked she opened the back door to grab her camera bag. She regarded the pair of hiking poles Cassie had given her with suspicion.

"One's fitted with a tripod head," Cassie said.

"Can't be a tripod when there's only one leg."

"You know what I mean, Mom. It's a monopod. Still it has a camera fitting. It steadies the camera."

Shelagh begrudgingly said okay. Not that she would change the way she did things. One more thing she'd need to carry with her. Now she considered the hiking poles, couldn't see any real benefit.

She walked at a steady slow pace, stopping for a breather at each kilometre marker. *Maybe I should have waited until Cassie could come with me. It's harder than when I was here with Jeremy. Maybe he'll come for the weekend and we could do this again.*

Then, suddenly, there was the windmill, one osprey head barely visible but poking above the rather sloppy accumulation of twigs and other building materials forming the nest. She looked skyward and caught sight of the other bird soaring high in a wide circle. *They knew I was coming,* she thought. *Must be a young one in the nest. It's getting late in the season. They'll let me know if they think I'm too close.* She looked back at the nest – the same structure Jeremy had first shown her – reinforced and modified each year with new materials with walls much higher and thicker than she remembered. The birds had added strands of plastic mesh that buttressed the side most exposed to the weather along with what looked like half a disposable aluminum pie plate. *Aluminum! I hope they don't get Alzheimer's. Poor Jack. I hope Karen comes tonight so we can talk.* Shelagh was at Cassie's this week so they could address their common concern that Jack no longer seemed capable to live on his own. The grease fire in his apartment kitchen confirmed their opinions. Inattention. Luckily the building handyman moved quickly to extinguish it. No damage done but he needed more care than she was willing or able to provide. She had taken to checking in on him on a semi-regular schedule lately now that they were both living in Ottawa again.

Shelagh leaned against a small tree, watching the comings and goings of the osprey pair. *My legs. I need to rest. I'm tired. Maybe I shouldn't have come. I'll just catch my breath. Oh, my chest.* She brought both arms across her chest. *There, that feels better.* She looked around for the blind she and Jeremy had built. *Built! We simply dragged roots, branches and logs and piled them.* That's where it was – she viewed the charred remains with disgust. *Why would someone light a bonfire out here? So dangerous.*

She searched the edge of the bush looking for more of the materials they'd used in the original blind. She dragged small deadfalls and branches. She piled everything haphazardly, annoyed she no longer had the arm strength to lift high enough to create significant walls. *The birds know I'm here. They're not stupid.* Shelagh pushed and kicked at her structure before she winced with pain and crumpled to the ground, instinctively holding her camera to her chest for its protection. *So tired … just so tired …*

70

AUGUST 1975 – HALIFAX

Jack guided Karen and Cassandra from the hotel down to South Street. He looked for familiar landmarks but stopped walking before they reached the Dalhousie University campus. He rubbed both temples with his fingers.

There's nothing along here I recognize, he thought. He glanced back down the street. "I was only here a short time and it was over thirty years ago but I thought I really got to know the place. I walked and walked everywhere. We were waiting to be shipped out so there wasn't much else to do."

"Until you met Mom." Karen raised her eyebrows.

Jack smiled. "We walked everywhere too, the two of us," he said then paused in reflection. *Didn't we, though. All along here, around every block. Shouldn't be surprised things are different. It's been thirty years. Disappointing though.* He took two big breaths to relax, the technique they'd taught him at the Y.

"It's good to be here with you, Dad. Too bad Mom didn't come."

"She's in the middle of a project, Cass. But maybe I can show you where she lived – Gorsebrook Barracks. Let's go back that way." *Right down there, I'm sure. I can imagine it so clearly. Almost see it.*

They walked back along South Street. "The side streets here used to be cobblestone," Jack said. *The hospital is new. The smoke shop was here … the tobacconist, Wally called it.*

"I'm going to get me a pipe," Wally had said. "You should get one. The chicks love a man with a pipe. It makes you look debonair."

"I'm a du Maurier man myself." Jack pulled a distinctive red cigarette case with gold stripes from his breast pocket.

We were all of twenty years old – pilots. We felt like the stars.

Now Jack grinned sheepishly. "I don't know why I should be surprised when things change. Somehow, Halifax remains with me as some kind of, I don't know … time thing. There must be a word." *The barracks was on the south side. The south side of South Street.*

"Maybe you're thinking time warp. But that's an Einstein relativity thingy." Cassie laughed. "It's like you're stuck in 1943."

"Like I'm frozen in time. One difference, though."

"What's that?"

"There used to be a fishy smell even this far up from the harbour."

"Dad, the sign on the school says Gorsebrook Junior High." Karen pointed.

"Well, at least we know we're in the neighbourhood."

"There's lots for us to do here." Karen smiled as she held her father's eyes. "Whatever else, I'm certain Citadel Hill is still there."

"We can be sure of that, K-G. Let's head in that direction." *Maybe the Citadel will be better.*

. . .

After lunch, they headed out again. It was only about half a mile before they joined the walking path off Sackville Street. Soon, they crossed the perimeter road skirting the site.

Jack paused before they started across the parking lot toward the main entrance. *I remember the grass covered ramparts. There sure wasn't a parking lot,* he thought as they moved through the cars and around signs and barriers toward the open gate in front of the cut stone entrance tunnel.

A lone ceremonial guard, dressed in red tunic, Black Watch kilt and Busby hat, snapped to attention, his rifle in order arms position. Cassandra offered him a cheeky salute. Once they were through the gate, they stopped. Jack pointed across the compound.

"We couldn't get in the way we came just now," he said. "In '43, I mean. We had to go around to the southeast corner. This part was secured because anti-aircraft protection for Halifax harbour was here. You'll understand the gun placement when we cross to that side and overlook the harbour."

"It hadn't occurred to me Halifax would need protection."

"Oh, but Cass, things were so strict we weren't even allowed to name Halifax in letters we wrote." Jack shrugged. "Bit of a joke though, when my dad died, my mom knew how to get in touch with me."

"She was probably able to do that through the Air Force."

Jack smiled as he looked at Cassandra. "Well of course, that's what she did. The call came through the Squadron Leader." They continued across the compound. Jack pointed out the munitions magazine and explained that another building had been used as a temporary barracks early in the war. As they wandered toward the side of the masonry fortress facing the Atlantic, Jack said, "We can climb onto that parapet." *And stand there just like Shelagh and I did. And look out over the harbour as we did, just before our first kiss.*

They overlooked the protected expanse of Halifax Harbour with its harbour islands, looked beyond The Narrows and the Macdonald Bridge connecting Halifax with Dartmouth, all the way to the Bedford Basin. And the other way out to the Atlantic.

"I had no idea the harbour was so large. But wait." Karen extended her arm, palm up toward her sister. "We have Cassandra Borden, noted geology expert, with us. Dr. Borden, tell us how retreating glaciers formed one of North America's largest natural harbours."

"Ah, Dr. Borden." Cassie bowed toward her sister. "You've hit upon the very topic I know nothing of. Oh sorry – of which I know nothing. Can't dangle our participles."

"What is wrong with you, woman?" Karen pretended to slap her forehead. "That was clearly a case of preposition dangling."

"But I can tell you one geological thing, though. That island out there –"

"Please continue, Dr. Borden."

"I will do exactly that when you stop interrupting me. That island ..." Cassie consulted the large display board. "Georges Island is a post-glacial drumlin."

"Wow, now that's just the sort of information I'll cherish the rest of my life."

Jack loved to watch them. He didn't need to participate. He enjoyed the mock competition. It hadn't always been pretend. When they were kids they were quite aggressive. He'd had to intervene on many occasions. But somewhere, maybe it was when they came home after two months working as camp counsellors, they'd transformed into allies and fast friends. Now it was good to be with them – good to laugh with them.

"The Narrows – anti-submarine netting was stretched across there," he said remembering. "A German U-boat did sink a ship just outside the harbour toward the end of the war. And ironically, the nets couldn't save the ships from themselves. There was at least one ship sunk manoeuvring to form a convoy. And another caught fire and sunk."

Jack stared off to the northeast searching for a building he couldn't find. *Must be behind those highrises. Those buildings weren't there. And now, Shelagh's not here either.*

▪ ▪ ▪

"That big white house." He had leaned over Shelagh's shoulder to point out where he was billeted. She grabbed his arm and pulled him into a hug.

"Maybe we could go there."

Jack looked at her.

"For some privacy," she said.

He laughed. "That's not what we would get there. Mrs. Buck is always home. She does serve a good cup of tea, though."

Shelagh punched him in the arm.

"Ouch!" Jack feigned pain and rubbed his uniformed sleeve. "We could go there if you like. You could meet my landlady."

71

AUGUST 1946 – BURGHEAD, SCOTLAND

Jack pushed Karen's pram along Sellar Street toward the harbour side of the peninsula. He wished Karen was a little older. Not a desire to hurry her through life but more that she might have a lasting memory of this opportunity to live in a Scottish fishing village.

Within days of her arrival, Shelagh had used her free time to explore accommodation possibilities offered by the villages and towns close to the base. She dismissed Elgin almost immediately. The size and layout of the town reminded her too much of Peterborough but she didn't say that when she wrote to Jack.

> Dear Jack & my darling Karen
>
> I miss you both like crazy. I guess I didn't realize how strong a bond there was between mother and daughter. I hope you two are doing fine.
>
> I have been searching for off-base housing for us. The natural place was Lossiemouth village but no decent accommodation for rent because it's so close to the base. They tell me the best places are scooped up as soon as they become available …

▪ ▪ ▪

She continued to explain that she'd set her mind on Burghead village, that she wasn't sure whether it was a peninsula, a point or an isthmus but she liked its long and narrow aspect, surrounded by water. She said she might sound as if she was prattling but she was excited to have found a second floor flat with windows looking toward the Moray Firth and beyond to the North Sea.

"Oh, many things have been seen from these windows, lass." Mrs. Kerr the landlady showed Shelagh how the windows opened. As soon as the breeze hit, Shelagh smelled, almost tasted, the sea air. She thought of Halifax ... and meeting Jack. "For your wee one I'd suggest Mrs. Douglas across the way. The red door up the street. Number eighteen. Course, she'd want to meet the wee bairn first – Karen, you say? But first missus, ye'll have had yer tea before you go back."

Shelagh had arrived in Burghead the first time on a bicycle borrowed from Pamela.

> Wouldn't you know, first person I run into at Lossie is Pamela Burroughs, Section Officer Burroughs, my CO. Some others from Allerton are here but not Mac. I guess she'd had enough. Another surprise, Katy Burns, my next-door neighbour in Vancouver, is stationed here in the real met office. Imagine that. Her family had moved to the interior so I didn't see her or any of her family when I was home. Probably not since I was posted to Edmonton.

Shelagh sorted out the bus schedule between Burghead and Lossiemouth. The RAF ran regular buses between Lossiemouth village and the base. She knew she couldn't always rely on good bike riding weather. She felt she should acquire her own bike as soon as possible though.

▪ ▪ ▪

Jack loved the two-bedroom flat with its overstuffed furniture. He appreciated that it was furnished and heating was included in the rental fee. He realized he'd lived in temporary quarters for much of his adult life but the concept of being a tenant was still foreign to him. His family and most of his friends grew up in homes they owned. "We'll buy a house when we're back in Peterborough." He leaned in to Karen. "But who knows when that'll be?"

Now he pushed the pram along Sellar Street past the stone houses with slate roofs he admired so much – stones hewn from quarries, he supposed. Not that the stone sizes were even. That was part of the beauty – hints of browns, dark greys and blacks with painted window boxes adding accent. Front doors opening immediately onto the street.

The previous day, he'd pushed Karen along the waterfront and the docks in the harbour. He pointed out trawlers, high-bowed, flat-bottomed cobles and sail-rigged fishing luggers moored at wharves and along the shore. He often picked up six-month-old Karen and held her close to his body to protect her from the almost constant wind when they were near the water. Other times he held her facing away from him as he described to her what they were looking at. He thought she enjoyed their almost daily outings. He had no idea what might register with an infant but hoped he might be contributing to lasting memories.

He felt strangely at home. All he knew of his family's Scots history was something his aunt had mentioned about his great-grandparents coming from Edinburgh to the United States in the late 1830s – then on to Canada within a few years.

When Jack first tried to show Karen the riches of the waterfront, she ignored his direction but pointed instead to a small boy, dressed in an oversized raincoat and what looked like an older sibling's Wellies, playing in a puddle of collected water at a low point on the wharf. Jack looked around for a parent. He thought the boy was probably about four years old and soon realized he was being watched by a young woman from behind the gate of a yard that backed on to the dock area. She seemed to recognize his concern and waved to him. Jack sensed Karen's fascination as she studied the boy's actions. He approached the puddle carefully, first splashing at the edge with the toe of one boot then retreating. Forward again but using only the same one foot to splash a little deeper into the water. Finally, after summoning up the courage to act, the boy splashed forward into the middle where he stomped with both feet. The boy laughed as he splashed himself. Jack realised why he was dressed as he was on an otherwise sunny day.

Today, Jack turned onto Grant Street ready to explore some of the shops. He left the pram on the sidewalk in front of one of the buildings and carried Karen into a small main street tea room – just a few round tables hardly seeming adequate for the four chairs around each.

He was surprised to notice Mrs. Kerr sitting with Mrs. Douglas. Ivy Kerr motioned him to come share their table.

"Aye, such a braw wee bairn. You and the wifie must come talk about babysitting."

"We will, Mrs. Douglas. Thank you. Right now, I'm happy to look after Karen. I'm not doing anything else yet."

Mrs. Douglas glanced around at the other tables before replying. They were mostly occupied by men. "'Twould be guid to see these layabouts tak' care o' thair bairns."

The two women laughed. Ivy Kerr leaned toward Jack and whispered, "Take care of their children." He smiled at the translation and nodded that he had understood.

Jack noticed the stares coming his way. A man looking after a child was obviously just as uncommon in these parts as it was in Canada. He didn't say it but thought how comfortable he felt being a father, how he hoped it would contribute to a lifelong close relationship with Karen. He thought some of the younger men looked toward him with interest. Mostly, the older men stared at him, and maybe the two women as well, with looks of distrust as if he had a role in reordering a social system already disrupted by strangers, wartime and continuing post-war restraints.

▪ ▪ ▪

Jack greeted Shelagh with a hug and a kiss as she reached the top of the stairs and walked into their flat. "Tomorrow, Karen and I will be off to explore the Pictish fort."

"What's that?"

"It's at the end of the main street. The Picts may have been the original people here."

"You mean like Indians at home?"

"Possibly, but they may have migrated from elsewhere."

"But I thought it was the Vikings. Isn't that what Mrs. Kerr told us?"

Jack raised his eyebrows. "Don't know but there are a number of theories. I should take the bus to Elgin one day, check out the library."

...

Jack wandered with Karen in his arms around the outside of the ruins of the Pictish fort. He maintained a descriptive monologue and accepted Karen's gurgles and coos in reply. He was startled to hear the unmistakable sound of four V-12 Rolls-Royce Merlin engines roaring in perfect synchrony. Every Lancaster pilot, every crew member and grounds crew had that sound imprinted in their brains. Jack turned seaward to watch as the familiar bomber continued its ascent above the water of the Moray Firth. He was almost transported back, back to the multi-instrumented cockpit, back to Wickenby but the feeling of Karen in his arms kept him grounded. *Those days are past,* he reminded himself. He held Karen up to see. He pointed. "That's the airplane Daddy used to fly," he said.

72

AUGUST 1975 – HALIFAX

Cassie interrupted Jack's thoughts. "What is it you're looking for, Dad?"

"Oh, I was hoping I could point out where I was billeted. Things have changed. Sometimes that seems a little sad. But down there is Pier 21. That's where we embarked and disembarked. Immigrants used to come through here. Out there would be where the Halifax Explosion happened. There's so much history here, Cass."

Cassie turned to Karen. "Remember in high school Miss Harper prattling on. This heading in the middle of the page. Now, in the margin in red … All format, no substance. No wonder I still believe the First World War happened all because Archduke Ferdinand was assassinated in Sarajevo."

"It sure could have been taught differently." Karen leaned against the stone wall. "But I can't complain, I got full marks by parroting back some approximation of what I thought I studied. Even if I didn't see its significance."

"When we get back to the hotel," Jack said, "I'm going to call Leon at the *Chronicle-Herald*. You remember him I'm sure. He's got time tomorrow to show us some sights and tell us some tales. Leon's an expert on the history of the city. He wrote a book about the survivors of the Halifax Explosion."

■ ■ ■

Leon Buck met them at the hotel after breakfast the next day.

"You're looking good," Jack said to the tall, grey-bearded man.

Leon shook hands with Jack then feigned a punch. "Not so bad yourself, lad." Leon deliberately looked Jack up and down. "Still playing tennis, I'd guess."

"I remember you visiting us especially at the cottage when we were kids," Karen said.

"Oh, for sure. We had good times when I worked for the *Star*."

"I was never sure whether you two were war buddies."

"No, no." Leon stood tall and rubbed his beard. "I was far too young." He laughed. "Truth is I'm in good shape now but I had scarlet fever as a teenager. When I tried to enlist, they said I had a heart murmur and wouldn't take me." He laughed again. "Biggest disappointment of my life. You see the girls only went for men in uniform –"

"Don't listen to that. Leon almost made it over as a war correspondent in 1945."

"Yeah, but wouldn't you know they ended the hostilities and wrecked my chance at fame –

Jack interrupted Leon. "Such nonsense. I was billeted with Leon's family while I was waiting to ship over. That's how we met."

"I can see you hit it off." Cassie was pleased with the good-natured jostling and repartee.

"Your dad used to write to my mom from overseas. She was so thrilled when he got married. Then he came by and stayed a couple of days when he got back."

"I know you stayed in touch but it's been a long time since we've seen you."

"We worked together at the *Star* when you girls were kids. I remember a birthday party. Yours maybe …" Leon looked at Karen.

Karen regarded Leon with renewed interest. "Yes," she said. "That rings a bell. Remember, Cass? Oh wait, you were miffed the party was for me."

"I'm sorry Shelagh didn't come. It would be nice to see her again."

"Oh," Jack said. "We seem to have our own priorities these days."

"I heard you quit the paper, Jack."

"As soon as I'm back from this trip, I'm writing my novel."

"Well, aren't we all?"

"I'm serious."

"We should talk about that. But for now, I have 'til noon. Then I have to head in to the paper." He turned to the girls. "Your dad said you were interested in Pier 21. Unfortunately, there's nothing to see there. It's barricaded off. Short-sighted policy, I think – hasn't been in use for about four years. There is somewhere I'm going to take you though. I know you've seen the harbour from the Hill but this'll give a different perspective."

▪ ▪ ▪

When Leon parked on Oxford Street, the others gazed across to the nearby stone church.

"Yep. That's First Baptist. I went there as a kid 'cause I lived right over here." He pointed to the white Cape Cod style house. "You can see it's getting crowded out by apartment buildings now. We sold it when my dad died but I know who lives there now. It's changed hands a few times, of course. Nobody stays put anymore."

Leon guided them across the street to the sidewalk in front of the house. Cassie pointed toward the windowless deep blue front door. But she was fascinated by the large octagonal stained-glass window immediately adjacent to the door.

"That window's amazing," she said.

"Yeah, that was a lot of fun as a kid. Whenever anyone came to the door, I'd make faces through the stained glass." Leon stretched his mouth sideways with his thumbs and crossed his eyes. "Just imagine what I looked like from this side."

"Normal for you," Jack said.

"Let's go into the back yard."

"Is that okay?"

Leon laughed. "A little secret, Cassie. I know the owner well." He pointed to the second floor. "That was my bedroom in the corner, both windows. Visualize this. December 1917. My mum's ten years old. In school. A blast. Louder than anything you've ever heard. Or felt. Some of the people I interviewed for my book said they felt the earth shake before they heard anything. As you can guess that definitely scared the crap out of them. My mum's school, just down the street – I'll point it out when we go back to the car – shook. The kids were sent home. I can't imagine – today, you couldn't be sure a parent would be home. Anyway, I don't know whether the school tried to determine if the city was under attack – it was wartime – before they dismissed the kids. My mum talked about being scared. I'd guess terrified."

"Wow." Karen looked at her father and Cassie. She could see that her dad knew the story.

Cassandra stood with her mouth open, her hands on her cheeks. "Right where we're standing." She shook her head.

"My mum was amazing. She seemed to focus on physical damage. She told us when she got home the house looked to be undamaged but the front door was cracked top to bottom and somehow wedged closed. All the windows on the second floor overlooking the harbour were shattered. But, as she told us kids, although her parents and older siblings knew some of the people who were killed, our extended family was safe. She always tried to focus on what was good."

"I'd really like to see your mother again. We still do Christmas cards but it's been awhile."

"Well, why don't I just knock and we'll go in for tea?"

Jack squinted at Leon.

"Oh, did I forget to tell you? Mum's the new owner."

"Really. Your mother's here?"

The door opened. "Well, it's Jack Borden, sure as I live." The trim but short woman with elegantly coiffed grey hair extended her hands toward Jack. "And these must be your daughters. How nice."

"Mrs. Buck. How wonderful to see you."

"Now Jack, you've known me long enough to call me Flora."

"Yes, well … Flora. Either way it's still wonderful to see you."

"Come in, come in," Leon said. "Don't just stand there stunned, Jack. C'mon girls."

Jack quickly introduced Karen and Cassandra.

"Yes, let's have some tea." Flora grinned at Jack. "Leon told me he was going to bring you over so I made some little sandwiches. I think your father used to humour me, girls, eating the *petits fours* I made for teatime." She looked quickly from Jack to Karen and Cassie. "Then he got a girlfriend and I hardly ever saw him. But your good wife didn't come with you?"

"No. I think you know she's a photographer. She does all our Christmas cards. There was a big Georgian Bay photo shoot that needed to be scheduled for August."

"Oh, I see." Flora looked inquiringly at Jack.

Leon ushered them to the breakfast nook overlooking the lower city and the harbour. "I've been regaling them with your explosion story."

"Did you get to the part about Aunt Peggy?"

"No, I needed to leave something for you to talk about."

Flora swatted Leon good-naturedly on his arm with her serviette. "Well," she said. "He probably told you the front door wasn't functional. So, coming from school, I had to go through the gate to the backyard. Old Dr. Ballard was coming out the garden door. I should be careful, shouldn't I, characterizing people. He probably wasn't as old as I am now. But he was old Dr. Ballard. My mother had called him over. He was our neighbour, you see. Mother had been feeding my baby sister, Margaret, using a glass baby bottle. That was a pretty new thing in 1917. I didn't pay much attention to Peggy. You two know what that's about." She smiled toward Karen and Cassie. "I don't think I'd gotten over my jealousy of having my status usurped by a whiner. I think she was about three or six months old. Anyway, with the blast, the bottle exploded. Shattered pieces of glass were everywhere in this room." She swirled her hand in illustration.

"Was the baby injured?"

"No, Karen. Luckily, either she had her eyes closed in contentment or her reflexes were that good. Dr. Ballard checked her over. Mum's miracle baby, she said for years afterward. He checked her eyes particularly. I imagine she put up an unholy fuss. But she was fine."

"What about your mother?"

"That's an interesting question, Karen. All attention was on Peggy. I wasn't home yet but I'm told Dr. Ballard was about to leave when he noticed blood on my mother's neck. Of course, it wasn't like today, women wore these high collars. The bleeding wasn't very apparent. He removed a large shard close to the jugular."

Karen shook her head. "That's amazing."

No one spoke for a few moments.

Then Jack asked Flora how she'd come to purchase the house.

"I retired three years ago. I was a teacher, you know. I have a decent pension. When Charles died I no longer wanted to live here." She looked at Jack. He nodded his understanding. "I tried an apartment but it was so … what would you say Leon?"

"Restricting."

"Yes, that's it, restricting. And you know, this wasn't Charles' house. I inherited it from my parents."

"Almost like a dowry," said Jack.

Flora laughed. "Oh, believe me, Jack, Charles knew I was worth marrying even without a dowry."

"Sorry. Stupid joke."

Flora tilted her head toward Leon. "Don't worry, Jack, I'm used to those. You know, my whole life was here," she continued. "Including the Explosion. My childhood. And Leon's childhood. I missed the house, the view, the history. I had a sudden desire … no, maybe more a need to keep it in the family. I don't know whether Leon will want it but I wanted to leave the possibility open. Especially now with real estate prices so high. I paid almost fifty thousand. Imagine."

"Unless you're tired of fish, there's a place on Argyle Street I often go for lunch," Leon said. "It's just across from the office. Mum can park there and we'll walk over. It's not far from the Lord Nelson, either, for you. Besides," Leon looked at everybody. "If you want to wet your whistle, they've got Alexander Keith's on draught."

"Now, Leon." Flora patted her son's hand. "Maybe the girls don't drink." She winked at Karen who in turn smiled slyly at Cassandra.

▪ ▪ ▪

At the restaurant, Leon told them of his interest in area history. "We've formed a group to advocate for preserving historic Halifax. Take Pier 21. It's an important site, not just for Halifax but for all of Canada. Of course, every level of government tries to dismiss us. They have no money, they say."

"Ain't that the truth?"

"But we're not going to be dismissed."

"That's good."

"I agree with you, Jack," Flora said. "I'm so glad Leon's involved in this."

"Anyway, the financial columnist at the paper says ignore them all. Let them squabble amongst themselves. He says for as long as he's been writing financial stuff governments have always been in cutback mode. He says they think that's their job."

"I know what you mean." Jack snorted.

"You know," Leon looked directly at Karen and Cassie. "He also says that interest rates will continue to go higher for the next couple of years. If either of you is thinking of taking on a mortgage, you should wait."

Jack laughed. "You think we'll see eight per cent mortgages again?"

"Hardly. Anyway, back to the program already in progress. The registers from Pier 21 are surely relevant to every immigrant family. Take my family. I pored through archival records to find verification of passage. Couldn't come up with anything. Then I was talking to this history professor at Dalhousie. I actually interviewed him for a story. We came here for a beer after. So he says to me, are you sure your name is Buck. Did he take me for daft? But he explained our great-grandparents were probably illiterate, didn't know how to spell their names. And the immigration clerks may not have been much better and wrote down something of what they thought they heard."

Leon paused to sip his beer. He looked pleased he had their rapt attention. "So, he asks where the family came from. When I say Poland, he rhymes off a list of Polish family names that have Buck in them."

"That happened a lot," Jack said. "Shortening, mishearing, misspelling."

"For sure. I've written a number of articles on that topic."

"What did you find out?"

"Bucovetsky."

"That's interesting. Are you going to write about your search?"

"No plans. Why?"

"I'm writing a novel, remember. Thinking about a man, finds his name isn't what he thinks it is, goes through legal machinations to change back, tries to make claims to family fortune in the old country. Something like that."

"You want to steal my story."

When he saw Leon's face fall, Jack beamed. "Gotcha. I'm not going to do that even though it would make good fiction."

"Actually, I don't have enough material for a memoir."

"Are you planning to do something with it?"

"Yeah, but maybe I should just let the great Jack Borden filch my ideas."

"Iain." It was Leon's turn to look confused. Jack continued. "Iain's my actual name. I'm toying with being Iain Borden for fiction. Stick with Jack for everyday use."

73

SEPTEMBER 1946 – BURGHEAD

Jack heard Shelagh's feet pounding on the stairs to their flat. Alarmed he moved quickly to meet her. She was beaming. She looked happier than Jack recalled seeing for months.

"Jack, Jack, good news." Her face was animated, smiling broadly, eyes alive, as she reached for his hug. "We're going to have a baby. I'm pregnant."

"Wow, sweetheart. That is good news." *Poor Karen. Having to share our attention so soon.*

"Doctor says end of March, first of April. I thought I was gaining a little weight. I haven't even felt sick."

"What's the air force think?"

"You silly man, of course you're the first person I've told."

"Of course." Jack nodded his head. So different from last time.

"I'm not planning to tell Pamela right off. Let her find out in due time. There's nothing strenuous about the job."

"What about the bus ride over to the base?"

"Well, that's the most strenuous part of my day. As long as the weather's good, I'll still ride my bike. Doctor says that's okay for now but I may need more rest later."

Jack continued to hold Shelagh. She'd folded into his arms, something she hadn't done for a while. *Feels good,* he thought. *Another child. I know she's counting on a boy.* Then he thought, *she must have known awhile.*

About two weeks previously, Shelagh was sitting looking out the large front windows when she turned to watch Karen lying on her stomach, reaching for the small teddy bear Jack had placed just outside her reach, kicking her legs, getting ready to crawl.

"You know, Jackie," she said. "A boy and a girl would be so perfect."

Sure, Jack thought, *we have built-in child care. Me. One's a handful.*

74

MAY 2007 – SUZANNE'S HOUSE, OTTAWA

"I'm glad we could finally get together." Suzanne Best carried a tray of snacks and two mugs of beer toward Karen who was sitting on a chaise lounge on Suzanne's garden patio.

"I'm curious about your bird houses," Karen said.

"Bluebird boxes."

"Here? In the middle of the city?"

"Well, I picked them up at a yard sale, cleaned and painted them, as you can see."

"What do you get?"

"Wrens. Noisy, early morning riser wrens. But damn it, Jim." Suzanne puffed herself up to full height and lowered her voice timbre. "I'm a doctor not an ornithologist."

Both women laughed. They clanked beer mugs.

"*Santé.*" Karen replied to Suzanne's toast then sipped her beer. "Oh, this tastes good."

"It's from a new local brewery – Beau's."

"You know, I don't drink beer very often. Even when I visit Cassie's place, it's usually red wine."

"I can switch you –"

"No, no. I like this. Takes me back to student days."

"Time flies, doesn't it," Suzanne said. "Has it really speeded up or is it just us?"

"Then there's my dad just sitting there. I wonder if time flies for him or just crawls."

"How is Jack? I haven't been to *La Maison* in a while."

"You know, Suzanne, he is so different every time I see him. Either I've come to grips with his deterioration and see him as normal, or –"

"Or what?"

"Or is it possible to recover from dementia?"

"Well, they have good and bad days, seemingly in and out but, you know, research shows –"

"Don't go all academic on me, Dr. Best."

Suzanne laughed then became serious again. "The short answer is no."

Karen and Suzanne continued to enjoy the deepening evening with an after-dinner late harvest Riesling.

"Instead of dessert," Suzanne had said. "You're such a carb counter."

"*Moi*? Carb counter?" Karen laughed then started to sing. "If I'd known you were coming, I woulda baked a cake … Hey, this is a perfect finish."

"Who says we're finished? There's still a few bottles of Beau's."

"This is such a great time of year – still daylight at eight o'clock, no insects and I don't need a sweater yet."

Suzanne had served marinated chicken breast pieces cooked on a skewer with red and green pepper and sweet onion chunks. While Suzanne barbequed Karen prepared stuffed baked potatoes. She'd become a fan of potato skins but had adapted a recipe she found to suit herself. The first time she prepared them she dutifully saved the scooped-out potato flesh for another use as the recipe suggested. But it reminded her of when she bought a juicer and saved the fruit and vegetable pulp for other uses also only to discard the castoffs after several days. She stopped juicing. Then she changed the potato technique, mashed the scoopings, added freshly made spinach dip and sharp cheddar cheese, stuffed the potato skins with this mixture, *et voilà* – stuffed baked potatoes. It was only later she discovered she was not the originator of this well-tested method.

After a few minutes of silence, Suzanne said, "You know, when I first saw your dad, he didn't know me. I realize it had been several years since we'd seen each other. Even when I explained who I was there was no recognition. But he covered verbally. That looked practiced to me, like he'd been used to covering for a while."

"It's funny, Suzanne. We do that ourselves. At what point does a seniors' moment become dementia?"

Suzanne laughed. "Absolutely. Sometimes I wonder whether it's simply because seniors are scrutinized for faulty responses and behaviours."

"He'd been slipping since before Mom died. And probably for a long time before that. He had a kitchen fire – became distracted. He forgot he was cooking."

. . .

Suzanne and Karen remained on the patio well past dusk. As the darkness deepened, Suzanne lit four patio torches.

"I've gotta trim those wicks." Black smoke plumed above the flickering yellow light straight up toward the sky.

"It's okay," Karen said. "We're not breathing it."

"I'll get the scissors." Suzanne headed into the house. When she came back she had a bottle of Sortilège and two brandy snifters.

"I thought you went for scissors."

"I got distracted. Tomorrow's another day." Suzanne poured the maple syrup whisky blend. "I was thinking again about our dementia discussion."

Karen nodded. "And –"

"It's a puzzler because he's so much different now. His cognitive test scores are almost normal. Anecdotally, there's some thought that consistent routine could help stabilize him. You see him regularly. That gives continuity. And I know you talk normally with him and don't revert to baby talk."

"Baby talk …"

"You know … patronizing, condescending." Suzanne changed to a mocking tone. "How are *we* doing today?" Then she asked, "Who diagnosed him, anyway?"

"Dr. Watson. I don't know him."

"Dr. Watson I presume. Was it Jock Watson?"

"Yeah, that's it."

"He's a good diagnostician. Alzheimer's expert."

"You know, Suzanne, I didn't even question it. I visited Mom more than Dad. He seemed so hard to get along with. That's why my mom left."

"That doesn't sound like your dad."

"It wasn't. I guess that's why a dementia diagnosis made perfect sense to me. Not that my mom was easy to live with. Dementia seemed a fitting explanation. But what explains how he is now?"

"Frankly, I don't know."

"Frankly, my dear ..." Both women laughed.

75

NOVEMBER 1946 – BURGHEAD

Shelagh looked tired when she arrived home.

"Hard day?" Jack asked.

"Yeah, it's the bus ride after all. It seems too long, stopping in each village."

"That's what you used to enjoy."

"Everything's so grey now."

"Yes, November's like that. Even at home it's my least favourite month."

"Jackie, there are good flats available in Lossiemouth now. Maybe we should move. I could manage the short ride to the base."

No. I like it here. Though it probably wouldn't make any difference to Karen. She's only nine months old. But Jack didn't say what he was thinking. Instead he said, "We could look."

■ ■ ■

"Sheils, I got a letter today from Rob. We may not need to move."

"We can't get away from him even here!"

"Listen. He has a friend in Aberdeen who has a car he would be willing to lend us. You wouldn't need to take the bus – I could drive you. And …" Jack was excited by the idea. "When it comes time, I could drive you to the hospital."

"I don't want to go to Elgin."

"I'm talking about driving you to work."

"Not that. When the baby's due, I want a bigger hospital."

"You know, Sheils, most women here have midwives deliver their babies. He could be born right here." Jack encompassed their salon with both arms.

"No."

Jack looked surprised.

"There are better hospitals in Inverness and Aberdeen."

"Well, I could certainly drive you there. Maybe Aberdeen – they have a medical school."

"Yes, Jackie. I would prefer that."

. . .

"What kind of car is it?" Shelagh looked out the window at the black four-door sedan.

Mrs. Douglas had taken care of Karen for the day so Jack could go to Aberdeen to fetch the car. The eighty-mile drive back took him about four hours.

"It's a 1940 Hillman – practically new. It was in storage for most of the war."

"And we can have it?"

"It's sad as it turns out. It was Rob's friend's brother's car – a Lancaster pilot who didn't come back. All these years they thought he was a POW but his body was identified in the summer."

"They should have sold the car."

"They wanted a keepsake – something that belonged to Teddy. Teddy, that was his name. Also, not many in this region can afford to buy a car yet."

"So, we have it for how long?"

"As long as we need it. Because I flew Lancasters."

"I hope you remember to thank Mr. Davies," she said stiffly.

"I will." Jack paused. "You'll like this. The man I talked to is a doctor – an obstetrician at the Aberdeen Royal Infirmary. I'm to drive you there next Saturday so he can examine you."

"Hey, just a minute! Am I hearing this right? You're choosing my doctor!"

"He's a specialist –"

"That's not the point."

"I thought you'd be pleased."

"You just don't get it."

"Does the base have an obstetrician on staff?" Jack was angry now.

"Really, Jackie. Is this just so your little boy will be born in the Royal Infirmary?"

Jack noticed Karen seated in her highchair, closely watching the whole interchange. He shook his head. "I'm sorry," he said finally. "I was just trying to help."

76

MAY 2007 – KINGSTON

Karen read Suzanne's name on the phone screen before she answered. "Hello there," she said. "Miss me already?"

"As if." Suzanne laughed. "I'm assuming you got home okay."

"Yeah. Lots of traffic on the 416. But I stopped in on Dad so I was a little later leaving Ottawa."

"Jack good?"

"Yeah really. I'm starting to think my idea of taking him to the UK may not be that crazy."

"Well," Suzanne said. "I've been thinking ... One of the reasons I called. What if Jack doesn't have dementia."

"What are you talking about? Just seniors' moments or something?"

Suzanne explained that she hadn't been able to sleep after Karen left. Had lain awake processing their weekend conversations and concerns. She described how she had gotten up from bed and spent over an hour checking her old psychology texts and looking for new information and trends on the Internet.

"And to answer your question, no, not seniors' moments but maybe delirium –"

Karen started to interrupt.

"Wait a minute. I really haven't formed a good argument but listen to me."

"Okay."

"He's in and out, alert sometimes, quite lucid. Then confused. Now the letters, the Internet. He has interests – maybe renewing previous attractions."

"Can he recover?"

"Oh definitely. You know, it's like what we were talking about, the difficulty diagnosing anything in the elderly. Forgetful episodes may just be forgetful episodes."

They continued to discuss Jack's nutrition levels, his hydration and electrolyte balance, his disinterest in things previously very important to him, the things that had bothered Suzanne right from the time Karen had first asked her to see Jack in her professional capacity.

"Where did this all start?" Karen asked.

"With the death of your mother."

"But they had lived apart for a long time when Mom died."

"That may be but they were important to each other. Neither had another relationship. They stayed in close touch."

"Couldn't live with each other. Couldn't live without each other. Here I thought they stayed civil for my and Cassie's sake. And for Cassie's kids. Thanks Suzanne. I'd love to accept that it may not be dementia. But I don't know if I'm ready to buy in yet except what you say makes some sense."

"*De rien. Pas de problème.*"

77

EARLY DECEMBER 1946 – RAF LOSSIEMOUTH

Pamela came out of her office as Shelagh was walking by. "Pearson, hold up," she called. "Pearson. Shelagh, when were you going to tell me you're pregnant?"

"I… uh, sorry ma'am. I don't know. I… uh, I wanted to be sure myself."

"What do you take me for? All I need to do is look at you and I'm sure. Come into the office." Pamela motioned her in. "Sit."

Neither woman said anything for a moment until Pamela pointed at Shelagh's swollen belly. "How long?"

"Almost six months."

"I figured you were pregnant. I've been trying to figure out protocol. It comes to this, Shelagh. You will be able to work until the end of January, then you'll have to resign."

"From the RCAF?"

"From the RCAF and, I think, the reserves."

"I can't do that. It's my life."

"The military does not allow two pregnancy leaves."

"But, Pamela –" Shelagh needed to collect her thoughts. She knew she was sounding panicky.

"It's Section Officer, Pearson."

"Yes, ma'am."

▪ ▪ ▪

"Then we'll go home," Jack said.

"Oh Jackie, I so much want the little one to be born in Scotland. Can't we stay, please?"

She's not even upset. Like it's a clean break and she can … we can … start over.

"Maybe we can move to Aberdeen, closer to the hospital. I do like Dr. MacIntyre so much better than stuffy old Burgess in Peterborough. It would make my mom so happy for the wee one to be born here. Maybe your mom too."

"My mother's family is from Ireland. Sheils, I don't mind staying a while but we'll have to go home sometime."

"Yes, yes, of course Jackie. But not just yet."

78

MAY 2007 – *LA MAISON ENSOLEILLÉE*

"I'm not sure, Robbie." Jack stopped at the water fountain.

"Why, Jack?"

"This trip is so important to Karen. She has big … umm …"

"Expectations?" Roberto stepped toward the nursing station and grabbed a Kleenex. "It's not a serviette but it'll have to do."

Jack dabbed his wet lips and wiped his forehead. "I can barely make it around the hallway."

"That's okay. That'll improve. We have plans for you."

"That's what I'm worried about."

"Don't be so concerned. Jeremy and I have entered a half-marathon. You know we won't just get up that morning and run it cold."

"I know that. You're both in good shape."

"Absolutely. We've been training already for a month. And that's what you're going to do also. You're going to train."

"I won't run any marathon."

"No, that's for Jeremy and me. Besides it's only a half-marathon." Roberto watched Jack's reaction to the half-marathon joke. He waved toward the hallway door. "Here comes Jeremy now."

"Hey Gramps."

"Hey Germ …" Jack glanced toward Roberto. "… um … Jeremy."

"Looks like you and Roberto are doing serious training."

"Like I said, I'm not running any marathon." Jack quipped.

"Nah, we won't make you do that. But are you ready to rumble?"

"Let me go in here first." Jack opened the washroom door. "I wouldn't want to be caught in no-man's land."

When Jack was gone, Roberto asked Jeremy whether he had talked with his sister.

"She's not sure she can get the time off. Something about post-tax season. Accountant speak."

"It's a unique opportunity. Jack won't be going again."

Jeremy blinked. "I hadn't thought of that. I need to explain that to Marianne."

79

JANUARY 1947 – BURGHEAD

Jack was surprised to see Fiona Douglas at Ivy Kerr's this early. He knew the two widows were almost constant companions – coffee, tea, shopping – but he thought he was getting a prompt start to his day. He assumed the women to be in their early sixties but was only guessing. He'd read in a magazine about life expectancy in Scotland. For the men, if he remembered correctly, it was shy of fifty years. He didn't know the comparison for Canada but had the notion that a man could expect to retire at sixty-five and live a few years beyond that. He didn't know why the two women were widows. Maybe war related. He felt it was too delicate a question to pose. In a village the size of Burghead, he could ask almost anyone but that offended his sense of propriety, privacy. Then he sometimes thought he could strategically ask either one of them about the other. But that opportunity never seemed to present itself.

Mrs. Douglas put her coffee cup down, turned her chair, placed her elbows on the kitchen table and looked intently at Jack. "It's the Burning of the Clavie," she said in answer to Jack's question about the busy excitement, ornamenting and trimming happening in the village.

"The what?" Jack asked.

"Th' Clavie, ma loon. Jist the Burnin` o' the Clavie. It's the Broch's new year."

Jack looked puzzled. He was anxious to get to the library to continue his research. He was excited to have a chance to work on his proposed article on the ancient Pictish people and this discussion with the women seemed to play right into it. Ivy Kerr smiled and placed her hand on Jack's forearm.

"Don't mind her, Jack my boy. That's her intent," Ivy said, hand still on Jack's arm. "To baffle you." To Mrs. Douglas she said, "Lave peer jimmy alane, Fiona. His puir brain is rattled enaw jist haen coffee wi' us twa."

Both women laughed. Jack had caught the mischievous twinkle in Fiona Douglas's eye. He realized she was just having fun. Not necessarily even at his expense there being no other audience. He glanced over to Karen, asleep, wrapped in a blanket on the daybed. He had brought Karen over to Mrs. Kerr's because he needed to catch the bus to Elgin.

"New Years," he said. "That we celebrated just last week."

"Aye, loon. War's ower. We'll celebrate anythin' aroon here. Ye can eay come tae th' parade, ma loon."

"She's pullin' yer leg, Jack," Ivy said. "She spiks the King's English guid as ony o's aroon here. We fall into our own dialect when it's convenient. She was a school teacher in Edinburgh, for pity's sake. And you know how soft they speak. English literature, do you please. Don't you mind her."

"They'd think ah wis stuck up if ah blether lik' ye. Th' wummin, ah mean. Doesn't maiter whit th' men think." Fiona slapped Jack's shoulder. Then she stood, clasped her hands in front. "Now class, the English literature of the sixteenth century is of particular importance to us this term as we study …" Eying Jack, both women chortled.

Jack smiled, picked up his coffee. "Tell me more about the Clavie," he said.

▪ ▪ ▪

"It'll be an exciting night," Jack told Shelagh later. "This is only the second Burning of the Clavie since the war."

"Why?" Shelagh asked.

"It's a bonfire, lass. The war. Blackout." Jack grinned then admitted he'd had the same conversation over at Ivy Kerr's. He related how Fiona Douglas had arranged for him to interview Jimmy McKenzie and Jock

Ralph, two of the local crew working to resurrect the tradition now that the war was over.

"Peep will talk with you," Fiona had said. "I know he's busy but he'll talk. I used to teach him. He'll do it for me."

"Peep?"

"Ah well, there's two Jimmy McKenzies, you see. Peep and Lichtie. Both on the Clavie crew."

80

JUNE 2007 – HEATHROW AIRPORT, LONDON, ENGLAND

Jack scanned the International Arrivals level at Heathrow airport. "I'm glad we're here, Karen. I was nervous about the flight."

"It was okay to be nervous."

"When will Cassandra get here?"

"There they are now, Dad." Karen watched through the windowed wall until Cassie and Tom turned the final corner. She waved to catch her sister's attention. "Cassie! Over here."

Cassandra turned to speak to Tom and pointed out Karen and Jack. She smiled broadly but shrugged her shoulders as she dragged her suitcase along the crowded passageway. Just too many other passengers to deke quickly through.

Tom saw Jeremy first. He was standing out of his mother's sightline. Tom touched his forehead in salute of recognition. Then he saw Marianne standing behind her brother. He nodded to her. Tom hadn't been certain Marianne was going to be able to make the trip. Her boss had been reluctant to allow her the time off. *Accountants,* he thought. *As if they run the world.*

Cassie went immediately to her father once she disentangled herself from the crowd.

"Dad." She hugged him and kissed both his cheeks. "It's so good to see you. Especially here."

"Well, my dear. I'm pleased as punch myself. Never thought I'd see England again. I only wish your mother were here too."

Karen greeted Tom with a hug then grabbed his hand to lead him toward Jack. "Dad, you know Tom."

"Yes, of course. Hello." Karen told me to be nice, Jack thought.

"Good to see you, Mr. Borden."

"Call me Jack." Jack paused. "Mr. Borden's my father."

Tom laughed. "I hear you, Jack."

Jack relaxed and smiled to himself. *Maybe he is okay.*

Jeremy strolled forward to join his family. "Hi, Mom."

"Jeremy." Cassie's eyes brimmed with tears. She melted into Jeremy's arms. "Oh, this is so perfect. Tom, look who's here …"

"I know," said Tom. He winked at Jeremy, allowed Cassie time with him before he greeted Jeremy with a hug himself. "You're not his only e-mail pal," he said to her. "Look who's with him."

"Marianne! Oh my lord. This is just so perfect."

. . .

Karen hugged her sister again. "I booked that cottage you suggested."

"Thanks, sis. That's where Tom and I stayed last year. It's pretty."

"A change from Kosova?"

"Yes. But it's still not a Georgian Bay cottage, K-G."

"I know – it's a house in the village."

Cassie smiled at her sister. "There are little shops."

"As if that would interest Dad!"

Karen raised her eyebrows. "Don't worry. We're going to do Dad things. Look at the two of them."

Jack and Tom were standing together at the car rental counter. Tom had encouraged Jack to accompany him to complete the paperwork for the pre-arranged vehicle. They seemed to be chatting amicably as they waited for the file to be retrieved. Jack's initially crossed arms were now at his side as he turned to face Tom. Even though she wasn't quite close enough, Cassie thought her dad's eyes showed a liveliness she hadn't seen for years.

Karen arranged a shuttle to take them to the vehicle pickup point. *Let's just get Dad out of this airport chaos*, she thought. *He'll need his energy for more important things.* Jeremy and Roberto had pitched in to prepare Jack physically to be here. She was grateful for that.

▪ ▪ ▪

Tom had reserved a Kia Sportage with enough room and comfortable seating for the six of them and their luggage.

"It's not a van is it, Jack?" he said.

"Tom told the girl at the counter … the woman at the counter, I mean." Jack paused for effect. He was pleased to see the smirks on their faces. "Anyway, Tom said he reserved a van. They couldn't find the reservation."

"Yeah," Tom said. "Turns out, a van's what a tradesman uses. You know, what we call a panel truck."

"Apparently we've rented a people mover," Jack said.

"Looks good to me, whatever it's called." Cassie stood hands on hips admiring the vehicle.

"Oh, and it's an automatic," Tom said. "That's a lesson I've learned."

Cassie took over the explanation. "First time Tom and I were here we reserved a rental car, not even thinking about the transmission. Not only the steering wheel on the wrong side but of course it was a standard …"

"Yeah, we flew into Glasgow airport. Immediately to the rental counter. Then, just imagine … haven't driven a standard for years, clutching, shifting with my left, first thing we encounter is a roundabout. Not only shifting with my wrong hand but driving on the wrong side of the road and … going in circles."

Cassie made a face. "That was the last time we didn't specify automatic."

"What about Kosova?" Jeremy asked.

"Oh we –" Tom and Cassandra started to answer in unison, looked at each other. Tom continued: "We don't drive there. It's too complicated – insurance, other stuff. Things are getting better but there are still a lot of accidents. We don't need that."

81

JUNE 2007 – NEWARK-ON-TRENT, NOTTINGHAMSHIRE

Emma's Cottage was more than Karen had hoped for – a four-bedroom house with modern kitchen, comfortable living room and library, back garden and a view from upstairs of the meandering River Trent.

"My thought is we can drive to Wickenby day after tomorrow." Karen was alone with Cassie stocking the refrigerator and kitchen shelves.

"You want to keep the old man in suspense, eh?"

"Nah, but you know as well as I do. He could use some down-time to get over the trip."

"We all could, I'm sure."

"Newark's a great town. We can wander over to Market Square. Just tourist it."

"Sounds good, sis."

▪ ▪ ▪

"We missed the Beer Festival by a couple of weeks." Tom showed Jeremy a tourist pamphlet. "Good news though, lots of pubs."

"I'm glad I came, Tom. I needed a break."

"I thought you might. That's an ambitious program you've undertaken."

"You and Mom were able to do it."

"Sure we did. I hate to say it but looking back it seems like it was a simpler time. Your field is so open ended. Knowledge expands so rapidly."

"Dinosaurs," Jeremy teased.

"Thanks. But not just that Jeremy. You have opportunities like the human genome project. Endless possibilities."

They stood looking over the red and white roofed tents of Market Square.

"Tom …"

Tom had just started to stroll toward one of the tents. He stopped. Turned to Jeremy.

"There's something … I mean I need to know something … about Mom … how she'd react."

Tom stood quietly.

"It's just … I don't know … I didn't know this'd be so difficult …"

"I'm listening, man."

"It's me and Roberto … we … we're getting an apartment …"

Tom didn't say anything immediately but he soon broke the silence. "You're a couple?"

Jeremy stepped back from Tom, looked away, his eyes blinking quickly.

Tom reached out, pulled Jeremy into a hug. "Hey, man. Don't worry about your mother. She'll be happy for you. Me too. We only met Roberto once but I liked him. Instinctively. Your grandpa thinks the world of him."

"What worries me is my dad. Not just you and Mom … Dad."

"Just take it one step at a time. Do it quietly. No dramatic announcements. First your mother."

Jeremy winced. "And Grandpa?"

"I don't know about Jack. Grandparents are cooler than you may think. And believe me, your mother will have no problem. She loves you, man. Talk with her about how to approach your dad and your grandpa."

"Do you have gay friends, Tom?"

"Everyone has." And Tom hugged him again.

82

JANUARY 1947 – BURGHEAD

"I'm so tired, Jackie," Shelagh said. Looking at her, Jack could see how strained she was.

"You'll soon be finished work," he said. "We can celebrate that as well. You'll have time to rest then."

"Only if you and Karen get out of the flat and leave me alone."

"I was hoping when you were home I could get some writing done. You know, so I can bring home the bacon now."

"Maybe Mrs. Kerr will still take her."

. . .

On Tuesday afternoon, a few days in advance of the big event, Jack watched the men put the finishing touches on the Clavie, the traditional tar-soaked half whisky barrel packed with tar- and creosote-saturated slivers and shavings of wood. The Clavie was then fastened to a four-foot pole, as Peep explained, held by a special nail that had been used for years before the war, rescued each year from the cooled remains of the charred mess. Then the lower barrel stave structure was completed so the burning tar barrel could be carried through the village by the Clavie King and the Clavie crew.

"Th' Clavie King an' each member ay th' Clavie Crew main be a Brocher," Peep told Jack.

"Must be what?"

"Born in Burghead."

▪ ▪ ▪

"You know," Ivy Kerr had said. "*The Northern Scot* always gives our Hogmanay a big centre spread in their newspaper. But it's just from Elgin. This renewed vigour after the war. That's just the sort of thing *The Scotsman* would be keen for. And your foreign paper back home as well."

Jack had thought immediately of Shelagh. "I'm planning to offer the Clavie story to *The Scotsman* in addition to *The Examiner*," he told her back in their flat. "It's spectacular from all I've heard. So to really do justice we need pictures. You could take some amazing photos to accompany the story. What do you think?"

Shelagh was slumped on the chesterfield. "I wonder." She sat up. "I'm sure I can borrow a camera from the base. Maybe a Speed Graphic would be the way to go – large format, you know."

Jack smiled at Shelagh's choice – a camera he was so familiar with from his days at *The Examiner*. "The picture quality would be great," he said.

"I wonder if we could get hold of some of that new Kodachrome film," Shelagh said.

"I doubt that'd be possible around here. A luxury item like that – not when food is still rationed."

"What about the photo shop in Elgin?"

"It's possible ... but maybe Ewan Sangster from *The Scotsman* is a better bet. There's bound to be film available in Edinburgh. I could get him to send it up by mail. Only problem Sheils, the newspapers print black and white."

"Then, we'll just submit my colour shots to one of the big magazines." Shelagh spread her hands in front of her face visualizing her photo spread.

▪ ▪ ▪

Jack and Shelagh left their flat shortly after dark. Jack decided to carry Karen, unsure what to expect. Fiona had shown him how to sling a blanket in front so he could carry Karen on his chest. She called it a Welsh blanket. Jack was sure that was some kind of slur. But he tried it and it worked.

By all accounts, the Clavie usually burned with flames shooting ten or more feet into the air. He didn't know whether this happened along the parade route or after it was placed in the destination clavie cairn . He didn't know what to expect an infant's reaction to be. He wanted to keep her safe. And warm – the wind had not dropped at sundown tonight. Temperature just above freezing but at least the daytime patchy drizzle had ended.

Jack was pleased Shelagh seemed engaged in the outing. She had borrowed two cameras and Jack had managed to have her magical Kodachrome film sent from Edinburgh. Before they left the apartment Shelagh handed Jack the Argus camera.

"You take the newspaper shots," she said. "I'll be pursuing art."

That's all I need, Jack thought. *But at least the camera's small. Just a 35mm.* He envisioned himself attempting to steady the camera with Karen slung across his chest.

They didn't venture very far from home at first but waited with the people lining King Street just a hundred yards from the Sellar Street flat. The crowd started to cheer as the spectacle of an approaching burning nest carried high in the air by three men advanced toward their corner. Jack knew from his research that smouldering ember fragments were dropped outside the village pubs to offer good luck for the new year. Other embers were dropped outside houses of prominent citizens, so when Jimmy McKenzie pointed to him and dropped a small piece of smouldering barrel stave before him, he was startled.

Jack touched his chest. "Me?"

"Fur th' wee bairn," Jimmy said. Then he pointed at Shelagh. "An' th' bairn suin tae come. Fur startin' yer new years fire. Tae keep th' witches awa'."

Jack wasn't sure how he expected Karen to react to the fire and boisterous crowd. She grabbed him tightly around the neck but otherwise was wide-eyed with wonder. Shelagh stood back, her large press camera ready to fire, framing her perfect shot. She was excited that Jack was able to get Kodachrome film from Edinburgh. She had snagged four powerful flashbulbs from the base so she knew she could light up the on-coming parade for a hand-held shot.

They knew they would not be able to have Kodachrome processed locally. They would need to send the exposed sheet film pack to Kodak in London. Shelagh would have time to decide which magazine she would approach with her colour transparencies. And as far as she was concerned Jack could do whatever he wanted with his news photo black-and-white shots.

"Let's go right to the fort. I'd like to get a shot of the clavie when they place it in the chimney," she said.

Jack checked Karen. "Sure," he said. "We can cut through town over to Grant Street and up. The crowd will stay with the clavie."

. . .

The marchers looked tired but exhilarated as they approached the end of the parade route at Doorie Hill and the final resting place for this year's Clavie on the stone altar in front of what Jack had come to know to be the ruins of the early Pictish fort. Several more men pushed in with hands and arms to help carry the flaming half barrel the last few yards up the hill. All the men who'd helped carry it through the streets were there for the final lift.

Shelagh had carried a heavy wooden tripod with her all evening, mounting the camera as she deemed necessary to create a steady platform to use with the slow-speed colour film. She assembled the tripod arrangement once again so she could capture silhouetted images against the flame background lighting up the harbour and the end of the peninsula projecting into the Moray Firth. Fire spilled over but flames still leapt robustly at least ten feet into the heavens.

. . .

Jack slipped out of the apartment early the next morning, Saturday, to return to the Pictish fort site. He was surprised to see about a dozen people in the near dawn combing through the scattered ash, picking the larger pieces of the charred remains. He approached one of the older men he remembered as one of the Clavie crew. "Jack Borden," he said as he offered his hand to the man.

"Och aye, Ah ken fa ye ur." Then he thrust his hand to grab Jack's. "Peter Robertson," he said.

"Why are people picking up those burnt bits?"

"These they will take back to their cottages. Stuff 'em up their chimneys to hold off spirits and witches for the year." Peter Robertson had switched to English. "For good luck, you see."

Folklore, Jack thought. *Superstition.* Then, with a shrug of his shoulders, he picked up a small chunk of charcoal himself. Double, double, toil and trouble. He shook his head. If it keeps the witches away.

As well as the luck scavengers, another of the Clavie crew rooted through the remains at the base of the altar, the Douro. Peter motioned Jack over to join the other man.

"I think you recognize the Clavie King," he said. "He must recover the nail."

"Got it." Jock Ralph showed Jack the now cooled large special nail that had fastened the symbolic new year and old year parts of the Clavie together. The nail would be used again in the ritual next January 11.

"Where were you?" Shelagh asked when Jack returned.

"You and Karen were both sound asleep. I didn't want to disturb you."

"I would have liked to go with you," she said when Jack described what he had done.

83

JUNE 2007 – WICKENBY AIRFIELD, LINCOLNSHIRE

Jeremy had been pleased Tom had asked if he wished to drive when they left that morning for Wickenby. He wanted the experience but hoped traffic would be light. They planned to bypass the City of Lincoln. They were going only about thirty miles.

As they passed by small farms getting close to Wickenby airfield, Jack straightened in his seat, looked out the window adjacent to him and leaned toward Cassie to see through her window as well.

Karen sat in the third-row seat with Marianne. All in the vehicle were silent but Karen was focussed on her dad. She sensed his growing anticipation. She hoped this excursion would turn out as well as she and Cassie had planned.

"Turn off A158 onto Lincoln Road," Tom said. "That should be at the flashing light up ahead. It's a B series road but we only need to travel about a half mile."

"Okay, I see the sign. It says Aerodrome."

"There's no road name on the map but we want Watery Lane."

"Watery Lane. Isn't that a hoot." Cassie leaned forward. "Well, Dad. Almost there."

Jack ducked to look through the windshield. His expression was deadpan. But his eyes were alive with emotion.

Jeremy drove into the parking lot near the only building. Tom helped Jack from his seat. All eyes were on Jack, watching his reaction. Jack rubbed his chin and nodded his head.

"I spent an important part of my life here," he said.

"How long were you here?"

"It's not the time, Tom. It's the memories, and a lifetime of friendship since." Jack pointed to the squat two storey white-stucco building. "That was the control tower. Looks just the same."

"Sign says there's a museum and a café." Karen pointed it out to her dad. "Anybody want a cuppa."

"Maybe in a minute." Jack walked back toward the road and peered toward some overgrown rubble across Watery Lane. "Let's look over there."

Tom quickly retrieved two walking sticks from the vehicle. Jack had refused his offer to buy a cane when they had wandered through Market Square but he took more interest when Tom stopped to examine hand-carved walking sticks. He told Jack he collected walking sticks and hiking poles.

"I've switched to adjustable poles when I'm hiking," he said. "I prefer to use two now. But I love these carved sticks. They're good for balance, poking in the underbrush and they just look first-rate. And hey, you can actually lean on it to rest."

"I like the look of this one."

"That looks good on you. That and a Tilley hat."

Jack laughed, looked at the shelf of hats in the display. "Looks like wool toques or baseball caps."

"What about this?" Tom held up a broad-brimmed cotton hat enclosed in bug netting.

"If we're dealing with midgies, I'm not going. Had enough of those when I took leave in the north. Those bloodsuckers were as bad as black-flies." Jack took an Irish fisherman's cap, placed it on his head, and turned to look at Tom. "How's this look?"

"Jaunty. Aye right. 'Tis you. Try it with the stick you like." Tom placed his hand on the shaft. "Grip it just under the wolf head."

▪ ▪ ▪

Now, Jack poked around in the underbrush. He'd always feared snakes. He remembered some horseplay involving a rather large grass snake so he knew the reptiles were native to the area. *Maybe that wasn't Wickenby,* he thought. *One of the training bases. We didn't have much time for foolishness once we were operational. I wonder if the village pub is still there. The Black Goat or something. Probably the Black Sheep.*

"Grandpa." Jeremy and Marianne had pushed on ahead. The other three were hanging back to make sure Jack was okay. "Grandpa." Marianne was running back toward him. She stopped and pointed toward Jeremy who was waving. "Right over there is the ruins of a … I guess Quonset hut … or is it Nissen hut?"

"Nissen hut. British base, you know."

Tom nudged Cassandra and indicated Jack with his head. "Give him some help," he said quietly. "Just be close. Don't make him feel you're hovering."

"When did you become such an expert on my dad?"

Tom raised his eyebrows but then relaxed his face into a smirk. "We also serve …"

When everyone had joined Jeremy, he showed them the still-standing frame of the hut. Most of the roof was gone. *Probably pieces scavenged*, he thought. Some remaining sections had actually rusted through in places. Part of the lower cinder block structure had collapsed or been pushed in. Graffiti marked the intact fragments of wall. Mostly modern intricate designs with a definite anti-war message. Make love, not war in red spray paint, peace signs, anti-nuclear weapons symbols in black. Stop war, no war, free Palestine overlapped, layers of messaging from immediate post-war to present-day.

Jack stiffened as he looked through the doorway. "Make love, not war," he said quietly. Jack didn't move into the structure although that had been his intention. "They have no idea what it was like," he said. "Because we fought they have the freedom to mock us."

Jeremy hesitated behind Jack, mistaking his grandfather's reticence for concern about his unsure footing if he ducked through the entranceway. "Do you want to come in with me?"

"I'd like to remember it as it was." Jack closed his eyes and bowed his head.

...

Upstairs in the museum they viewed the Wickenby Memorial Collection. Cassie pointed out the corner control tower, still functioning, responsible for the still active runway surfaces. "I think of a control tower as a tower, high up over the airport."

"We didn't want that," Jack responded. "For safety. This is high ground already. We didn't want to provide the Germans such an obvious target."

"You should give the museum a copy of *Assaulting Happy Valley*, Gramps. Most of the books displayed here are memoirs."

"That's the point, memoirs. *Happy Valley* is fiction."

"But Dad, Wickenby is alive, almost a character, in your story. I think Jeremy's right."

"Thanks, Mom."

"I'll ... maybe it's a good idea. I'll see once we're home."

Cassie looked toward Jeremy. He slipped off his small backpack, unzipped its main compartment and drew out a copy of Jack's novel.

"I just happen to have a copy if you'd like to donate it."

Jack accepted the book from Jeremy. "Where'd you get this? It's ... um ... like new. It's been out of print for years."

Jeremy simply smiled, cocked his head, shrugged his shoulders. "We have our ways."

...

Tom, Cassandra and Karen spread out through the small room examining the displays. Jeremy and Marianne accompanied Jack while he spoke to a volunteer about donating artefacts, in this case, his book. Following that, Jack parked himself on a chair in front of an old short-wave radio set with a pair of attached headphones. Marianne turned away and rejoined the others. Jeremy stayed by Jack's side.

"Thank you, kiddo. That was a nice thing you did, bringing the book." Jack reached up to pat Jeremy on the shoulder. He picked up the headphones, examined them while he spoke. "You spent a lot of time yesterday in quiet conversation with everybody." Jack twiddled the knobs on the radio. "Everybody but me, that is. Looked pretty serious."

Jeremy's face lost its easy-going smile. He didn't know how to respond.

"You know, if it's about you and Roberto …" Jack turned in his chair to face Jeremy.

Jeremy didn't say anything.

"Look, the world's changed. I don't understand much anymore. But I do know love and friendship." Jack smiled. "The last time you put me through my paces, you both seemed nervous – like you wanted to say something. If all that walking did anything for me, it pumped more oxygen to my brain. I may be old but I'm aware. So, I asked Robbie and he told me."

"Told you what?"

"You're going to be apartment mates."

Jeremy relaxed. He didn't realize how tense he'd been.

"And the rest of the stuff too."

"What rest?" Jeremy thought he may have relaxed his guard prematurely.

"Oh, the stuff you've been telling the others." Jack laughed. "Here you thought you were hiding things from your grandpa but I already knew."

Once again Jeremy didn't trust himself to respond – he wasn't really sure what the rest of the stuff was.

"Like I told you, I don't necessarily understand. But I need to ask you …"

"Yes."

"Does this make Robbie my grandson-in-law?" This time Jack slapped Jeremy on the back. "He's helped me a lot, kiddo, Germ man. I like Roberto. He helped me get my mind back – with that yellow stuff, you know. I only wish the best for the two of you – the absolute best."

This time Jeremy wasn't worried about Jack's sense of decorum as he hugged him. "I love you, Gramps."

"Me too, Germy."

▪ ▪ ▪

Now, Jack stood back from the airfield. "There's only two runways operational," he said. Jeremy and Marianne had come out of the museum with him while the others stayed behind. "We had three plus a full perimeter track. We were able to move aircraft into position to prepare for departure along the perimeter track while others were already taking off." Jack waved his arm to the south. "The runways were a mile long. Way beyond the current tarmac. Just small planes now."

Jack was pleased his grandchildren were there. He knew they couldn't possibly share his sense of being there, being part of history – couldn't experience his feelings of triumph and loss. But he was glad they were with him. The image of the airfield remained burnt into his memory – essential to know every inch for night time takeoffs and landings. So vivid to him even though runway remnants were overgrown. Nature had taken all these years to push grasses and scrub bushes through the broken concrete. Jack pointed across farm fields, out to the horizon south of where they stood. "Look out as far as you can see." Jeremy and Marianne followed his direction. "Through the mist." The three of them stood in silence. Then Jeremy looked at Marianne. They peered into the distance.

"Maybe it's my imagination. Right on the skyline. Like maybe two towers." Marianne shaded her eyes with her hand.

"There are three but we can only see two from here." Jack turned toward the source of a familiar four-cylinder engine thrum. Sounding slightly irregular yet somehow poised a vintage Tiger Moth accelerated toward takeoff. Jack nodded his head approvingly. Those biplane trainers were already ten years old when he learned to fly in them. Yet almost sixty-five years since then, there they were. Still going strong.

▪ ▪ ▪

Mission twenty-eight. Ruhr Valley. Only two more after this. Suddenly a shudder. We're hit. Pulsating. Reverberating. Anti-aircraft artillery fire heavy. Stay on target. Release bomb load. Eight-thousand pounder. We're rocked again. Hard. Jonesy looks at me. The blast right under our seats. Bomb bay. Mick screams. I fight to steady the plane.

Jonesy yells to Mick. "You okay?"

"I'm hit. My leg."

I sense more than see Jonesy kneel to stretch toward the bomb bay hatch. Too dark to see detail. Slight red glow from the instrument panel. Damage report first. "Ack-ack fragments through the turret, Bordsie. Shattered port side." Then he tends to Mick. "There's no room. I can't get down with you. Show me."

"Leg's cramping. Hit above the knee. Don't feel anything."

"Unzip your leg."

"Wha –"

"The pant leg. Unzip it," Jonesy says. "Any blood?"

"Yeah."

"Leave it, Mick! Don't pull it out! Tie it off." Flash of white. Jonesy pulls off his silk scarf and flips it down to Mick. "Above the wound. Tight. You don't wanna lose more blood."

We're losing altitude. Flaps and rudders working freely. All engines operational. Mick's hit. Trapped. No room. Look after the plane, I tell myself. I turn to my navigator. "Time to the coast."

"Twenty-seven minutes at current speed and altitude. Then another thirty home."

"He okay, Jonesy?"

"Shock. But okay." Jonesy kneels to speak with Mick again. "Hey, Mick. We'll pull you out when we're over the Channel. Keep still. Still as you can." I see him squeeze Mick's shoulders. "You'll be fine," he says. "We'll get you home. Good work, lad. You'll get a citation."

"Posthumous."

"Don't talk that way. Bordsie's got the engines humming full throttle. We're gonna make it."

▪ ▪ ▪

"Grandpa?" Marianne put her hand on Jack's arm. "You okay?"

Jack was startled. "Yeah." His heart was pounding. He was sweating. "Just remembering."

They paused a moment then Jeremy asked quietly, "Do you want to tell us?"

Jack hesitated, took several deep breaths. "It was so real," he said then recounted what he'd been remembering. A very dark night – took off from Wickenby in the remnants of daylight. The squadron amassed with others – hundreds of Lancasters as far as the eye could see, all in formation. But now it was dark, new moon. Mission completed and back over the Channel on the way home. Jack peering toward the coastline. Same as other dark nights. But this was different – urgent today – Mick wounded. The longest twenty-seven minutes of his life. Then the silhouette of cliffs, the coast of England just when Dave said it would appear. Inland, flying low, he imagined the towers. "I broke radio silence. First to my crew. Home safe, boys. Mick's injured. Then, Flight leader, request landing priority. One wounded. Get me medics and an ambulance."

Jeremy interrupted. "You told me your whole crew made it through the war."

"The medics cleaned up Mick's wound. Gave him some sort of injection. He walked with a limp for a while. Didn't miss a mission."

"How come?" Marianne said.

"Repairs took a couple of days. He had time to recover. Next flight, he eased himself through the side crew door and into his turret. Never let on how stiff and sore he was. I wasn't going to say anything. Didn't want a replacement. He wanted to finish with our crew. We were so close."

So close. Two to go. Each mission more dangerous. Right into the heart of Germany. Non-stop strategic bombing. Destroy the supply lines – factories, train yards, airports. We had the upper hand in the air. They weren't giving up – tenaciously defending. Relentless anti-aircraft artillery fire. So close to going home. Never been hit before. Mick so vulnerable in his turret. Mid-upper and tail gunners sitting ducks in their turrets. At least one of our squadron aircraft lost every outing. Captured, killed – we didn't know.

"What made you think of this now?" Jeremy asked.

"The towers. Once I could recognize them through the dark, I knew we were home. Our dark beacon."

"What we see on the horizon. That's –"

"Lincoln Cathedral," Jack said. "Safely home."

THE END

CPSIA information can be obtained
at www.ICGtesting.com
Printed in the USA
LVOW11s0012300318
571699LV00001B/3/P